THE TYPHON AFFAIR

A MAC SISCO NOVEL

THE TYPHON AFFAIR

A MAC SISCO NOVEL

BY

LOU EARLE

PHiR Publishing
San Antonio

PHiR Publishing
San Antonio, TX
phirpublishing.com

ISBN: 979-8-9867452-4-4
Library of Congress Control Number: 2022922069

Printed in the United States of America

For my brother, Larry, whose enthusiasm was a beacon of motivation.

CHAPTER ONE

The Signal

The Director of the National Security Agency, Admiral James Clausen was an early riser, but 3:45 am was at least two hours before he normally delicately left his wife's side to begin his morning jog. Fortunately, a forty-year career in the Navy had trained him to be a very light sleeper and his wife the exact opposite. He grabbed the cell phone that had disturbed his slumber and when he saw the caller ID, he accepted the call and quickly moved into his study. "Mac, what's wrong?" Clausen asked urgently.

Mac Sisco answered, the tension obvious in his voice. "I just received a text from an unknown source." Clausen waited patiently for the rest of the answer. "Admiral, there was only four words in the text, WE ARE ALIVE-JASMINE."

"Meet me at the building in one hour. I'll let my night teams know we're coming and to be on the alert," the Admiral answered as he rang off and headed for the shower.

Mac Sisco was one of NSA's very few and elite Special Ops Agents. This small group was outside the bubble of the Agency's normal intelligence gathering approach. NSA was all about intercepting signal and human communications and was far and away the best in the world at what they did. However, from time to time, there was a need to verify and validate their sigint data and to do that they needed human intelligence. That was Sisco's job and he was the best Clausen had ever known and that included the folks over at CIA and DIA. Sisco was a fit thirty-five-year-old who at six feet one and 180 pounds looked more like a young real estate broker from Texas than a lethal weapon. His standard attire was jeans, a polo shirt, his favorite custom full quill Ostrich boots and occasionally a Larry Mahan hat to top off the effect. He was strikingly good looking with an angular jaw and short straight auburn hair. And while his boyish good looks and subtle Texas drawl drew the attention of the ladies, he was seldom perceived as any kind of threat. In fact, his easy, low-key approach was downright disarming.

Mac's physical strength came from years of rock climbing and a disciplined fitness regime. But the agent's mental toughness was what really set him apart. He was a master problem solver and strategist and his unorthodox ways to extricate himself and his teams never ceased to surprise those with whom he worked. Mac's training had been long, deep and brutal with military experience in Afghanistan and rigorous Seal training during his military service. He had even graduated number one in his class in his multi-agency special operations courses and survival skills. Yes, Sisco was the real deal and a very important asset to NSA.

Only days before, Mac had successfully completed one of his most challenging assignments as the leader of Team Apogee, an international group of five of the best agents on the planet. They averted a worldwide crisis organized by a global cabal called Typhon. Although Typhon was still being dismantled by the good guys, Mac's team had taken out the Typhon leadership, or so they thought. Typhon's leader, Peter Gunderson, a financier and well-known billionaire, perished in a fire when a gas explosion tore apart his mansion in Bryn Mawr, Pa., while Gunderson was sleeping and burned it to the ground. DNA on the site verified Gunderson's identity.

The rest of Typhon's senior leadership including Peter Gunderson's son, Jefferey Gunderson and his two colleagues Nicholi Krishinko and Wart Von Stemp perished along with an ex- MI-6 agent, Jasmine Snow who it was believed was working with Typhon. Their private jet went down in a violent storm over the South China Sea. NSA was able to absolutely confirm these findings after an extensive international search was unable to find any evidence of the crash. However, the aircraft suddenly dropped off the grid and the weather supported this conclusion.

Mac's Team Apogee was instrumental in discovering many of the details of Typhon's global activities and identified the principles. Their field role was now ended, and the team was due to depart the next day. But now it seemed that everyone may have jumped the gun. Mac's text message was ominous. It might be nothing. Just a random spam or a joke by an admirer trying to get his attention. Or it might be something entirely different and Admiral Clausen was taking it very seriously.

◆

An hour later Mac cleared security at the NSA headquarters in Ft. Meade, Maryland and went straight to the ninth floor. Clausen was in his office on the secure line with the door open when Mac arrived. The Admiral waved him to a chair in front of his massive walnut desk and continued his conversation. "Yes, Bob, I need your team to pull out all the stops on this intercept. I'll have Mac send you the text and you can start running the big servers against the messages we've scraped over the last several hours. Hopefully, we grabbed the source of it since it was an international connection. OK, Bob keep me updated." The Admiral broke the connection and turned to Mac who was already forwarding the text to Bob Worthington, head of NSA's codes and ciphers group.

"I know what you're thinking Mac," said the Admiral "and I am very concerned you may be right. But why such a cryptic message?"

"I don't know," Mac answered, "but I have a theory."

"Shoot," said Clausen.

"Well, what if the Typhon goons discovered the tracker I put in Jasmine's purse? They were already suspicious of her and they may have destroyed the tracker and then confined her. Somehow, she must have had a way to get that text out but had no time to send more. If anyone could pull this off, it would be Jasmine."

"It's a reasonable theory, but are you sure this isn't just a random spam or joke?"

"No, I can't be certain of that, but I have no idea who would do that. I just have this gut feeling that this message actually came from Jasmine. I can't shake it," Mac said in earnest.

No one spoke as the two men imagined the implications of this new information. Finally, Admiral Clausen broke the silence. "Well Mac, if you're right, you know what this means."

"Yes Sir, I sure do. It means Typhon is still in play and Team Apogee must be reinstated!"

"It also means that everything we presumed may be false, despite all our alleged evidence," exclaimed Clausen. "I am afraid, we have been played and Typhon is alive and well. We'll dig into this text, but based on your hunch and my skepticism, I am reinstating your team and putting Apogee back online. All FACIT code word level security protocols are re-invoked. I will intensify my internal investigations into our mole theory and inform President Holbrook and the NATCOG members that we need to put the pedal to the metal. Get the word to your team to cancel their departures and meet back here at 2 pm today to strategize on next steps."

"Yes Sir, I am on it," Mac promised enthusiastically as he strode out of the office, a man on a mission!

◆

Every member of Team Apogee awoke to the same message from their leader. It simply said, "change of plans. Cancel departures and meet at my house at 10 am, Sisco." One by one they arrived, full of anticipation and excitement. Something big had happened over night and everything had changed, and they were barely able to contain themselves.

Elaine Warsaw, true to her British punctuality arrived at 9:30 am. She had spent the morning cancelling a month's worth of speeches at conferences and universities across the globe. As one of the world's experts on societal engineering, she was in great demand. And while the cancellations were regrettable, she much preferred the surreal excitement of working with Mac Sisco.

Peter Singe, Mac's pilot and problem solver extraordinaire arrived next. Peter had put off a consulting gig back in Tokyo but was happy to delay the long-haul flight and was actually itching to get back in the fight.

Pat Curry, the big Australian on the team was delighted when he got Mac's message. His financial duties down under were typically pretty mundane and he loved working with the high performing squad where the challenges were always off the charts.

Carrie Swan was the tech wizard and a free spirit and for Carrie schedules were best left to computers. Nonetheless, she still managed to time her ten-mile morning run to finish at Mac's front door five minutes before the meeting.

Commander Joe Franklin, ex-Navy Seal was certainly used to being prompt, but since his retirement had come to enjoy sleeping in. Joe was responsible for operations and general backup, had been Mac's mentor in the old days and always had his back. He was five minutes late and was immediately penalized for his tardiness by serving everyone more coffee, a chore he happily endured.

They were the best in the world in their specialties and equally accomplished in clandestine special operations. But more important than their individual competencies was that as a team their capabilities had proven to be much more than the sum of the parts. They were loyal, fearless and flexible and failure was not in their vocabulary. They trusted each other with their lives and had deep respect for Mac Sisco. He was tough, but fair and always put the team first and for them that was what great leadership was all about.

"Thanks for dropping everything and meeting this morning," Mac began after everyone was seated.

"No problem," quipped Joe Franklin. "I had to get up to answer your text message anyway."

Mac smiled, "ok Franklin, for that smart-ass remark, you get to stay on coffee duty." The room filled with smiles and chuckles as the big Seal laughed out loud. "But seriously," Mac continued, "early this morning I received a text message from an unknown source with only four words in it, "WE ARE ALIVE-JASMINE." There were gasps and expressions of surprise across the room.

"Oh shit," Franklin said, "Jasmine is alive!"

"That is my assumption," answered Mac.

"This has got to be some kind of sick joke from some crazy kook," exclaimed Pat.

"Maybe, but I have a gut feeling about this," Mac responded.

"Don't you think that's jumping the gun a bit," questioned Peter.

"Mac, being a behavioral scientist, I tend to agree with Peter," intoned Elaine. "Our personal relationships with Jasmine naturally create biases that can sway our logic and turn desires into hunches."

"Well, I'm with Mac on this one," interrupted Carrie. "Jasmine is uncanny at extricating herself from impossible situations. I mean, we never even really could confirm that her plane crashed."

Mac turned to Joe. "Joe, where is your head on this?"

"My head is all about faith guys. I never thought she was dead to begin with!"

"So what now Cap," Franklin continued. "We've got to convince the Admiral."

"Done deal, Joe," Mac exclaimed. "He was my first call this morning. I met with him at the building at 4:30 am. He agreed with my hunch and started the wheels turning. The cipher teams have been working on intercepting the source for five hours already. There is too much at stake to ignore this new wrinkle. All our assumptions about Typhon's leadership's deaths may well be incorrect. It may even have been a setup to throw us off the track."

"Holy kangaroo, it sounds like we're back in the saddle again," roared Pat Curry.

"Yes, we are," said Mac, "and we meet with the Admiral at 2 pm today to get Team Apogee's new orders."

◆

"Sir, I just got the results of our intercept scans for the source of Mac's text that we discussed earlier this morning," said Admiral James Clausen to the President of the United States.

"Well Jim, what do we know? Has Typhon regrown its heads," asked President Holbrook.

"It appears, they have Sir. The source of the message is a mobile phone located in Auckland, New Zealand."

"Wasn't that one of the destinations your team predicted Typhon's plane was headed before you lost the signal?" asked the POTUS.

"Affirmative," answered Clausen. "Based on this latest intel, I also believe it is highly probable that Peter Gunderson is also still alive and likely set up an alternate Typhon HQ."

"This is very disturbing Jim. It seems like we are right back to square one," said the President.

Clausen expected the critique but wasn't fazed. This wasn't his first rodeo and it wouldn't be his last. "Actually Sir, given the situation, we're very fortunate."

"How so?" asked Holbrook, surprised.

"Well, Sir, they didn't get away with the ruse. Furthermore, since they believe we think their leadership is dead, we may have gained the element of surprise. We even have a pretty good idea where they are."

"I see your point James, touché," chuckled Holbrook.

"I am reinstating Team Apogee and the field operation immediately, Sir," continued Clausen. "They have already convened in my conference room to receive their new orders and will be deployed to New Zealand by 1700 hours. My C&C team is currently working on narrowing down the mobile phone's specific location and we have a safe house set up in Auckland, already provisioned to support their op."

"As always Jim you are out in front. Good work. I will inform the NATCOG members and the National Security Council."

"I would strongly advise against that Mr. President," warned Clausen.

"I'm listening," Holbrook responded.

"Two reasons," said the Admiral. "First, we're in the very preliminary phase of this operation and a lot can change. But more importantly, we believe we may have leaks here in the Agency and possibly elsewhere. I am implementing our LIP protocol here and I recommend you surreptitiously do the same for anyone engaged in the Apogee mission at a FACIT level. We should coordinate these actions carefully, so I'll confirm with you when we initiate our actions."

"I agree with your recommendations, Jim," said the President. "I'll alert my assistant to expect your call."

"Thank you, sir," said Clausen as he hung up the secure line and strode out of his office to meet with Team Apogee.

♦

The Director's Executive conference room went quiet when Clausen unceremoniously entered. "I'll keep this short and sweet, ladies and gentlemen," he said as he opened the meeting. "You've got a lot to do between now and 1700 and a long ride after that on your way to Auckland, New Zealand. This will be a play-by-play action plan. That means you all need to call the audibles and develop it on the fly. NSA will provide logistical and intel support. By the time you land after eighteen hours airtime, we should have compiled detailed information on what we believe is Typhon's new HQ. Once you're underway, I'll provide an interim status on our progress and we will be in contact with additional guidance and support as you assess the situation on the ground. Your safe house will be stocked with tactical gear and supplies. Any other special requirements can be obtained from our Army installation on the island through the General in charge. He has been briefed on your mission as has our New Zealand embassy."

"We believe Typhon may have detailed information about your mission and capabilities and we must assume they may even know we have uncovered their subterfuge. In any case, you can assume they will be very prepared and have significant offensive and defensive capacity. We also believe that their entire leadership has convened there, so this represents our best opportunity to neutralize the organization and that is our mission. It is absolutely imperative that we behead Typhon once and for all," Clausen finished fervently. "God speed and good luck."

CHAPTER TWO

THE LIP

Admiral James Clausen had logged over four decades working every kind of counter espionage activity on the planet and this was certainly not his first security breach. But several aspects of this situation were challenging. First, there was very little time. It was important to expose the bad actors quickly to protect the field operation and to eliminate any constraints to NSA's activities. Additionally, any missteps could jeopardize the field op and the team and could also set back the overall Apogee mission. Finally, it was simply intolerable for the Admiral to allow any treasonous actors to skate on his watch. Needless to say, Clausen had plenty of incentives to squash this thing and take no prisoners. As he struggled to control his visceral anger and frustration over his predicament, he knew what he needed to do.

The process was fondly called the LIP, for Leak Identification Process and he had helped develop its use across Homeland Security including the CIA, DIA, FBI and NSA. First, he needed to determine the most likely points of disclosure. That meant identifying specific individuals who had access to the most sensitive and leverage-able information about Apogee. In order to narrow the list, he had to focus on potential vulnerability to influence or bribes. That list would then be vetted thoroughly by analyzing personal financials, hobbies, acquaintances, historical engagements and lifestyle for anomalies. The resultant targets would then be subject to an invisible custom incrimination trial/test whose outcome would either exonerate or incriminate them. By tomorrow COB he needed to begin that implementation and, if properly developed and deployed, he should begin to ID his traitors within forty-eight hours.

After four hours sleep and one hour on the phone from his home in Bethesda, Md., Clausen connected with a small group of his most trusted colleagues inside and outside the agency through whom he could execute the LIP and any other immediate pre-cleanse imperatives. He also sent a secure text message to President Holbrook expressing his urgent need to conduct a thirty-minute FYEO (For Yours Eyes Only) briefing at 0700. By 0630, he had already received a confirmation of his call as he stepped onto the 9th floor of the building in Ft. Meade, Md. Clausen purposely scheduled the call early to avoid any staff interactions. Martin would be the first to arrive at 0745 and by then his call would be over.

At precisely 0700, he dialed the private number for POTUS on his secure grey phone. Holbrook picked up immediately. "Morning Jim," the President said, "I imagine the shit is hitting the fan."

"Good morning Mr. President," answered Clausen respectfully, "you might say that." Twenty minutes later, having completed his update, Clausen asked, "are there any other questions or instructions, Mr. President?"

"No, Jim, I get the gist and will execute top level LIP actions at the White House, NSC and other Apogee assets on your timeline. I suggest we schedule another call in forty-eight hours, same logistics."

"Yes Sir, Mr. President," the Admiral responded.

"And Jim…"

"Yes, Mr. President?"

"Watch your back. I have a feeling this could get ugly!"

At 0745 that morning, right on schedule, Admiral Clausen heard his Executive Assistant Martin Stabler unlock his office door to begin another day and thought to himself, *now it begins.* Clausen had no reason to mistrust Stabler, nor did he believe that he was culpable, but he was certainly among those who had to be assessed. His handling of all the most sensitive data, coupled with his unprecedented access to the Director and his personal engagements made him a unique target for influence. Of course, Stabler knew this better than anyone and was interviewed and polygraphed periodically for exactly that reason. His personal information showed no evidence of malfeasance or particular vulnerability other than an extravagant vacation or two, but all within the LIP guidelines. One of Clausen's early morning calls on the way to his office was to his Chief of Security, who owned the LIP Protocol for the agency, to develop the most effective trial for Martin. Now, as Martin was brewing his first cup of coffee, Clausen reviewed the Top-Secret FACET e-mail describing his Security Officer's recommendations.

At exactly 0800, like clockwork, Stabler gently knocked on Clausen's door. The Admiral answered, "enter."

Martin opened the big walnut paneled door and stepped in. "Sir," he asked, "can I get you a cup of coffee."

"No thanks Martin," responded Clausen pleasantly. I got in a little early for a call with POTUS and already made myself a cup."

"Very good, Sir."

The Admiral continued, "but come on in and take a seat and let's get our daily update out of the way." After Stabler had reviewed all his action items from the prior day, he sat patiently waiting for his boss to make his assignments. Clausen rattled through a dozen tasks and follow-ups as Stabler dutifully jotted notes into his iPad.

When the Admiral finally paused, as if finished, Stabler asked, "anything else Admiral?"

Clausen leaned forward intensely and said, "yes actually Martin, there is one more important item. I need you to follow up on a very sensitive matter that President Holbrook brought to my attention."

Martin sat up a little straighter to indicate his total concentration to his superior.

The Admiral continued, "there is evidence suggesting that Peter Gunderson, the alleged leader of Typhon, was not killed in the explosion and fire at his residence in the suburbs of Philadelphia."

"But how is that possible, Sir? The report stated that his DNA was definitively identified at the scene," exclaimed Stabler.

"Yes, that's true," answered Clausen, "but we have an eyewitness who saw Gunderson leaving the residence several hours earlier carrying a suitcase and apparently never returned." Martin was stunned at this news. He knew from his last communication with Gunderson about the Apogee plans that he would be vacating the residence for a new HQ and would fake his death so there would be no follow up.

The Admiral continued, interrupting his frantic thoughts, "I need you to get up to Bryn Mawr, Pa. and personally interview this individual, verify these claims and immediately report back to me. If Gunderson is still alive, we need to get on his trail while it's reasonably hot. I will text you the witness' contact info, a photo and the restaurant where he agreed to meet before you leave. The meeting is scheduled tonight at 6 pm. Do not divulge any of this to anyone. The witness is already freaked out about talking with us. The only reason he is willing to meet is because once we have verified or discredited his story, he knows he is no longer at risk."

Stabler was already sweating by the time he left Clausen's office. He needed to get to Peter Gunderson fast. If his story was really credible and the Agency believed it, Gunderson was screwed. Stabler didn't have a clue what Gunderson would do, but he knew he needed to get rid of this hot potato. This shit was above his pay grade! Just then his mobile phone buzzed as the Admiral's text was delivered and Stabler had everything he needed. Thirty minutes later he pulled into the driveway of his two-story colonial in Laurel, Maryland.

He quickly went into his home office and retrieved a second mobile phone. Like its brother, this back up was loaded with an identical Typhon app providing him secure communications with Gunderson using one-time pad encryption and was only for emergencies. To ensure that forwarding Clausen's text information couldn't be traced back to him, he pulled up that text and took a photo on the back up mobile. After adding the detail of Clausen's conversation in a new text with the image attached, he hit send. The die was cast, he had done his part. He thought to himself, *I hope that SOB doesn't call or contact me, but he knew that would never happen.* Across the street and a block away, a grey, nondescript Chevy sedan with tinted windows sat silently parked against the curb. Inside two NSA field agents sat patiently waiting for Martin Stabler to make his next move.

♦

8,800 miles away in Auckland, it was four am the next day when Stabler's urgent message popped up on Peter Gunderson's mobile as he was sleeping. Gunderson's video call with Jefferey the prior evening had been disturbing. Not only were both his son and Von Stemp injured, but also, they had burned up valuable time with little return. Gunderson could see little benefit in continuing the search and destroy mission against Apogee under these circumstances. The prudent option was to bring his team to Auckland and re-group. Besides, this new situation convinced him that Chaos was a go and he needed all hands on deck to make that happen.

The Jasmine woman might be a wrinkle, but he would deal with that in due course. She was of little concern and could be dispatched quickly if needed. He had already alerted his Asian region and the Australian and New Zealand branches of Typhon to send their Elite Chaos Teams to Auckland to bolster his resources. They would bivouac on the ranch not far from the main compound and provide all the security he would need. Jefferey had begrudgingly concurred with his plan. It was obvious they wanted to avenge their losses and do some serious damage to Apogee's team. He certainly couldn't blame them, but that would just have to wait. Once Chaos was operational, he would give them that chance. Who knows, he might even join them and have some real fun for a change being back in the field.

Now, as the magnificent glow of a down under sunrise began to illuminate the breathtaking landscape of Gunderson's Ardyh Ranch, he groggily awoke, still fighting the enormous shift in time zones. His attention was immediately driven to the blinking red light on his cell phone alerting him to an urgent message. Grabbing the device, he quickly pulled himself up to a sitting position as he leaned back against the imported Texas Cedar headboard spanning the end of the king-sized bed. Opening Stabler's urgent email, he rapidly read the frantic note, his face darkening. How could this be true, he asked himself. He had taken great precautions and considered every detail. He searched his memory of that day trying to recall if there had been any irregularities. None that he could remember. He replayed his departure over and over in his mind, examining every detail as he left the residence and entered the limo, but couldn't recall any breach of security. He had left before his grounds keepers and regular staff had arrived and the entrance itself was not visible from the lane running by the mansion's gates. There were only two possibilities, he conjectured, either one of his workers had arrived early and observed him leaving or his Typhon security team, in this case his driver, had betrayed him and given him up to the agency. Whichever the case, he had no time to investigate. Even now, it might be too late.

Peter Gunderson knew better than anyone that the credibility of his death was absolutely crucial. If that fabrication were discovered, he would be relentlessly hunted whether Typhon succeeded or not. He simply couldn't allow that. Of the two possible explanations, Gunderson knew he could only act on one. With two dozen employees on the property daily, he simply didn't have the time to identify the source. But if it was his driver, he might still stop up the leak. His odds were about even and that was a lot better than zero. Without a moment more hesitation, Gunderson dialed a number he knew from memory and explained what he needed done.

◆

Stabler left in midafternoon for his meeting in Bryn Mawr. At a little over 120 miles, he could easily arrive in less than three hours and have plenty of time to scout out the place. He also wanted to check out the ruins of Gunderson's residence just to make his own impressions. Clausen had set the meeting at 6 pm, but told Stabler not to arrive until 6:30 pm, so that the source could get comfortable before he arrived. *The guy must really be skittish*, Martin thought. Stabler considered falsifying his report to the Admiral, if the evidence looked credible, but he knew that couldn't work because the source could easily dispute him and might even have physical proof. No, he had to ride it out, but the good news was that he would still be out in front of the information and could keep Gunderson in the loop. And there was a silver lining, his stock value was rising fast and he figured it wouldn't be long before his price followed.

Stabler circled the main line property several times and finally decided to take a closer look. He pulled up to the massive gate and identified himself to the Police officer guarding the entrance. On his drive down, he had requested Clausen to clear the red tape and the officer quickly waved him through. He cruised slowly up the winding cobblestone drive, tall pines soaring majestically on both sides until opening up onto the mansion's manicured grounds. In the distance, he could see the smoldering rubble of what, only a day before, had been one of Philadelphia's most elegant edifices.

Now, as he closed on the scene, it reminded him of the photos he'd seen of European cities bombed out by the Germans during the Second World War. Several large stone chimneys jutted into the still smoking afternoon air. A few exterior walls followed broken geometric patterns like the sides of a maze never finished. The rest was, well, just gone! But one thing was certain; no one could have survived this holocaust. Nothing more to see here, he thought and started back down the drive to his rendezvous with destiny. The plan was to meet his guest at an outside table at the White Dog Cafe on Lancaster Pike in Haverford, another main line village just a few miles southeast of Bryn Mawr. His leaker would be wearing a Philadelphia Philly's ball Cap with the brim pointed backwards.

An hour before Stabler arrived at the White Dog; a grey sedan pulled into its parking lot and grabbed a spot between several other cars near the entrance. Inside the vehicle two NSA counter terrorist field agents carefully scanned the restaurant and its perimeter. The traffic was beginning to pick up as the happy hour and early dining crowd began to arrive. But profiling was at the top of their skill set and they knew what they were looking for. At 5:45 pm, one of the agents left the car and grabbed an outside table. He pulled a Philadelphia Philly's cap out of his pocket and put it on backwards and ordered a beer. At 6:10 pm, a black SUV pulled into the White Dog's parking lot and a middle-aged man with short slightly graying sideburns and Ray Ban dark glasses got out and entered the restaurant. Minutes later he stepped outside on the terrace and approached the agent's table and took the opposite chair.

"Good evening," he said, "my name is Martin Stabler. Admiral Clausen sent me to meet with you. Sorry for being here a little early, but there was less traffic than I thought."

The agent calmly looked up and smiled at the would-be assassin and replied, "no problem, that's ok, we won't be staying long, as his partner strode up to join them."

At precisely 6:30 pm Martin Stabler drove up to the restaurant as directed. He parked his car near the entrance, and anxiously scanned the outside diners, but saw no one fitting the description. By 7:00 pm, he decided something had to be amiss. He went into the restaurant and inquired if anyone had come in wearing a Philly's ball cap, to which the Maître d' laughed and proclaimed, "are you kidding me, that's all we see in here this time of year." Disgusted, Stabler returned to his car and dialed Clausen's direct line.

He got the Admiral's voice mail and left a message. "Sir," he recorded, "the guy looks like a no show. I'll wait an hour and see if he arrives, unless I hear different from you. I have a feeling this guy's story is bogus."

Admiral Clausen listened to the voice mail from his assistant and sighed. The LIP had worked just as designed. Minutes earlier he had finished a call with his LIP field team who had provided him with an update on the Stabler operation. The agents reported that they now had an individual in custody who had fraudulently represented himself as Martin Stabler and were bringing him into the agency for questioning. So far, he refused to provide even his name, but they were already running a check on his identity and by the time they had returned to Ft. Meade, they expected to have much more information and would check back in with Clausen then.

The Admiral rubbed his tired eyes and leaned back in the big leather chair as he considered next steps. So Martin was a mole, but maybe not the only one, so they had to keep working the LIP protocol. That said, they needed to take advantage of this revelation. That meant keeping up the ruse. Martin could not know of his exposure. Furthermore, they needed to create a narrative that the eyewitness had died in a freak accident so that Peter Gunderson would believe that his assassin had succeeded, and his secret was still safe. Of course, Gunderson would attempt to contact the assassin, who would either never respond or would do so under agency control. Worst case, Gunderson would assume his plan had worked even if he was somewhat troubled by the lack of his contract killer's confirmation.

Martin would return and make his report, which Clausen would accept, and within twenty-four hours the news of the witness' untimely death would put an end to the whole saga. Clausen's challenge now was to very carefully craft information that he would feed to Stabler that advantaged Apogee and took down Typhon. For that plan, he needed to closely coordinate with Mac and his team. Before contacting Mac though, he had one more call to make. He dialed in the number of his Operations Director on duty overseeing Apogee's daily intelligence gathering. He needed to know about their progress and any updates.

Following that conversation, Clausen grabbed his secure grey phone and dialed in Sisco's number. Mac picked up immediately. "Yes Admiral," Sisco briskly responded. The Admiral explained the LIP operations being conducted throughout the Apogee structure and in particular the details of the Stabler findings.

Mac responded, "Admiral, I am truly sorry about Stabler. He certainly played his part well."

"Yes, he did, answered Clausen and the scary part is that if Typhon can get that deep into our intelligence organizations, how many more are there?"

"You're right, of course," Mac responded, "and the president sure called this one. Sir," Mac continued, "do we have any news on tracking Jasmine's mobile"

"Yes we do," Clausen said positively. "I just got an update from downstairs. My guys say the coordinates from that mobile put her in a location which we strongly believe is her final destination and more than likely Gunderson's new headquarters. We're in the process of pinning down the exact address, topography and terrain and any other details that we need to build a penetration strategy. I'll get that to you as soon as we have it which should be by the time you and the team land in Auckland."

Mac committed to reconnecting with Clausen via a secure video link once they had arrived at the safe house to finalize their plans.

Before hanging up, Mac asked, "Admiral, has your team come up with anything about this Chaos reference we overheard?"

"Nothing yet," said Clausen, "but one idea we're kicking around is to link it to its scientific meaning, the Chaos Theory. It deals with nonlinear things that are effectively impossible to predict or control. As I understand it, these phenomena are often described by fractal mathematics, which captures the infinite complexity of nature. If we are right, Typhon is about to set in motion a series of additional fractal systems that will operate out of control and without any rationale predictability. Once initiated, these actions may cascade and become virtually unstoppable. That is why it is so critical that you intervene now in Auckland. We must understand Typhon's fractal roadmap and deter these actions wherever we can."

CHAPTER THREE

DISCOVERY

As the plane hurtled earthward, its passengers were pressed back into their seats like astronauts on lift off. Jasmine knew enough to lean forward with her head between her knees. The maneuver saved her from being pulverized by airborne debris rocketing aft. The sound was deafening now, and it seemed inevitable that the jet would be torn apart long before it made planet fall. She managed a quick glance out the window and it seemed something was different. It was subtle but there. It was almost imperceptible, but she was sure that the ugly deep purple sky had brightened. She risked pressing her face against the window and peered out intently. Yes, she was right. The sky was clearing. She could see holes in the cloud cover beneath her and then far below a great mass of water.

And then it hit her as she recalled the pilot's warning about evading the storm by either climbing or diving. They weren't crashing, the pilot was taking the plane down to escape the weather. Before she could even debate her theory, she felt the plane shutter as it began to level off. Once again gravity began to shift as the aircraft regained stable flight. She turned her gaze upward and could see the massive dark clouds already beginning to recede as they shot out from under the tempest above them. At first, she hadn't even noticed that the alarms had ceased and then the cabin intercom buzzed. "Please everyone, stay in your seats. A crew member is coming to assist you. If you have sustained any injuries and are able to notify them, please do so. Our sincere apologies for the extreme measures we took to escape the weather. We were caught in a rapidly forming upper altitude disturbance which could only be avoided by an emergency decent. I must be candid when I tell you that we were very fortunate to have enough elevation to dive out of it. We are currently assessing all our systems, but it appears that we had no damage and unless we have any serious injuries, we should be able to complete our flight to Auckland."

Two flight attendants that had been strapped in at the front of the passenger cabin suddenly appeared. They looked as shaken as she was by the frightening episode but were doing their best to deal with the situation. "Are you alright?" the female attendant asked Jasmine as she carefully grabbed the seat back to steady herself.

"Yes, I think so," Snow responded hesitantly as she flexed her arms and legs for any discomfort.

The attendant handed her a bottle of water and a small towel and said, "please stay in your seat until we have cleaned up the cabin. There is quite a bit of debris and sharp shards of glass and plastic that are strewn in the aisle way."

"How are the other passengers?" Snow asked, concern in her voice.

Just then, she heard Krishinko's deep baritone from behind her.

"Son of a bitch," he groaned. "Will somebody get me a towel to wipe the blood from my head and some ice for the swelling." The attendant turned and rushed to Krishinko's seat in the rear of the plane.

"What happened Nicholi?" Gunderson yelled from further back in the cabin.

"Somebody's bag hit me in the head when we went into the dive. It hit me so hard, I was knocked out cold for a moment. The damn thing is heavier than a sack of ball bearings," he moaned.

"How bad is it?" Von Stemp chimed in.

"I'll live said the big Russian, but it really pisses me off. Wait till I find the bastard that owns this sack of shit!"

Snow gasped, hearing this banter as she stared at the adjacent seat where her large leather bag once sat. Without even thinking, she loosened her belt enough to turn around and peer over her seat back and stare apologetically at Krishinko wincing as the flight attendant administered to his head wound.

"Nicholi, that would be my leather satchel. I'm sorry you were injured, but I did not anticipate that it would become a weapon of mass destruction."

The Typhon agent glared back and responded, "Snow, you've already got two strikes against you. There had better not be any more bullshit from you or I will personally even the score!"

Thirty minutes later the cabin had been cleaned up and they were in clear sky. The ride had smoothed out and Gunderson had moved forward to check on Krishinko's condition and was sitting beside him in the aisle seat. Nicholi was still fuming about the incident and had picked up the large handbag showing his boss the weight of it as he hefted it up in the air. Gunderson, in an effort to mollify the Russian, took the bag from Krishinko shaking it violently to assess its mass and items began to fall out of the partially open zipper. As he reached down to retrieve them he noticed one peculiar item on the cabin floor.

"What the hell," he said out loud.

Krishinko, who was staring out the window turned and asked, "what is it Jefferey?" Gunderson put his hand to his lips in a gesture of silence as he picked up a small pellet and leaned forward to get a better look at it.

Gunderson had been on the dark side for a long time and he knew immediately what he had discovered. It was a highly sophisticated tracker and the implications were very bad. Typhon was being tracked and if he didn't stop it, it would lead someone right to Typhon's new clandestine headquarters.

Krishinko stared wide-eyed at the device and said in a low voice, barely audible even in the close quarters, "well shit Jefferey, we're leading the enemy right to our camp!"

"How do you want to handle it," Nicholi asked urgently.

"We need to turn this catastrophe into an advantage," Gunderson responded angrily. "First we contain it by destroying the device and then I stop all communication from this aircraft. This has to be the NSA. The technology is very advanced. If the signal suddenly goes dark, they will start looking for us at our last location which right now is over the South China Sea. They will connect the severe weather with the disappearance of the tracker and after a search will quickly conclude that we perished in the storms. Their little subterfuge will backfire beautifully. With my father's fake death from the gas explosion and our unfortunate demise, they will believe Typhon is now aimlessly leaderless. Even if they later discover their error, the pressure from their ground agents will be suspended and we will have gained time and the advantage of surprise."

Krishinko smiled broadly despite his aching head and whispered, "that's brilliant boss! Your old man is gonna love it."

Gunderson wasted no time making his way forward and entered the pilot's cabin. A few moments later he returned to his seat.

As he passed her, Jasmine called out, "what's up Jefferey, are all systems still go?"

"Aside from some minor damage to the passenger cabin's interior, everything appears to be functioning normally," he answered pleasantly. Snow was immediately suspicious. *That was certainly not a Gunderson response,* she thought. *Something was going on and it couldn't be good.*

Gunderson took his seat and Nicholi immediately pressed him, "what's the situation, Jefferey?"

"I wanted to get our exact location and inform the captain that we are operating completely incommunicado from now on. This plane is about to cease to exist. We were already flying without electronic beacons on and are scheduled to land at a private airstrip in NZ. And now the coup d'état," he exclaimed as he ground the tiny pellet under the heel of his boot exposing the frayed circuitry.

"What about the woman?" Krishinko asked.

Jefferey took a moment contemplating the question and then said, "we say nothing about finding the tracker. Information is power and we're not going to give her any of that. Besides, there are two possibilities. Either she is in on it with NSA and knew about the device and even planned to let us capture her so that she could track us. Or NSA planted the tracker in her handbag without her knowledge because they couldn't trust her and believed she was working with us."

"Obviously, we can't trust her either," exclaimed Nicholi.

"That is certain," nodded Gunderson. "Also, Nicholi, let's keep this confidential even from Wart. He gets very worked up and in his current state, I need him focused on the mission, not on revenge. That will come soon enough. When we rejoin my father in Auckland, I am sure that he'll want to personally interrogate Miss Snow and decide how to use her to our advantage. Are we clear?"

Krishinko nodded. "Yes Sir, I understand."

Snow could feel the shift in Gunderson's demeanor on his way back from the pilot's cabin and it worried her a lot. She had an uncanny ability to read situations and was almost flawless in her insights, especially when it concerned her survival. Somehow, she had to find out what the bloody hell was going on. She knew they didn't trust her and that was probably not going to change. She needed to find a way out of this, and her best option was to somehow contact Sisco. He might not trust her either, but at least he had scruples. These thugs would kill her without hesitation or regret. But it had to wait until they had reached their destination wherever that might be.

The landing was smooth and uneventful. They remained on the plane until the big jet was carefully towed into a large hanger. Once they disembarked, they were escorted to a private waiting room. There was a well-stocked bar around which the Typhon agents immediately gathered ignoring her.

Snow turned to Krishinko and said, "I am truly sorry Nicholi about the handbag incident."

Krishinko just growled and said, "right."

She sighed, *so much for making amends,* she thought. "Would you mind awfully returning my bag," she asked to no one in particular.

Krishinko, glanced at Gunderson with a questioning look, but Jefferey ignored him and jumped in. "Of course, Ms. Snow, but please pay better attention to your belongings from now on."

Retrieving the bag from his boss, Von Stemp grumbled, "here Snow, try not to lose it again," as he strode to the unisex bathroom and disappeared inside. Minutes later he returned and made his way back to the bar in search of another beer.

After fifteen minutes, Gunderson impatient declared, "Nicholi, I'm going to go check on what's holding things up. Keep Ms. Snow company while I step away." Krishinko nodded and turned back and drained the last of his beer, before retrieving another from the small refrigerator behind the bar.

Snow got up from her chair and announced, "I have got to use the loo, Nicholi. You can guard the door if you want," she quipped smiling. Nicholi sneered but nodded without a word. Jasmine did need to use the bathroom but hoped she might stumble on something useful by chance. As she walked towards the stall, she noticed a cell phone perched on the sink's edge. Her heart leaped as she grabbed the device and tapped its screen. *Oh joy,* she thought, *no password required.* Next, she glanced at the header and was rewarded with another break. She had a cell circuit and internet access. *OK, what's next,* she thought urgently. *Where in hell am I?* She quickly tapped on the map application on the home screen and the curser began its search of the globe finally zooming in on a rural location about seventy-five miles from Auckland, New Zealand.

Suddenly, Krishinko banged on the door and bellowed, "come on Snow, you have thirty seconds and if you don't come out, I'm coming in." In a panic Jasmine pulled up the text messaging app and keyed in

Mac Sisco's mobile phone number which he had shared back in London the first night they met. Krishinko banged on the door harder.

"Time's up Snow," he yelled. Jasmine desperately keyed in four words and hit send. The text message disappeared and was immediately replaced with the designation, delivered. She immediately deleted the message from the phone and replaced it where it was. She stepped into the stall and flushed the toilet and raced to the door. Calmly she opened it and greeted Krishinko staring down with an irritated look on his face.

She smiled and said, "Nicholi, it's a little more complicated for us ladies you know," as she moved around him and took her seat again.

Gunderson returned and announced that their transportation had arrived, and it was time to leave. As they headed for the exit, Snow noticed that Wart was patting his pockets and seemed to be looking for something. He stopped, scratched his head and then headed for the bathroom.

"Gunderson yelled, "come on Wart, we're out of here."

Von Stemp shot back, "be right there boss," and disappeared into the head returning almost instantly with his cell phone gripped in his hand.

Gunderson looked at Krishinko and asked exasperated, "does that guy have a bladder problem or what?"

CHAPTER FOUR

DOWN UNDER

Peter Gunderson greeted his embattled team as they arrived at the new NZ HQ and directed them to their quarters to get cleaned up and rest for a couple hours before dinner. Snow was escorted to a separate guest area of the house and directed not to leave her suite unless she was escorted. Gunderson had been cordial, but firm and informed her that she was considered marginalized until cleared by him and that process, he warned, would be executed soon enough.

Earlier that day Gunderson had sent Stabler a note demanding an update on his trip to Philadelphia and had received a one-sentence response, no show. He smiled as he dialed his contractor for confirmation on the hit but got no response. Not unusual so soon after a termination, he surmised. He'd probably get the final payment demand before anything else. *Might as well check the media,* he thought. Accidents are usually pretty good copy. He scanned the usual sources and found nothing. But soon after drilling down to local media, he came upon a headline in the Patch-Bryn Mawr-Gladwyne Local News; *Bryn Mawr Resident Killed When Car Jumps Guardrail on Entrance to Schuylkill Expressway.* The day and time matched up and there were no other accidental deaths reported in the area that day. Gunderson relaxed and breathed a sigh of relief. It looked like his little escapade had worked as planned and he remained in the history books.

Snow had not been invited to that night's dinner and had been served her meal in her room. Guards had been posted at all the exits from her suite and while she had not been interrogated or abused, she was a prisoner, nonetheless. She was frankly very confused by their distrust. Their only communication with her had been their warning about the US intelligence initiative and their instruction for her to join them in Paris. They had no knowledge of her tryst with Sisco in London or journey with him to the Apogee safe house in Paris, so why be skeptical of her loyalty. Unless of course, they had somehow learned of her activities. But how? At any rate, she could easily explain all that and she would. She literally had no choice. It had been her only play and she had gotten away with it. They should be thanking her, not imprisoning her. Now she could play the game for their benefit. She needed to convince her hosts that she was still and always had been on their team.

As Snow was stewing over her predicament, Peter Gunderson was holding court with his team on the terrace following a potpourri of New Zealand seafood. After partaking of green shell Mussels as an appetizer and Kaikoura, the country's famous delectable crayfish, the four men sat comfortably ensconced in large wicker chairs sipping brandy in the waning sunlight peeking over the mountains. As expected, the elder Gunderson took the lead. "Alright gentlemen," he began, "let me begin by saying that I elected to delay initiating Chaos, but only for a few days to allow us to properly prepare. Let me be very clear, the last few days have convinced me more than ever that we can ill afford to delay that action given the increasing pressure of our adversaries. While I have some concerns that this premature launch is risky, my current assessment of Typhon's global progress indicates that it is actually tracking very well.

When one examines the primary drivers of societal unrest, all are now bearing significant fruit." Gunderson then launched into an uncharacteristically professorial tone as he described the state of the planet.

"Across the globe," Gunderson lectured, "with uncanny consistency, progressive practices driven by unions, parents, grade schools and universities are rapidly changing the educational landscape worldwide. Traditional curricula focused on the arts and STEM are quickly being replaced by a new orientation on social equity, critical race theory, cancel culture and identity politics. Almost overnight the world's youth from K-12 to PhDs are being reprogrammed into embracing anti-nationalistic policies and adopting authoritarian ideologies and an anarchist governance.

"Long-standing traditions, historical precedent and proven governing structures are being systematically attacked. Statues are felled as history is erased, police are defunded, and the rule of law is being dismantled with impunity. Open borders, mob rule and the eradication of individual rights are fast becoming the new standard in many countries. Objective journalism has long since been replaced with biased, opinion-based and filtered content that has little resemblance to the truth and even less respect for facts. The unmistakably common theme that dominates all these shifts is the unrelenting pressure by a small and powerful elite class to establish the servitude of the masses. Typhon has been methodically driving these shifts for decades and once the tipping point has been achieved will conveniently ride into the fray as the white night to lead the masses out of their misery. Yes, it is happening just as we planned it and we are now on the cusp of success."

Having finished his tutorial, Gunderson, picked up his snifter, swirled its contents gently and took a modest sip of his brandy.

Seeing his opportunity, Jefferey interjected, "Sir, if things are doing so well, why do we need to take chances with Chaos?"

The senior Gunderson responded, "fair question, Jefferey. Our problem is that at this juncture we didn't anticipate being identified or having any major counter initiatives launched against us. Our models did consider that possibility and that is why Chaos was designed as a contingent deterrent, but it was not anticipated for at least another year."

"I see," his son responded.

"So what is the risk of launching it early," asked Krishinko.

Gunderson became visibly more intense as he answered. "Also a fair question, but before I can explain that I need to take you beyond the basics you already know about Chaos and do a deeper dive into its implementation and consequences."

"What I am about to tell you was only meant to be disclosed when and if Chaos was to be deployed. I am the only one who is familiar with all its details and only upon my death or its implementation would other select members of Typhon be briefed. The reasons for this strict compartmentalization will soon become apparent," Gunderson stressed.

Taking another delicate sip of his cordial, he continued. "As you have been informed already, Chaos is a program whose primary purpose is to accelerate Typhon's activities by orders of magnitude. What you don't understand is how that is accomplished and the results that it precipitates. A little history is required here," Gunderson went on. "Typhon's entire strategy is founded on the Chaos theory, a mathematical theory of nonlinear changes which are characterized by unpredictability."

"Over the years," he continued, "we have used a series of mini Butterfly Effects very sparingly to catalyze Typhon's global disruptions. These tiny aberrations were carefully modeled, and countless simulations were run to understand the permutations and combinations that might result. But implementing Chaos is like Typhon on steroids. The fractals in Chaos are enormously powerful and unpredictable and when they occur simultaneously, the results can be magnified even more. Launching a single fractal could quickly get out of control. Launching many of them is likely impossible to manage. So you see," Gunderson sighed, "Chaos is a crap shoot under the best of circumstances."

"So what's the upside, and the downside?" asked Jefferey.

"The upside is that Typhon accelerates along planned lines and we can manage it and achieve control decades faster," Peter Gunderson responded.

"And the downside?" his son pressed.

His father paused and then answered gravely, "the downside is that we lose total control with outcomes that could be catastrophic worldwide. I'm talking about a global economic meltdown, unpredictable shifts in governance across most societies, armed regional conflicts and even nuclear war among major players. All our work would be for naught and we would lose our opportunity to control mankind's future."

Von Stemp had been quiet up till now, but couldn't help but ask, "Mr. Gunderson, what's a hypothetical example of one of these fractals?"

"Wart," Gunderson answered, "I'll do better than that. I'll describe one of our actual planned Chaos fractal actions. Understand, the Chaos plan was developed in tandem with Typhon's strategy over quite a few years. Some parts of it are templates waiting to be completed; others are defined down to a tactical level. The plan, however, is dynamic and is always in flux. Over the next few days we will work on setting the priorities and filling in the blanks and then we will launch Chaos at the level of intensity required to ensure Typhon cannot be stopped by anyone or anything! So Wart, in answer to your question, one of our fractal operations is to assassinate the Prime Minister of Israel."

Even the three hard-core terrorists couldn't hide their dismay as they assimilated this answer. Gunderson continued undeterred and said, "and that op is among the more conservative prime fractals that head up the list. So, starting tomorrow, we will begin to fill in the blanks for over 100 Chaos actions. Each one will be prioritized and sequenced. Each one will be modeled for outcomes and each outcome will be vetted for contraindications with other actions much like you would assess the risks of taking multiple drugs. We will begin at 10:00 am tomorrow morning in the computer center, which is in the adjacent communications building. Jefferey, you and I will be breakfasting with Ms. Snow at 7:00 am, followed by a private session with the three of us from 8:00 am to 9:30 am in my study in the residence. It is long past the time for her to convince us which team she's on."

♦

Snow awoke from a troubled sleep to the soft chime of the guest phone on the mahogany nightstand next to her bed. She lifted the handset and a voice message intoned, "Ms. Snow please join my father and me in the main dining room for breakfast at 7 am, Jefferey Gunderson." Jasmine glanced at the intricately carved grandmother clock as it began its melodious chiming, 6 am. After a quick shower, she donned the casual field outfit she had packed in the small duffle she had brought a lifetime ago in London. She needed to look like a serious agent, so she went light on the makeup, pulled her jet-black hair back and donned a brown turtleneck, beige kakis and work boots and headed for the door. It was locked from the outside. *Nice trick,* she thought, *locking your guests in, that's one kind of paranoid.* A light tap on the door and it swung noiselessly in, now entirely filled by an enormous figure that beckoned her to follow him.

Peter Gunderson and his son were already seated sipping large mugs of steaming coffee as Jasmine approached their table. "Well, good morning Ms. Snow," Peter said graciously as he rose to pull her chair out. "I hope you slept well?" he asked.

"Very well," she lied, "thank you."

"I hope you're hungry," Peter continued. "Our chef prepared a wonderful breakfast buffet."

Actually, she was starving, since it had been pretty slim pickings on the jet. Once the three had filled their plates and returned to the table, Gunderson again initiated the conversation.

"Ms. Snow, I would appreciate you telling me about your operation since you took over our London office and specifically what transpired over the last couple days."

Snow spent the rest of the breakfast hour describing her work since being hired. It was pretty innocuous stuff, but both men appeared very intent as she droned on. Before she could begin describing her last few days, Peter said, "excuse me Ms. Snow, but why don't we repair to my study and we'll continue our discussion. The staff will be clearing our table and we will be less disturbed there. We have fresh coffee service there or you are welcome to bring yours with you," he politely offered.

Gunderson's study, like most of his spaces, was large and opulent. The decor was warm with lots of exotic wood pieces and oversized chairs and a massive stone fireplace at one end. One wall had a double glass slider that opened up to a large brick patio guarded be a simple low wrought iron fence just inside a neatly trimmed boxwood hedge. The view of the manicured lawn and swaying grass fields running all the way to the distant mountains was, in a word, magnificent.

Once seated in the study, Gunderson requested, "please continue Ms. Snow."

"As I was saying," she complied, "the day before I received Wart's first message about the U.S. intelligence intervention, I was taking my lunch break on a walk near my office, when I was approached by a stranger. He was asking for directions and we struck up a conversation. We spent about an hour together and before I returned to my office, he asked me to dinner that night."

Over the course of the next hour, Snow described every detail of her time with Mac Sisco including his admission of his real objective and his identity. While she didn't go into any detail, she readily acknowledged their brief tryst and the planning they had done together in London, the meeting with Joe Franklin in Paris and their plan to ambush the Typhon team in their safe house.

She finished her soliloquy by saying, "once Sisco fessed up, I had no option but to convince him that I would turn. If I couldn't convince him, I would have been arrested and interrogated. Even with my training, I might have given up something. Plus," she went on earnestly, "I figured I might be able to stay in the field and screw up their op and save your asses, which by the way, I did."

"What do you mean by that?" Jefferey challenged.

"When I came into your safe house, I could have easily blown your whole gig," she countered. "I was armed when I entered the living room and you and Wart were sitting on your butts like we were all there for tea. Even after you disarmed me, I wasn't shackled, so at any time, including during your altercation with Franklin, I could have easily signaled Sisco to rush the joint while I kept you guys busy. I mean, at that point, two of you were injured and Krishinko was trying to pick you up off the floor!"

"Why didn't you alert us about Apogee being there when you first entered?" asked Jefferey accusingly.

"Jefferey," she fired back, "you should know the answer to that."

"What do you mean?" he asked irritated.

"Well, you took my comms which were in place when I entered. If I had said a word about Franklin and Sisco being outside, I would have blown the operation, including your surprise."

Peter had been listening carefully, evaluating every nuance. He saw no tells. She was confident, firm, even arrogant. There were no pauses or hesitations and her story was solid and the logic sound.

"Look gentlemen," she said as she got his attention, "consider this, if I weren't dedicated to Typhon, I could have easily taken down Wart, the one arm bandit, on the way to the chopper. I could have messed with Krishinko, the guy trying to do complex pilot shit at the controls. I could even have doubled back on you Jefferey, the guy occupied with a prisoner who had already clocked him with his hands tied, or just headed for the hills. So you see, I had numerous opportunities to ruin your plans and I didn't. How do you explain that?" Jasmine asked.

Peter Gunderson paused, then pressed a button on his mobile and out of nowhere Snow's hulking guard appeared and stood silently by the door to the study.

"Ms. Snow, you are nothing if not convincing and though I would like to believe you, there is too much at stake to err on this matter," Peter stated firmly.

"We need to do some additional research, now that we have your whole story and even if you check out, I am going to have to be convinced that you are worth the trouble."

Gunderson turned to the big guard and ordered, "please escort Ms. Snow back to her suite."

As Snow turned to leave, she addressed Peter Gunderson, "Mr. Gunderson, don't wait too long. Whatever you're doing next, I can assure you, I could help. I've been in this business a long time and I know a lot about how your enemies operate on both sides of the pond."

♦

When Mac and the team arrived in Auckland, they checked in with the NZ U.S. Consultant General on their logistics. They had set up camp in the Lighter Quay Complex on the eastern side of the Viaduct Harbour. The weary travelers gathered in the large great room overlooking the Harbor, enjoying the warm breeze wafting in through the open French doors to the expansive terrace. It was late afternoon and everyone with favorite beverage in hand from the well-stocked bar, relaxed for the first time after the brutal flight.

Mac waited patiently as the conversation began to trail off and almost apologetically tapped his frosted glass of Steinlager to get everyone's attention. He cleared his throat and began. "I am glad that we are back together at this juncture of the operation, because I believe that our most challenging work is still ahead. Now that I have dispensed with the melodramatic portion of my lecture, let me bring everyone up to speed on where we are and then we can begin to figure out where we're going from here."

Over the next hour Mac reviewed the salient details of the operation, first from 50,000 feet and then summarized each of the sub-assignments, allowing further explanations from each of the sub-teams and open discussion. The dialogue was thoughtful and productive, but most of the questions revolved around their new mystery partner, Jasmine Snow. Mac and Franklin tag teamed on this topic, both being completely frank about their trepidation and the ambiguous challenge she presented. The room fell uncharacteristically silent as Mac concluded the update.

Swan was the first to chime in, "Mac, just to clarify, do we know exactly where Ms. Snow is right now and what kind of logistics we're dealing with?"

"Yes and no," Mac answered. "We know based on the GPS coordinates that her location is about an hour or so drive from here, near the Brunderwyn Ranges. The NSA team is matching the location with NZ real estate records to determine if and how the geography has been developed to give us specifics. They're also scheduling high altitude imaging as soon as one of our satellites is in position, but that might take twenty-four hours. I also requested the Agency to deploy high altitude drone surveillance for images and potential intervention as a last resort. If this is Typhon's new HQ, we really need to recover as much intel as we can, so deploying a Predator with Hellfire missiles is not our preferred outcome."

"At this point," Mac continued, "I think we all need some serious shut eye, since I have a feeling we may not see much of that for a while. Hopefully, by tomorrow, we should have most of our data and can build our plan. So," Mac concluded, "let's meet for breakfast at 0700 tomorrow and plan to start our work at 0800 sharp."

CHAPTER FIVE

CHAOS

James Clausen waited patiently outside the Oval Office for his invitation to enter. President Holbrook was known for his punctuality and as the ornate Grandfathers clock in the hall struck its fifth chime on its way to ten, the big door quietly opened, and Clausen was waived in.

"Come on in and take a load off," invited President Steven Holbrook, smiling at his old friend, as he approached Clausen to shake his hand. "How about some coffee," he offered.

"That would be wonderful," replied Clausen, "I'll add it to the three cups I've already consumed, if you'll excuse me if I suddenly start climbing the walls." Holbrook laughed heartily and took a seat behind his desk.

"Jim, because of the nature of our discussion today and the LIP work we are both doing, I have taken the liberty of inviting Leon Fowler, Deputy Director, NSC. Leon has been personally managing the coordination of our NSC activities and is also heading up our LIP protocol."

"Yes, I know Leon," replied Clausen. "I'm sure his insight would be very helpful."

The President pressed on his intercom and announced, "please ask Leon to come in."

Moments later, after the gratuities, the three men took their seats around the colonial coffee table to discuss the fate of America.

President Holbrook opened the discussion, turning to the Admiral and asked, "Jim, please give us an update on NSA's LIP status." Clausen proceeded to outline the Stabler investigation and its results. He included his planned charade of feeding Stabler inaccurate information designed to expose and disrupt Typhon.

"This is great work, Jim," exclaimed the President.

Fowler enthusiastically agreed. "I wish I could report as much success," Fowler admitted meekly. "We currently have five ops in play in our phase one run, but so far none of them have identified any wrongdoing. We plan to run another LIP action and expand it to target ten additional secondary level assets once our phase one runs are exhausted."

"My expectation," continued Fowler, "is that this threat has so many tentacles that we'll flush out several moles before we run out of prospects. I am very interested, Admiral," Fowler continued, "in what kinds of dis-information are you planning to feed Stabler to counter Typhon? It seems to me that dovetailing with your obfuscation might be a good strategy."

"To be candid, Leon, we haven't gotten that far yet," replied Clausen, "but I anticipate a recommendation from my team very soon and will keep you in the loop on our progress."

"That would be great," Fowler said, gratefully.

Clausen turned to the President and asked, "Sir can we move on to NATCOG and the global M initiatives?"

"Certainly," responded the President. "My outreach was reasonably successful. We are now at over 100 countries who have formally joined our coalition, and more are on the way. The EU is still recalcitrant even though we now have more than half their members enrolled. France and Germany continue to flagellate themselves over the decision, but my guess is that they will be late to the party and may miss it altogether. NATCOG members have agreed to a series of common preemptive actions focused primarily on strengthening their governing structures. They will also be assessing and eliminating their vulnerabilities and countering the prime disruptions we are all experiencing, such as fake media, educational practices focused on social engineering and critical race theory, cancel culture and revisionist activism as well as the ramped attacks on the rule of law. All the members have also expressed a strong concern about the growing globalism that threatens their sovereignty."

Turning to Leon, the President asked, "do you have anything to add?"

"Your description is spot on," Fowler said. "I would say, in addition, the real power of the way NATCOG members are approaching their specific challenges is to do it their local way. This means that there will be many different approaches from which we can all learn. As a result, we should know quickly, what solutions work and why."

"Yes," the president agreed, "it's a good model. Have we seen any particular actions that are working," he continued.

"Well, it's obviously still early, Mr. President, but your own executive action on prohibiting certain educational programs in federal agencies that promote anti-American concepts or terrorist principles are being replicated in several other countries."

Admiral Clausen added, "also Sir, re-introducing patriotic educational practices like the Pledge of Allegiance, etc. supports an overall theme of nationalism that has been sorely lacking. I might also add, your executive action of enforcing and strengthening the penalty for defacing federal property and statues has had an immediate effect here and abroad."

"What about the media, any progress there," the President asked.

Fowler shook his head, "unfortunately no. Oh, there are members who have taken draconian measures to mute their media, but we can't employ those actions here, of course, even if we wanted to. That said, many countries are considering actions against the social media companies for their biased censorship."

"All in all, a lot of good work and it's a beginning, but I fear in some ways it may be too little too late," the President sighed.

"We certainly can't afford to lose any more ground, that is for sure," agreed Admiral Clausen.

"How about on your end Admiral," Fowler asked. "How are we doing with the Apogee team?"

"Actually, the team has made significant progress in the short time it has been active," Clausen replied. "How much do you know Leon, so I don't cover old ground?"

"I think I am up to speed through Set Three for two of the teams," Fowler answered, "but I haven't heard how the international activity went."

Clausen spent the next thirty minutes describing Mac and Joe Franklin's activities through the Paris operation.

"What about the MI-6 woman, can she be trusted?" Fowler asked.

"At this point, we can't say. Her story is entirely feasible and probably true. What we can't judge is what her real intent is and because we can't trust her implicitly, we must consider her on the dark side."

Before Clausen could go on, Leon exclaimed, "the intel you garnered in New York and the Cayman Islands was enormously valuable to us and our allies, but it sounds like, unfortunately, the Paris operation missed the mark."

"I have to disagree Leon," responded Clausen. "I haven't quite finished the story. You see, Mac planted a bug on Ms. Snow and the Agency tracked it until it mysteriously stopped functioning somewhere over the South China Sea. We originally assumed that the aircraft was lost in a storm, but several days later Mac Sisco received an unsourced text indicating she was alive. NSA was then able to intercept the source of the text and track it to what appears to be, its final destination. Even as we speak," the Admiral continued, "we are overflying the area, gathering aerials and the entire team is already on station and preparing an assault plan."

Fowler looked stunned as he exclaimed, "well I'll be damned Admiral, my apologies. I would sure hate to be on the other side. Your guys seem to beat the odds every time. It's certainly a good thing you can block Stabler from feeding Typhon any valid intel or Gunderson would already know about your attack."

"Your right about that," answered Clausen. "That's why it's so crucial that we keep Martin from knowing his cover has been blown and continue our LIP protocol actions to ferret out any other traitors. We have no margin of error. We simply can't afford to allow Typhon any advanced insights into what we are planning."

President Holbrook interjected, "Admiral Clausen is on the mark as always, Leon. Even if we can neutralize Typhon, we may not be able to stop what they have started, especially if his theories on Chaos are correct."

"What exactly are those theories Admiral?" Fowler asked. Once again, Clausen took the floor and updated the Deputy Director of the NSC on NSA's hypothesis on Chaos.

Again, Fowler's jaw dropped in surprise at the scale of the problem.

"Mr. President, if the Admiral is correct, how should we deal with the NATCOG members?"

Holbrook answered solemnly, "of course we must immediately inform them. But we would be premature to do that yet, since we are still speculating. Any leaks could cause a worldwide panic, which would be catastrophic and only exacerbate the already combustible environment."

"Yes Mr. President, I agree," responded Fowler.

"That said," countered Holbrook, "I would rather pull the trigger too soon than too late and I will. We need to give our allies notice so that they can prepare, especially in deepening their security."

More than anyone, James Clausen understood all this and its implications. The ball was clearly in his court and he would soon have to make a call one way or the other.

"Yes," Clausen responded, "Typhon's Chaos may well include some very severe measures including assassinassions of heads of state, country level insurrections, significant mass terrorist attacks and even biological interventions on select targets or en mass. Once any of this begins and expands, we will have an uncontrollable worldwide panic from which there might be no defense or recovery."

Clausen continued gravely, "I have instructed my agency team to make a final recommendation on Chaos and its likely implications within forty-eight hours and I am pushing Team Apogee to execute their plan within that same timeframe." Both Holbrook and Fowler nodded and agreed to meet again prior to any final action as the meeting came to an end. There was nothing more to say. It was up to Clausen now!

◆

Leon Fowler left the oval office without making any of his usual rounds visiting with staff and executive office dignitaries, as was his usual custom. He had much to do and little time to do it. Fowler had been in public service his entire adult career and at just forty-two years old was on the fast track in the bubble that was Washington, D.C. His recent appointment to Deputy Director of the NSC put him in constant touch with all the real movers and shakers in government. Even more important, was his status and the relationships he was making with the intelligence community. Not only was he on a first name basis with the directors of the FBI, CIA, DIA, NSA, Justice Department and Homeland Security, but he had been careful to work down the chain of command in each agency as well. Yes, his career was skyrocketing, and he had to keep it that way, at least for a while.

The problem was that Fowler's ambition was only exceeded by his impatience and he didn't plan to spend his years on screwing around with Washington politics. He wanted it all and soon and he needed a clear path with high odds and Leon Fowler figured that path was through Typhon. He had been looking for just this kind of break for the last year. He was perfectly positioned in the NSC and when he was first briefed on POTUS' plans and the NSC role, he knew this was his chance and he wouldn't squander it. At first, he had believed that he could use Typhon as his launching point to catapult his career in D.C. But as he gained more insight into what Typhon was doing and their real probability of pulling it off, he arrived at a very different conclusion. The fact was, there would be a winner and a loser and Leon Fowler was going to make sure he was a very major player on the winner's team.

It had been way too risky to begin a direct dialogue with Typhon until the time was absolutely right. And that time appeared to be fast approaching. To make that happen, two things had to be in place. First, he had to be able to maintain his anonymity as he worked both sides. This was critical to guarantee that he would benefit, no matter who prevailed. It also was crucial to protect his personal security, since both organizations would eliminate him without a second thought if necessary. Secondly, he needed to have the right leverage with Typhon and that meant providing them with invaluable information that would readily be traded for wealth, power, stature and preferably all three when the time came. Today's meeting had been the final key to everything. The first challenge, maintaining his confidentiality, had been a serious conundrum. Everything he did was monitored and he had struggled with a way around it. He had to be able to communicate directly with Peter Gunderson to make his pitch. But in today's meeting, the answer had been conveniently dropped in his lap, Stabler!

Of course Leon knew Martin Stabler and had actually shared drinks and an occasional dinner out with the Admiral's assistant as part of his networking agenda, but he had not been updated about his treasonous acts until today. Now he saw clearly how he could use Stabler as a conduit to Gunderson. He had already texted Martin; inviting him to have a drink at a local watering hole that evening after work and had gotten a return thumbs up. He would use that opportunity to inform him that his cover was blown and that his future looked very grim unless he played ball with Leon. He would explain that he would keep quiet about his disclosure so long as Stabler would work with him, including sending encrypted messages to Gunderson. If Martin did as he was told, Fowler would keep him in the loop, so he could bolt at the right time and avoid arrest or if Typhon prevailed. Fowler would help make sure he was taken care of. If Martin did not comply, Fowler would ensure that he was quickly arrested and begin a new life behind bars.

It was perfect, Martin not only knew Peter Gunderson, but had a way to get to him and get his attention. Leon would take it from there. The second item, his bargaining chip, was of, course, not just the future value of Leon's position on the NSC and how that would benefit Typhon, but the immediate information regarding NATCOG's and NSA's plans, including the imminent attack on Typhon's new headquarters. If Gunderson had advanced information about the impending assault, he could not only defend his HQ, but maybe even capture the NSA team. It would also allow him the opportunity to build a legal case against the U.S. assault and provide him time to execute any contingencies he might have planned, including launching this alleged

Chaos operation. Leon smiled, only a couple of steps and his future was golden, no matter what the outcome!

◆

At 6:00 pm that evening Martin Stabler walked through the doors of Oliver's Old Town Bar in Laurel, Md. and spied Leon Fowler seated in a booth at the back of the bar sipping a pint of dark beer. Martin had been excited to get the invitation from the Deputy Director and though they were acquaintances, he didn't know him well. It was rare to have someone of Fowler's stature invite you for drinks unless there was a good reason. Martin was dying of curiosity. Maybe Fowler was going to recruit him for a new position. He walked up to the booth and took a seat as Fowler reached out to shake his hand.

"Nice to see you again Martin," greeted Fowler, "it's been a while."

"Yes it has," responded Stabler, "great to see you too, Leon."

"Sorry, I started without you," Fowler said, "it's been a long day."

"No worries," replied Stabler. "I'll just step up to the bar and grab a quick Mic."

"So, what's been going on?" Fowler asked when Stabler had taken his seat, beer in hand.

"Actually, as I am sure you know, quite a bit," Stabler replied.

"Right," answered Fowler, "same for me. I would say things are beginning to heat up rapidly," he continued.

"You could say that again," Stabler agreed.

"Actually, that is the reason I wanted to meet with you Martin," Fowler replied, leaning forward and lowering his voice.

Stabler's countenance darkened as he detected a sense of menace in the other man's voice.

"Hold on Leon, you know we can't discuss any details about our work, so I regret I won't be able to have that kind of conversation."

"I am afraid you have no choice, Martin," Fowler shot back, "and I can assure you it is in your best interest to listen to me very carefully."

Martin put up his hand in objection and began to rise from the booth, when Leon said calmly, "your cover as a Typhon informant has been blown, Martin!"

In that moment Martin's vision began to blur and the room began to spin as he collapsed back to the leather-cushioned bench. "What are you talking about?" he objected in a meager attempt to deny such an absurd accusation.

"Don't bother," replied Fowler, growling. "Clausen ran an LIP on you and you failed miserably. That was what your little trip to Pennsylvania was all about. Clausen had a team of counter terrorist agents surveil the whole gig. And before you even arrived, they picked up an imposter, posing as you, to meet the imaginary witness and do the hit. They already have him in custody and are grilling him as we speak. I don't imagine he will last long, but it doesn't matter because Clausen knows you exposed the whole thing to Gunderson in advance."

Fowler almost felt sorry for this loser, as he stared into the vacant eyes of a man destroyed. But, in life there are sheep and there are wolves and Stabler was just one of the herd.

"Oh my God," came the muffled groan as Stabler covered his face with his hands.

"Calm down Martin," commanded Fowler, "how would you like a lifeline?"

Stabler looked up, eyes swollen, "what do you mean?"

"Well Martin, as it turns out I may be able to throw you a preserver."

Confused, Stabler blurted out, "a preserver?"

"Yes Martin," if you do exactly what I say, you might survive this whole ordeal. In fact, you might even come out on top, as it were."

"What kind of things?" Stabler asked hopefully.

"I am interested in communicating with the top dog in Typhon, who I believe to be Mr. Peter Gunderson and you apparently have a direct line to him. Furthermore, you seem to be able to connect with him in a way that avoids discovery, which is also a necessity for me, Martin. Is that something you can do for me?"

"Yes," Martin stammered, "I think I can arrange that."

"You think or you can?" demanded Fowler harshly.

"I can, I can," stuttered Martin quickly. "But how can you help me? Clausen and others now know I am an informant. How can you undo that?" he asked, perplexed.

"I can't undo your stupidity, Martin, but what I can do is to give you advanced warning before they make a move on you."

"But even if I can avoid arrest, where can I run, where can I hide?" Stabler asked, again appearing to lose it.

"That's part of my negotiation with Gunderson," smiled Leon. "I will ensure that you are taken care of. Even if Typhon were to fail, they obviously possess enormous resources all over the world and as a part of my deal, they will provide you the cover you need to start a new life. I may even be able to parlay a top slot for you in their organization."

Stabler's mind was racing, could this work? Maybe, but two things were deal breakers and he had to be sure they were solid.

Stabler, straightened up, trying to regain his composure and asked, "OK, Leon, you have clearly gotten my attention, but please answer two questions." Fowler nodded in agreement.

"First," Martin continued, "how are you going to convince Gunderson to play ball with you and what's in it for you?"

Fowler grinned and asked, "Martin, did you have any trouble working a lucrative deal with Gunderson?"

"Uh, no. I didn't even negotiate because his offer was so good," responded Martin.

"Wouldn't you say my position and access to information is off the charts more than yours?" Fowler continued.

"Yes, I see your point," Stabler answered embarrassed.

"As far as the second part of that question, my objective is not your concern, nor is it relevant to your situation. Is that all Martin?"

Stabler's eyes narrowed, "but how can I trust you?" he blurted out.

Fowler's grin turned cruel as he replied, "well Martin you can't, but what choice do you have. If you try to make a deal with Clausen and play both sides in a plea bargain or attempt to implicate me in any way, I will crush you. Remember, you have committed treason against your country and that is punishable by life in prison or death and I am the Deputy Director of the National Security Council of the U.S. I wonder who my friends in Washington will believe."

Stabler had his answers and he had no options. This was the best deal he would ever get, and he knew it.

"Alright then, do we have an agreement?" Fowler asked again.

Stabler, now thoroughly defeated, nodded and said, "yes we do Leon."

"Wonderful," laughed Fowler, "now let's order another drink and celebrate our new partnership and get down to business and I'll layout what you need to do."

It really hadn't taken that long. Fowler congratulated himself as he strapped into his Porsche 911 Turbo and accelerated out of the tavern parking lot. They had only needed another forty-five minutes to conclude their planning. He had learned exactly how Martin communicated with Gunderson and was convinced that it was indeed secure. The backup mobile was also useful for tactical communications and might come in handy. He had to hand it to Gunderson, he was a top tier operator for sure and he had a feeling that this capability was just the tip of the iceberg for Typhon. Fowler had already drafted a succinct message to Gunderson and provided it to Stabler with the mandate to get it to Gunderson the next morning. In it he included his personal introduction and outlined the terms of his agreement and the urgent timeline required for a response. In essence, Gunderson, needed to agree to Fowler's offer and respond quickly so that Leon could deliver his urgent intelligence. Leon was counting on the fact that the leverage of his position and the urgent nature of his information would be too enticing for Gunderson to ignore. *Only time would tell,* he thought to himself, but it wouldn't be long. At exactly 2 pm tomorrow, Stabler would encrypt his note to Gunderson and minutes later, 9,000 miles away, Gunderson would have a decision to make.

◆

He was already on his second cup of coffee at 8:30 am a day later when Peter Gunderson's emergency notification alerted him. Expecting a call from either his contract hit man or Stabler confirming the kill, he grabbed his mobile, and quickly retrieved the message. As he read the message his eyes widened in surprise. This was indeed an unexpected opportunity, he thought. Over the years, Typhon had recruited some extraordinary resources, but few were positioned as well as Mr. Fowler, nor had any presumed to demand these kinds of terms. Even more outrageous was the need to make a decision and reply in two hours because the intel was so time sensitive. In some ways Gunderson felt like he was being held hostage, but if the information was as critical to Typhon's success as Fowler bragged, then maybe it all made sense.

The one demand that did add credence to Fowler's deal was that it included a commitment for Typhon to bring him into their operation at a level no less than a direct report to Gunderson himself. That intrigued Gunderson. This guy was willing to throw away a significant career, give up his country and go to work for Typhon. Fascinating! He was one cocky SOB. Gunderson would have to take some risk to get the answer and $100 million was just the down payment.

Ninety minutes later, Martin Stabler received an encrypted message from P. Gunderson to L. Fowler but did not decrypt it in his office. He left a note for the Admiral that he was taking a late lunch and left the building and drove home. There he retrieved a recently purchased burn phone and called an unlisted number.

A voice quickly answered, "yes Martin."

Martin replied, "I just received a message from Gunderson."

"Please read it to me," answered Fowler.

Stabler read the note carefully, "Mr. Fowler, I agree to all your terms and will forward the upfront fee to your designated institution immediately. If your information validates as accurate and commensurate, Typhon will honor the remaining terms. Please acknowledge, to finalize your agreement."

Fowler could hardly contain his excitement as he struggled to reply, "please acknowledge my agreement, Martin, and send the intelligence information we discussed immediately. We certainly want it all to be actionable so that Mr. Gunderson gets what he is paying for," Fowler directed as he closed the call.

"Damn," he said out loud after hanging up, "that was easier than I expected." *I hope I didn't low-ball my offer. No,* he thought, *beauty is in the eye of the beholder* and it remained to be seen if Gunderson would appreciate the beauty of his intel as much as he did. Oh well, worst case, $100 million for his trouble and best case, a half billion and a new job. Not bad for a couple days work, he whistled. All he needed now was to confirm the deposit and everything was a go.

At 10:30 am NZ time that morning Gunderson received confirmation of his new partnership and instructed one of his Swiss Banks to transfer $100 million into a private account in the Cayman Islands. Thirty minutes later, his computer alerted him to another message from L. Fowler via M. Stabler's encryption program at the National Security Agency. Gunderson immediately instructed the system to pull up the message and began reading.

Once again, there were several folders identified with brief headers. The first of them was entitled, Overview - Immediate Threat

Assessment. He opened the folder and began reading. The report focused on three major threats to Typhon's immediate activities. The first described the discovery of Martin Stabler's relationship with Typhon through a Leak Information Process (LIP) conducted by Admiral James Clausen, Director, NSA. It detailed the case and the setup as well as the arrest of Typhon's contract hit man. There was no mention in the overview or later in the detail about NSA's insights into exactly what Stabler had disclosed to Typhon. It also included the NSA strategy to keep Stabler in play and feed him fraudulent information to disrupt Typhon's actions.

The second threat referenced Chaos. Apparently, in the skirmish between Jefferey Gunderson and his team and Sisco and Franklin, the U.S. agents had overheard the reference to Chaos and reported it to Clausen who had assigned an agency team to do a deep dive and come up with some theories about it. Fowler reported that during the NSC meeting he attended, Clausen briefed POTUS that NSA's best guess was that it could be an extension of the Chaos Theory but were still working on the details.

The third threat took Gunderson's breath away. Team Apogee had planted a bug on the MI-6 woman and had tracked her travel to New Zealand. At that very hour that team was in Auckland, location unknown, planning their next move against Gunderson and his organization. No specific timetable was set, but it was anticipated that they would act very soon. Gunderson wasted no time as he grabbed his mobile and hit the speed dial for his son.

"Yes sir," came back the immediate response.

"Jefferey," Peter Gunderson snarled, "get Krishinko and Von Stemp and get over to my office right away. We have a serious problem!"

CHAPTER SIX

TWISTS AND TURNS

The news was not good as the Apogee team poured over the aerial photos of the property officially registered as the Ardyh Ranch. The (LEO) low earth orbit images from the KH-11 satellite that had been transmitted to the team from Joint Defense Facility Pine Gap in Australia were amazingly sharp. Further detail had also been provided by a Predator Drone over flight. There was no question about the challenge they faced. There were well over a hundred armed militants camped out strategically on the 500 acres with a concentration of them guarding the perimeter of a large compound. There was a half dozen buildings situated on a plateau at the center of the ranch. It would take a small army to overcome that force and any overt attack would eliminate the only advantage they had, stealth.

The team spent the better part of their first day in Auckland mulling over exactly what their mission was. The news from NSA regarding Chaos and their theory of what it might encompass complicated matters as well. The Agency reasoned that most of Chaos' disruptions would already be in stasis waiting for the trigger that would set them off. In all likelihood, Gunderson would have programmed numerous triggers that would initiate these actions automatically. They could be event-based, time-based, command-based or even combinations that would be almost impossible to determine or deactivate. If this was true, there was only one mission approach. They needed to uncover all the Chaos plan details in time to prevent their activation. Of course, that information would most certainly be recorded somewhere. It would be much too detailed to be held in one's head, even for a paranoid egomaniac like Gunderson and access to that data was likely to be somewhere on the compound. And then there was Gunderson and his lieutenants. They would also possess a thorough understanding of Chaos, its targets and its schedule.

Mac and the team knew an aggressive assault could be launched with a single phone call. A couple of MQ-9 Reaper drones cruising in at 230 mph armed with up to four Hellfire missiles or Paveway II or GBU-12 bombs each could incinerate the entire plateau in minutes. But while that would cut the head off the serpent, it wouldn't stop Typhon. Mac also knew that Peter Gunderson would understand all this and would have designed Chaos and his own security accordingly.

Mac had broken the team into the same twosomes as their last assignments with each working on different aspects of the problem and it was time to get a read out and pull all the pieces together.

He broke into the buzz of conversation and said, "OK guys, let's see where we are. Let me overview the mission first and then we can discuss the elements and barriers. Our objective is to recover the Chaos Plan that, of course, assumes that NSA is correct in their hypothesis. The mission can only be accomplished by a stealth operation. If all else fails and we determine Typhon's leaders are expendable and there is value in taking out the HQ, I will call in a Reaper to do the work. It will already be staged from Pine Gap and be on station, so once I make the call, we need to be off the property within fifteen minutes."

"OK," Mac instructed, "let's start with how we get onto the property without being detected. Pat and Carrie, what have you got?"

"We really have only one option, Mac," responded Curry, "and that is to HALO jump in."

"And we need to do it at night," added Swan. "It takes way too long, and the risk is too great to hike in. They have bad guys everywhere and even one slip up and we're made, not to mention they outnumber us fifteen to one."

Curry further emphasized, "we need to come in high to avoid detection as well as ground fire."

"Makes sense," said Mac, "but how do we navigate to the plateau from 25,000 feet?"

"Well first," Swan answered, "the drop zone will be modeled considering wind speed so that our dive will position us directly over the target when we deploy our chutes at 3,000 feet."

"Then we'll navigate to the target two ways," Curry interjected. "Based on our nocturnal aerials, the compound uses powerful perimeter security lighting all night. The place will be lit up like a circus. Also, as a backup we will each be equipped with a fancy military GPS navigation system that can very precisely guide us to the residence's coordinates."

"OK, how do we get past the perimeter security guards?" Mac asked.

Swan, smiled and said, "that is for Peter and Elaine to answer, thankfully."

Elaine Warsaw responded in her very British accent, "indeed it is, and the answer is, we don't!"

"Ha, Ha," laughed Franklin, "good answer Elaine, but seriously how do we get past their twenty or so guards?"

Peter Singe piped in, "Joe, Elaine is right, we don't get past them because we can't get past them." Joe looked dumbstruck but waited for the explanation he knew had to be coming.

Singe went on, "we have to land on the roof of the residence. It has a very slight pitch because of the high winds that blow through on occasion and there are no lights shining upwards, so it is completely shrouded in darkness."

"That does call for some pretty tight precision on the landing," Mac stated.

"Yes it does indeed," Warsaw responded, "but it eliminates a whole raft of difficulties. Our biggest challenge will be to accomplish it quietly and contain our chutes rapidly," she finished.

"It also means that the wind on the plateau at the time we land needs to be below ten mph."

Curry asked, "not to ask the obvious, but what is the average wind this time of year up there?"

"Actually," Singe said, "we are quite fortunate. In this season, the winds are generally mild, from five to fifteen mph. Also, at night the wind dies down and its lowest point is at about 2 am. We have reviewed the weather data over the last thirty days, and it supports that historical trend. We have also checked the forecast for the next week and it looks calm, at least for the next three or four days."

"It seems so far our approach has been literally preordained," Mac observed. "It's like there is only one path we can take and that is the one you guys have developed. So, how do we penetrate from the roof?" he asked.

"Peter, you want to take that one," Warsaw offered.

"Sure," he replied, "we have two options. There are four skylights on the roof that can be breeched. According to the original house plans, they are constructed of thick glass, which can be cut with a portable laser and suctioned off. While the roof is relatively high, it is a one-story edifice and we can deploy down a grapple line from there. That is also our way off the side of the home if we determine that the skylights are not feasible once we are on sight."

"Guys, that is some terrific stuff you have put together," Mac exclaimed.

"No kidding," agreed Franklin, "but one thing is for sure, this is going to have to be perfectly executed or we are toast!"

"That is true," said Mac, "and we haven't even started the real work."

Everyone nodded grimly, but Warsaw always the cheery one, said, "but think of how many insurmountable obstacles we've already conquered."

Mac smiled appreciatively and said, "thanks Elaine, for bringing well deserved optimism back to the fore. OK, Joe, let's talk about finding Chaos."

"Right," responded Franklin, as he reviewed his notes. "So here's the deal," the big Seal explained. "According to the builder's plans for the residence that the Agency acquired, the main building is 25,000 square feet. The most obvious location for securing confidential records is in Peter Gunderson's private office vault or in his computer and communications center, which is a building adjacent to the residence. At two am, the principals will most likely be in their private suites. We have no specific intel on how many guards may be in the residence, but we can assume that every member including Jasmine Snow has a personal security guard assigned to their space. That would be at least six guards and we imagine at least another four are general security inside the main house."

Singe said, "that's a lot of muscle. I can't wait to hear how we neutralize all these bad actors without alerting anyone."

"Our approach follows the same logic as yours," Franklin explained. "Mac and I basically eliminated all the approaches that would not work and were left with only one that could be successful. The architectural plans identify where all the power and HVAC systems are. Once we penetrate the residence, I will immediately enter their utility room and diffuse an incapacitating gas into the HVAC system. The gas will take less than five minutes to permeate the entire residence and in under ten minutes all the residents without a mask will fall unconscious. Once the gas stops, the effects last thirty minutes and then those affected will begin to recover."

"Wow," Curry said, "I really like this, so far no blood and guts stuff."

Mac said, "that's kind of a critical success factor for this entire op. Any major skirmish alerts the entire hostile force and we can't let that happen or be around if it does."

"So, what are the assignments, once everyone is snoozing?" asked Swan.

"You and Pat make a short run to the Computer center and do your usual stuff. Locate the files and pull the drives so we can extricate with the data," Mac responded. "Peter, you and Elaine secure the principals, Peter Gunderson, Jefferey Gunderson, Nicholi Krishinko and Wart Von Stemp. Zip tie them and gag them with duct tape and meet us at the exit across from the helicopter hanger building identified in the builder's drawings. Joe and I will secure all the guards the same way and Joe will then join Elaine and Peter to help control our captives. Peter, once Joe relieves you, make it to the hanger and check out the helicopter. Our NSA intel identified the chopper from NZ airport records as a Sikorsky S-76D helicopter similar to the one we borrowed from LeMaster and Peter piloted. It will be tight, but we can get all of us on board for a rapid exit."

"Where will you be Mac?" Warsaw asked.

"I will find Snow and bring her out and meet you guys at the exit point."

Franklin, looked up and asked, "will she come out in chains?" The whole team's attention turned to their boss as he replied.

"That is my current plan," he answered soberly.

"You know it all sounds peachy," said Swan, "but pulling that chopper out of the hanger, firing it up and loading all our sorry asses on board is not exactly a stealthy exercise. How are we dealing with the Typhon vigilantes in the meantime?"

"That's the other reason we have the MQ-9 Reaper on station," Mac replied. "Once we are in the hanger, I will alert the folks at Pine Gap and the fireworks will begin. I imagine the Typhon folks will be too busy to worry about our little interruption."

♦

Peter Gunderson stalked the room like a caged animal as his team dealt with the latest intelligence from Leon Fowler. The information had stopped short of the specific location of the Apogee team; so sending a kill team to take them out was not yet possible. Unless he could go on the offensive, Gunderson knew that the Agency team would soon make a play. He and his team had run the scenarios and aside from a massive assault, they could not construct another option. There was just no way a small team could penetrate their defenses. They had too many resources on the grounds and around the compound. Any manned air assault could be averted using surface to air missiles or ground weapons. If the U.S. were crazy enough to destroy the compound, it would only delay Chaos for a few days until his global triggers began to automatically activate. Of course, that didn't mean there weren't productive actions he should take.

The first was obvious; relocate crucial leadership to another location until the crisis was over. Gunderson was no coward and the idea of relocating was repugnant, but it was a prudent move and actually reinforced the idea that he, in fact, had died in Philadelphia. After a fiery debate with his subordinates who favored the idea, he finally acquiesced, and it was agreed he would vacate the ranch early in the morning with a digital copy of the encrypted Typhon and Chaos plans. He would travel off road to the Mangawhai coast where his 250-foot yacht, Calamity, would be moored, having travelled up from Auckland's harbor. The craft was of course registered under a pseudonym, so Gunderson would remain in the wind until his team had dealt with this untimely irritation.

They would remain at the ranch on high alert with their squadrons of Typhon troops to greet their uninvited guests. Actually, all three were chomping at the bit for another shot at Team Apogee. He had little doubt about the outcome this time. Either way, it wouldn't be long, they had completed most of the Chaos planning and what remained he could finish at sea. In the meantime, he would press his new partner Mr. Fowler to get him a location in Auckland where Sisco and his team were held up. If they got that information before the American moved on Typhon, and he could launch a counterattack, all the better.

◆

Jasmine Snow was climbing the walls. It had been over twenty-four hours since her meeting with the Gunderson boys and she had no idea where she stood. She had misjudged Peter Gunderson's paranoia and unless she could assuage his distrust, she had no doubt he would discard her like damaged goods. Her problem was, she had no idea how to do that. Even though she had disclosed the entire Sisco affair, it hadn't been enough to gain his trust and she didn't understand that. She had nothing left to bargain with. Unless she could come up with an answer very soon, she had to escape somehow. She was also keenly aware that if Mac and his team caught up with Typhon, she would be caught in the crossfire.

Jasmine had been in the game a long time and she knew the longer she delayed, the less options she would have. She shrugged and said, "bloody hell, I've got to move now." Getting by the hulk outside her door was not realistic, so she opened the slider to her terrace and innocently stepped outside to get some air. Several guards were stationed at intervals across the illuminated, manicured lawn. Their primary focus was away from the house, but periodically they turned to observe the residence. She returned to her suite, laced up her work boots, grabbed a beer and strolled back outside as if to enjoy the star filled, late evening sky. After a few minutes, she purposely dropped the beer mug on the ground, shattering the glass. As the sound reverberated off the building, she loudly cursed, "oh shit!" The closest guard quickly turned and stared at her as she yelled out, "sorry, just dropped my damn beer! I guess, I've had enough for the evening," she garbled as she staggered back into her suite, leaving the patio door open.

She retired to the bedroom, switching off the lights as she went. She grabbed the TV remote and tuned in on the late-night news. She waited a few more minutes and turned off the bedroom lights as well. The suite went dark. Finally, she placed the two king sized pillows under the covers simulating a person sleeping and moved silently into the suite's kitchen. There she retrieved two steak knives with serrated edges and crept to the terrace doorway. Her first inclination had been to sneak up behind the guard, slit his throat and make a run for it across the lawn and away from the residence, but she knew that was very high risk. She peeked out the door, looking left and right along the side of the house, and noticed for the first time that most of the windows were dark. *That was the answer,* she thought. Hug the wall and follow it until you find another entrance to the house, then navigate your way to an unguarded exit.

Snow held her breath and very slowly edged out of her suite and along the darkened side of the house, pressing her body into its field stone wall. The first entrance was an identical suite that she ignored. Its entrance would be on her same hall and too close to where her guard was stationed. She continued on, passing up two more suites for the same reason. Further down the side of the house she could see it angle as it began to form its horseshoe shape. Any entrance after that bend was likely to have an exit invisible to the guard. Just before the bend was another guard casually smoking a cigarette while strangely tapping his foot up and down rhythmically. As she approached, she realized why. He had ear buds in and was completely engrossed listening to the music. *Wow, what a break,* she thought as she slid around the corner and out of his view.

The next suite was locked, but the one after it had the slider opened slightly and its screen closed. Looking down this side, more of the rooms had lights on so this had to be it. She crossed its terrace and peered into the darkened room. Someone was definitely staying there, but they were not in the living room. She gently tried to open the screen door and it smoothly slid to the side. Snow stepped inside and closed the screen. She waited until her eyes had adjusted to the darker space and moved deeper into the room, her attention on the bedroom on her left. There was no sound. She heard no slow breathing or other signs of life, so she advanced quickly to the entrance door and opened it soundlessly. A bright shaft of light shot into the suite from the widening crack, as she looked left and right down the long hall. No guards were in view, but she had no choice but to go left away from the big sentry outside her suite.

She continued to move down the hall as quickly as she dared, stopping every few feet to listen for voices, but heard none. It wasn't long, however, when the architecture changed and the rooms no longer appeared to be suites, but other functional spaces. As she carefully rounded another curve, she began to hear low muffled voices coming from the next room. As much as she wanted to retreat, she had no alternative but to pass the closed door without giving herself away. As she approached the door the voices became more distinct and she clearly recognized the autocratic growl of Peter Gunderson. What she heard next literally stopped her in her tracks.

"I am not going to run away like some coward just because a plebeian bureaucrat from NSA shows up," Gunderson snarled.

"Sir," intoned Nicholi Krishinko, "there is no reason for you to remain here. We can have a couple of the guys take you cross-country in the all-terrain vehicle down to the Mangawhai coast where you can board the Calamity unseen. Once you're out to sea, you'll be untraceable and can manage Chaos from there."

"Nicholi is right Dad," Jefferey Gunderson interrupted. "Even with all our security, it's too risky for you to stay. Besides," he continued, "we want another shot at these assholes."

"Yeh," Von Stemp agreed, "it's payback time!"

"Alright, I'll go," said Gunderson, "but I don't like it, especially at this critical juncture. Just make sure you stay in touch and this time, don't screw up, kill those sons of bitches."

"What about the woman?" asked Jefferey.

Gunderson paused and then answered, "she actually might be telling the truth, but there's just no way to be sure, so I'd terminate her. But I'll leave that to you, kill her or keep her; it's your choice. Jefferey, contact my Captain on the Calamity and tell him to get her underway and rendezvous with me at the proper coordinates. I'll contact him from shore, when I get there, so he can send a tender in to pick me up. I'll get my gear and the digital files and plan to leave here at 2 am this morning."

The message was clear, Jasmine had to move fast and get clear of this place. She moved quickly down the hall until she came to a large open foyer leading to the main entrance. She approached the large double doors, opened one slightly and looked out. A large stone porte cochère extended outward and offered good cover. Strangely, she saw no guards, probably because they didn't believe that any interloper would exploit such an obvious entrance. She rushed out the entrance and hid in the shadows behind one of the massive columns.

Across the drive, only about thirty feet away was a large garage that clearly was her next best cover and she sprinted to its door and disappeared inside. Huge overhead lights hung from a high ceiling, but only a few were on, giving the large expanse a dim appearance with long eerie silhouettes of assorted farm equipment, exotic cars and utility vehicles. Thankfully, this time of night, the entire building was unoccupied, so she had the luxury of investigating the vehicles for keys as she considered a high-speed escape. Some of the heavy equipment could be operated, but that wouldn't help her. Even if she had found practical transportation, she realized the impossibility of out running the sentries or their AK 47's. Disgusted, she climbed into one of the vehicles to rest and figure something out.

There had to be an answer, she thought as the kernel of an idea began to gnaw at her. What was it? It was something she heard Gunderson say, but what the hell was it? Damn, it was just out of reach. Frustrated, she put her hands on the wheel of the big four-wheel drive Hummer and then it hit her. This was her way out. Gunderson had agreed to leave the compound in a four-wheel drive vehicle and drive cross-country. This Hummer had to be that vehicle and it was leaving in two hours across his ranch property, bypassing all the guards and troops all the way to the coast and no one would stop him or check him. He was the boss! *Clear sailing all the way,* she thought. She just had to find a place to hide. Excited,

Jasmine scrambled into the back seat. It was huge, but no cubbyholes even for a midget like her. Since this was a military issued vehicle, there was actually a third seat too and behind that was a storage area with a canvas cover buttoned to the sides and back to conceal stored items. She first tested the third seat to see if she could hide under it if she lowered it down. She found she could wedge herself halfway under the seat but would still be exposed unless she covered herself with something. Not bad, but not great either. Then she got out of the car and walked around to the back of the Hummer and lowering the gate and peered underneath the luggage cover. This would work as long as no one looked there.

Could she take the chance? She imagined the scenario at 2 am, when Gunderson and his security guards arrived at the Hummer. There would probably be no more than two of them and the boss. The guards would sit up front and Gunderson would sit in the second seat. It hadn't sounded like he would be packing much, so it was logical that he would put his luggage either beside him on the second seat or behind him in the third one. Odds were in her favor that no one would want to go to the trouble of undoing the canvas in the back-luggage compartment. But just in case they did, she needed some insurance. She finally found what she was after in a pickup truck parked at the rear of the garage. She pulled two large dusty blankets from the back seat and carried them back to the Hummer. Jumping up onto its rear gate, she crawled gingerly into the pitch-black compartment pulling the blankets in with her. She turned back and pulled the lower gate up, then unfastened two buttons on the canvas to allow her to grab the upper door and pull it down and locked it from the inside. Struggling, she redid the buttons and moved forward into a prone position against the back seat. Snow knew this was her best shot and she had done all she could as she pulled the dusty covers over her head and began a long and fretful wait.

She awoke from a fitful sleep, her eyes popping open feeling the slight movement of the vehicle and the sound of one of the doors opening.

"Sir, shall I put your belongings in the seat with you or in the back?" came a voice only a few feet away.

"My luggage can go in the compartment in the back and I'll hold on to my briefcase," Gunderson answered. Snows' heart was in her throat. Shit, she was about to be made! Seconds later, as she tightly gripped one of the steak knives at the ready, she heard the guard pushing down on the back gate handle to open it to no avail.

"What's the hold up?" Gunderson asked impatiently.

"Sorry Sir, the back compartment is locked, and I have to get the key to open it," answered the guard.

"Forget it, just throw it in the seat behind me. I want to get moving," Gunderson commanded. Snow counted the doors as they closed and breathed a sigh of relief as she heard the garage door grind open and the big Hummer slowly pulled away out into the fields on its way to the coast.

CHAPTER SEVEN

LAUNCH

Fowler was just stepping out of the shower at 7 am when his recently purchased burn phone rang. Wrapping himself in a towel, he crossed into his bedroom and retrieved the mobile phone. Seeing the caller ID, he answered, "yes Martin?"

"Leon, something's going on," Stabler said in a panic. "It sounds like your heads up to Gunderson has moved Typhon into action."

"What do you know and what do they need now?" Fowler barked, impatiently.

"I just received a request from Gunderson for the address of Team Apogee's location in Auckland," Stabler replied. "I assume Typhon is about to launch a preemptive strike on Clausen's team."

"So, what's the problem, Martin?" asked Fowler.

"Leon, I don't know that address and I'm out of the loop, remember. Furthermore, even if I could come up with an excuse to request that info, Clausen would give me a fake address, so I would feed it to Sisco, and Typhon would be conveniently ambushed. And by the way Leon, bad intel to Typhon means goodbye to both our futures."

"OK, fair points Martin, obviously somehow I have got to get this information from Clausen or POTUS. That is going to be delicate. How soon do they need it?" Fowler asked.

"That's the second part of the problem," Martin answered, "yesterday!"

"That's what I was afraid of," Fowler said irritated, "but it makes sense now that they have actionable intel. They want to attack Sisco and team before he attacks them and have the advantage of surprise."

Fowler knew that his entire arrangement would be tested by this latest request. He should have seen this coming and gotten the detail in the meeting with Holbrook and Clausen, but even then, he had to be careful of pressing beyond need-to-know policy.

"OK, Martin, get back to Gunderson and tell him I'll get him the information within two hours."

"How in hell do you intend to do that Leon?" Stabler asked.

"Frankly, I don't know yet, but I'll think of a way. Stay cool and stay tuned and be ready to respond the second I contact you," he directed as he hung up the phone. Fowler dressed quickly and poured himself some black coffee to help kick him into gear before he left for his office. On the one-hour commute into D.C. he wracked his brain to come up with a line he could use with President Holbrook or Admiral Clausen that wouldn't create any suspicions and by the time he pulled into the underground parking lot at his office, he thought he might just have an angle.

Fowler had always had a gift at solving problems. Ever since he was a kid, he loved to solve puzzles and could not resist a challenge no matter how tough it was. One of his favorite techniques was to turn the problem on its head and come at it from a different angle. That is what had been the trick that had given him his idea. He had thought about why Typhon needed the address and it was obvious, surprise and urgency of action.

He also thought about the risk of exposing himself by inquiring into this sensitive detail with Clausen or the president. How could he accomplish both goals. The answer was to create the urgency and surprise without even asking the question directly. The fact was, he didn't need the address. He just needed to set up the ambush.

Leon smiled, coffee in hand, he left his car and took the elevator to the ground floor. Instead of heading up to his office, he went to the lobby and exited the building so he could get a good cell signal and dialed Stabler.

"Yes sir," came the immediate answer.

"Martin, listen carefully. I want you to use whatever ruse you want to ask Clausen where Sisco and his team are located in Auckland but make it credible. You are already exposed, so he won't be that concerned about telling you."

"Whoa, Leon," objected Stabler, "we already went over this, he won't give me the actual address, he'll feed me a fake location to throw Typhon off."

"Exactly," answered Fowler, "that is what we want him to do."

"What," stammered Martin, "I am not following you at all, Leon."

"Martin, he knows you will report the address to Typhon so that they can mount a strike on Team Apogee, right?"

"Yes," said Stabler in a measured tone.

Fowler continued, "and what will they do, Martin?"

"They will stake out the property and set up a counter ambush for Typhon," answered Stabler, still mulling over the operation.

"Right again, Martin. But unbeknownst to Clausen and Apogee is that Typhon will already know this whole thing is a fake to set them up and they will actually be there before Sisco and pull a reverse by ambushing his team."

Stabler was stunned, *this could actually work,* he thought. "I've got to say, Leon, that is brilliant. But one concern bothers me."

"And that is?" asked Fowler.

"Once Typhon takes out Clausen's team, isn't he going to figure there is another leak somewhere and accelerate his LIP work?"

"Sure he is Martin and I will drive that effort in the NSC to add to our cover. And remember Martin, you can assume that anything you get from Clausen is either irrelevant or bullshit. So, have you got all that, Martin?" continued Fowler.

"Yes I do. I'll get to Clausen within the hour and send Gunderson the fake address ASAP," he replied.

"And let me know when it's done Martin," Fowler ordered. "I expect it will come up in my next update with POTUS and Clausen." Leon Fowler hung up, threw his empty coffee cup in a trashcan by his building and confidently strode up the steps to his office secure in the knowledge that his next payment was all but guaranteed.

◆

The big Hummer moved across the rough terrain like an angry predator, clawing up the ridges and bumping wildly through the switchbacks. Snow planted her feet against one side of the compartment and her arms against the other to keep from flying into the air. After over an hour the torturous terrain finally seemed to be behind them and the ride smoothed out, giving her some relief. There had been little exchange between the passengers during this interval, but now, she heard some conversation. The guards finished updating Gunderson on their ETA. Apparently, they still had a couple hours to go, but they would make good time because the worst stretch was over.

She had already considered the next step in her escape. It made sense that, when they arrived at their destination, the guards would leave the Hummer unattended to help Gunderson hook up with the tender. That would be her chance to bolt. If the keys were still in the ignition, she could opt to steal the vehicle and make a run for it. She discarded that idea almost immediately. It would tip them off and they would call in reinforcements immediately. Besides, she needed them to be ignorant of her whereabouts. Soon enough they would discover she was missing, and they would assume she was still in the proximity of the compound. That is where they would conduct a search. No, she needed to stay in the wind for now. That was her best way to stay alive. Hopefully, there would be enough cover for her to slip away into the outback and hike to the nearest town where she could figure out what to do next.

Snow's thoughts were suddenly interrupted when she heard Gunderson ask the driver, "does the cell service improve as we get closer to the coast, I can't afford to be out of touch with the ranch for very long?"

"Yes sir," came the reply. "Actually, it should start getting stronger within the next few miles as we get closer to some of the more populated areas," said the guard.

"Good," responded Gunderson emphatically. She put her ear up against the partition that separated her from the third seat so she could hear more clearly and listened.

Ten minutes later, she heard a ringtone from a mobile phone up front. No one answered, but the ringing stopped, so she assumed it must be a text alert.

Then she heard the guard's voice again, "I'm getting four bars Sir, so you should be good to go on your mobile."

Gunderson answered, "yes, I just got a text, so I should be able to connect with Ardyh."

A moment later, Gunderson began to speak again. "Jefferey, I think things are looking up. I just got a text from our man, Leon Fowler, in D.C. and he has setup an ambush for your team with Team Apogee. It's quite ingenious actually," Gunderson continued. "Fowler couldn't risk any kind of overt query regarding Sisco's Auckland location, so he had Stabler ask the question and of course, knowing that Stabler is a leaker, Admiral Clausen fed him a false location where they could ambush you."

Gunderson read the address to Jefferey from the text. "So now we know exactly where these guys will be, and you can take them out." There was a pause as Gunderson went silent and then he spoke again, "no, Fowler doesn't know the exact time they will stake out the place, but he figures it will be as soon as tomorrow morning before sunrise. I would say, get your team in place around 4 am." Another pause and Snow heard Gunderson speak again.

"Good, I agree, take our best boys guarding the ranch on the operation. I think six to eight of them with you and Nicholi should be able to handle Sisco's team, especially since they won't see it coming. Take Von Stemp but hold him off if he isn't fit. I don't need any more screw-ups. If you can take Sisco alive do it, but don't jeopardize the op.

Oh, and if you can pull it off, try to let Von Stemp take out Franklin, otherwise we'll never get his head back in the game."

The conversation ended and Gunderson, in a more positive tone than usual said to the guards, "OK, boys, get me the hell to the coast, I have a boat to catch."

Snow pulled back away from the partition, her mind racing. *What the bloody hell was going on,* she thought *and how could she use this information to her advantage?*

◆

It was late into the night when Team Apogee had finally worked out all the details of their assault and had agreed to sleep in until 9 am the next morning before preparing all their gear. The operation was planned for the next day. They couldn't wait any longer.

Mac was first up and put the coffee on to brew. It would be a long day and a longer night, he knew, so he was glad they had all gotten some shuteye. As he poured his first cup, he heard a text alert from his mobile on the counter. He picked up his cell and began to read the text, his face clouding. It was from Clausen and it was a doozy! After he finished reading the text for the second time, he closed the app and rubbing his stubble beard, he thought about what the hell they were going to do about it.

It was not surprising that the entire team was already congregating around the coffee pot even before 0900. That was pretty typical of pre-op jitters. Mac waited until everyone was settled at the large dining room table and had finished gorging themselves on scrambled eggs and bacon with muffins, skillfully prepared by Franklin and Curry, before he cleared his throat and got their attention.

"Everyone looks well rested," he opened positively. The group nodded in unison as he continued, "early this morning I received new information from the Admiral which may offer some options for us. It seems that Martin Stabler attempted to identify our location here in Auckland with the obvious intent of passing it on to Typhon so they could take us out. Clausen used that opportunity to feed Stabler a different address to setup an ambush opportunity for us. Of course we don't know when or exactly how they will execute this assault, but we can make some assumptions and if we're right we could reverse the game on them."

"So," Mac continued, "we need to decide which way we want to play this. Suggestions?" he asked. The silence was palpable as each member of the team mulled over their options. Mac smiled and said, "now don't everyone chime in at once."

Peter Singe was the first to comment. "It seems to me that we only have a few options. We can make some assumptions about when their attack would take place and take up surveillance in advance of our estimate. Or we can ignore the whole trap and move forward with our current plan."

Joe exclaimed, "that about sums it up, I'd say."

Curry spoke next and asked, "well where do we want to conduct our little party, on their turf or ours?"

"That depends on how the op goes down," answered Mac. "If we really surprise them, here in town, that's huge."

"That won't be easy to do if we don't know when or even if they're coming," Warsaw pointed out.

"Yeh," Singe said, "we might sit there for days and they don't show. Based on this Chaos problem, we don't have any time to waste. The other disadvantage of moving on them here is that we don't know if the principals will be part of the assault, so no prisoners to interrogate. They may just send a whole bunch of goons down here to do the dirty work," he concluded.

"Before we get all lathered up about the negatives, I think we should also consider how risky our current plan is," said Warsaw. "Remember how we all agreed that we had to execute perfectly to succeed. Well, just to remind us all of that challenge let me recap. We will be dropping from the sky at 25,000 feet to land on the roof of a building without making a sound, surrounded by hundreds of heavily armed thugs on alert and exiting in their chopper with five prisoners. All that has to be perfectly coordinated with an MQ-9 Reaper firing targeted Hellfire missiles. Nothing to it," she concluded dramatically!

"Yep, that about sums it up," Franklin repeated once again, as the whole team chuckled under their breaths.

Mac couldn't help but smile, but it was true. It was a tough call, but maybe there was a way to split the difference. "Thank you for providing that contrast Elaine," he said seriously. "But maybe there is a way to have our cake and eat it too." They all turned to him with interest. He continued, "our planned operation goes off tomorrow morning at midnight from here so that we can be on station by 2 am. Why not set up surveillance at the fake site early this evening, say around dusk? We can spare two of our team. If Typhon shows up, we can elect to engage or not. If they don't show up by then, we execute our original plan."

"Makes sense," Curry said.

"Yes," agreed Singe, 'it really provides us with all the options." One by one the rest of the team nodded in agreement.

"OK, let's get our prep done and we'll do a final run through at 4 pm before an early dinner," Mac concluded.

◆

Snow could tell it was still dark as the Hummer finally pulled to a stop.

"Sir," the voice of one of the guards boomed, "we are at our coordinates."

Gunderson responded, "good, how far to the water?"

"About 100 yards," the guard replied.

"I'm contacting the captain now to see if they are here," Gunderson replied.

A moment later, Snow heard Gunderson ask, "Captain Reynolds, we have arrived, are you in position? Excellent, how soon can I expect the tender? All right," he continued, "we'll guide them in with a beacon. Oh and Captain, be ready to get underway for open sea as soon as I'm on board," Gunderson commanded.

This was it, Jasmine thought. The question was, would both guards assist Gunderson as he met the tender or would one remain behind. She remained still as she listened for their next move.

Gunderson had just finished the call and said, "ok boys, the tender should be here in about ten minutes and we need to guide them into the beach, so bring your spotlight and my luggage and let's get down to the water. Once I get out to the yacht, I'll contact you and you can head back to the ranch."

Jasmine breathed a silent sigh of relief. It seemed her luck was still holding. She heard three doors open and then close as the passengers retrieved the luggage and began their short trek to the water's edge. She waited about five minutes before extricating herself from her blankets and undid the canvas to unlock and open the top and bottom doors of the back compartment. She carefully crawled out of the back of the Hummer and stared into the brightening dawn. The truck was parked facing the water and provided cover from the beach. She made certain the compartment was still locked as she gently closed the doors. It would have been a dead giveaway if one of the guards had noticed it unlocked. Looking away from the beach, in the dim light, she could make out low brush and dunes a short distance away. Another break, she thought. She could use the cover of the Hummer to sprint straight back to the dunes and hide until the guards started their return trip.

The sand was soft here, so even her footprints would not give her away. Suddenly, she heard a voice barely above the crashing waves and peeked around the back fender.

"Sir, I'll run back to the car and get it," said the guard as he turned and jogged towards her. *Bloody hell*, she thought, and turned and sprinted for the closest dune that kept the Hummer between her and the guard, but she knew she wouldn't make it. Just before the man was coming into view, she dove into a prone position behind a low bush ten feet from the dune and lay very still. The guard rounded the hood of the Hummer and headed for the back door. Opening it, he retrieved a brief case and closed the door. He was directly facing her and seemed to hesitate as he casually scanned the dunes, almost like a tourist on vacation.

Then another insistent voice stuttered through the crashing surf as Gunderson yelled, "did you find it?"

"Yes Sir," snapped the guard coming out of his momentary reverie as he turned and trudged back through the deep sand to his boss. She again waited for her heart to stop pounding, as if she feared her assailants could hear it. She was about to crawl to the dune, when she heard another sound, this time a gasoline engine. The tender was arriving, definitely time for her to bug out of this place once and for all.

CHAPTER EIGHT

PASSING IN THE NIGHT

Jefferey was itching to get on with the operation to ambush Sisco and his team. But he decided to wait until breakfast to update Krishinko and Von Stemp. For what was coming, they would need the rest and so would he. At 7 am he met his two colleagues for breakfast and briefed them on his father's call and although they had agreed enthusiastically with the plan, Von Stemp was visceral about his desire to engage in the action and get the first shot at Franklin. Jefferey had acquiesced to his request, but warned him that if he showed any vulnerability, all bets were off. With that settled, the three men set about the task of planning their attack and identified the eight elite militants that would accompany them. Their best crew were the ones guarding the house inside and a few of those outside. By early afternoon they had rounded them up and instructed them on the operation.

As the three sat down to eat a late lunch, one of Jefferey's lieutenants came to their table and announced, "Mr. Gunderson, may I have a private word with you?"

Jefferey looked up surprised and answered, "of course and standing up, walked with his guard into the adjacent kitchen.

"Sir," the guard said, "the woman is missing!"

"What," Gunderson replied in dismay. "How could that be?"

The guard answered, "we didn't check her room this morning, because she always eats breakfast and even lunch from the cupboard in her room. But we always check her right after lunch, and she was gone. I have already checked with all our perimeter people and her terrace guard saw her last night at about 11 pm on the terrace drinking. He said she was drunk and went to bed before midnight. She never came out again and her hall guard never saw her either. No vehicles are missing so wherever she is; she is on foot and can't get far. We are currently scouring the immediate grounds and will find her."

Gunderson was furious and fired back, "you had better find her fast or your ass is in deep shit! And let me know immediately when you do."

The guard mumbled, "Yes Sir," as he sheepishly turned and left.

Once back at the table, both Krishinko and Von Stemp looked at him expectantly.

"What's up," asked Krishinko.

"The woman has disappeared," Jefferey spat out.

"Oh shit," said Von Stemp in surprise.

Gunderson proceeded to describe the details of Snow's disappearance.

Krishinko said, "boy, none of that makes sense, there are a lot of guards around the house."

"I know," Gunderson agreed, "but somehow she pulled it off. We clearly underestimated her."

"Does this change our plans in anyway?" Von Stemp asked, concerned.

"Well, it could a little," Gunderson, said. "I want to be here when they bring her in, so I can find out how she escaped and then personally take my father's advice. So," he continued, "let's do this. We'll send an advance team ahead to set up the assault positions and the three of us will join them for the operation at the site at 4 am. Get your gear together. We'll have an early dinner, get some rest before the operation and leave the ranch at 3:30 am by chopper for the fifteen-minute run to Auckland. I'll have one of the advance team pick us up at the private hanger and we'll all be in position for the attack on Apogee on schedule." Gunderson rose to leave and reminded, "I'll see you back here for dinner at 6 pm."

♦

Just before dark, Pat Curry and Carrie Swan left the team to take up their posts at the fake residence. It was only about twenty minutes away so they could acquire the best vantages before the sun went down. Directly across from the large condo was a multilevel parking garage which provided an unobstructed view of the entrance and part of one side of the structure. Armed with night vision binoculars and active comms back to Sisco, they selected a secluded spot behind a large column and waited. Soon the sun disappeared like a brilliant yellow orb diving into the ocean and was soon replaced by a spectacular star filled canopy.

Lights soon began popping on throughout the area, first in adjacent residences and restaurants followed by tardy streetlights adding to the attractive ambiance of Auckland's active nightlife scene. The sidewalk in front of the condo began to pick up traffic as the dinner hour approached, but the two agents observed no suspicious activity. By 7 pm, the dinner crowd began to be replaced by the bar shift, but still no indication of questionable activities. Swan had been on comms with Mac several times during the surveillance to provide status reports and just before 8 pm she checked in again.

Mac came online, "Carrie, any change?" he asked.

"Nope, just another quiet evening in paradise," she quipped. "We haven't even seen so much as a bar brawl or more than a half dozen specimens over six feet anywhere near the condo. We even changed positions to get a different view of the building and nothing. It looks like tonight is a bust," she concluded.

"OK," responded Mac, "that settles it. We go with the original plan. Stick around another half hour, just to be sure then come on back and we'll finish our prep and head out to the private field for wheels up at 1:00 am."

◆

By 6 pm, Gunderson's search parties had still not located Jasmine Snow and darkness was fast closing in on the ranch. By the time he sat down for dinner with his two lieutenants, Gunderson's mood had soured even more. Both men were reticent to bring up the issue, as they took in the scowl on their boss' face.

Finally, Krishinko asked, "Jefferey, are we still on schedule?"

Gunderson, nodded angrily, "yeh, but I have left orders to contact me immediately as soon as we re-capture that little bitch. But none of that bullshit will delay our operation against Sisco. We will join our guys in Auckland to take those assholes down. I have instructed the advance team to depart the ranch at midnight and establish their positions around the condo by 2 am. It's over an hour's drive, so they need to allow another 45 minutes to get in place. They'll keep an eye on the residence until we join them between 3:30 - 4:00 am. By this time tomorrow, Team Apogee will be destroyed, and Ms. Snow will be history," Jefferey concluded.

Finishing their meal, the three Typhon terrorists agreed to meet at the hanger at 3:30 am for their short flight to Auckland and the payback they had all been looking forward to.

◆

Snow hid behind a large dune while observing Peter Gunderson's departure on the tender and then waited until the two guards got the call that their boss was secure on his yacht. As she peered over the top of the sand, she could see the large boat in the distance begin steaming out to sea. Minutes later the two guards climbed back into the big Hummer and headed back to Ardyh Ranch.

The sun was rising quickly, and the temperature was too as the sweat began to glisten on her face and arms. She had no idea where she was or which way she should go, but she did have an ace in the hole. Her captors had taken her mobile phone, but left her with her sports watch and the Garmin 6X plus had GPS and mapping features built in. She quickly pulled up her position on the map and saw that she was about fourteen miles from Te Hana, which was a sixty-minute drive to Auckland. *First things first*, she thought, she needed to get to civilization, and it looked like Te Hana was her first stop. The only road was inland, so she set off in that direction. The going was slow until she got out of the thick sand in favor of hard rocky soil and could pick up her pace. Almost an hour later she joined up with the Kaiwaka Mangawhai Rd. and followed it until it intersected with New Zealand State Highway 1, running due south through Te Hana, on its way into Auckland.

She had broken into a slow jog to eat up the miles to Te Hana and by the time she approached the small Maori town, she was dripping with sweat and parched. She followed her trusty Garmin's directions off the highway to one of the town's popular stops, the Te Hana Cafe on Rt. 316. She was incredibly thirsty and suddenly realized that she was also almost weak from not eating in almost twenty-four hours. Fortunately, she had the foresight to always hide cash on her person for emergencies and she had no less than three hidden caches of bills sewn into both her light coat and camo pants, so she wouldn't be begging for scraps.

After devouring her meal in short order, she inquired into transportation to Auckland and was told that she could rent a car or take a bus. The car was faster, but Snow was paranoid about being tracked by Typhon and the next bus was leaving at about 10:30 am and would put her in Auckland around noon. Although there was an hour wait, she opted for the bus and spent the time drinking coffee and brainstorming her next move.

The bus departed right on time and had few passengers, allowing her to take a solitary seat near the back. She had spent her wait time reviewing all that had happened since her meeting with Sisco in London. She had quickly arrived at the uncomfortable conclusion that no matter how convincing she was, neither Typhon nor the Apogee Team had any good reason to trust her. What had been her best defense had created her worst outcome. For both, the stakes were so high that her elimination was clearly their best option. It seemed the only practical course of action was to run. Maybe, over time everyone would forget about her and she could regain some semblance of a normal life. But she knew in her heart that was unlikely. She imagined the first several years of constantly looking over her shoulders for the threat that seemed inevitable, the moving from city to city, country to country and then one day, the discovery that would surely end in her death. She couldn't go through that. Better to face the music now and give it her best shot. *Stick with the Brit's famous, stiff upper lip,* she thought.

She began to doze off as the miles flew by, still without a plan or even a good idea to calm her. In her dreams, she imagined Typhon fast on her heels, unrelenting, as they tracked her every move, getting ever closer. In vivid detail, she could see Jefferey Gunderson stalking her until finally she was cornered in a narrow alley, as he approached brandishing a large knife, an evil grin on his face. With only feet between them, she screamed out, rushing at him to turn the tables as the big blade came up to meet her.

The bus hit a bump as it turned into the Lamination Services Station in Auckland and pulled to a stop. she bolted out of her nightmare; sweat thick on her face and neck. She looked at her watch, 12:07 pm. Now what, she asked herself as she rose to disembark behind the few other riders. She almost staggered off the last few steps of the bus, suddenly realizing how exhausted she was. She needed to hold up somewhere secure, rest and recuperate at least for a few hours and maybe her brain would work better. As the bus pulled away, she glanced around for an answer, her eyes coming to rest on a sign directly across Albert Street from where she stood, less than fifty feet away. Surf N Snow

Backpackers, Rooms and Dorms for Rent. *Hallelujah*, she thought, perfect, a hostel, the one place that no one would ever look for her.

At $15.00 per night, it wasn't exactly the Hilton, but then Snow didn't intend to stay long. She needed to get a few badly needed hours of shuteye and then she could concentrate on the rest of her life. Her head barely hit the pillow before she was deep in a, thankfully, dreamless sleep. Six hours later, she groggily opened her eyes as the angle of the sun beamed in through the un-shaded window. Pulling herself up and checking her watch, she realized her power nap had turned into a bit of a marathon. After washing her face and reviving herself, she actually felt human again. Returning to the bedroom she sat down in the single cushioned chair next to the window and looked out on Albert St. as the last golden rays of the brilliant sun began to retreat towards the other side of the earth. In her mind, she picked up where she had left off on the bus until she got to Peter Gunderson's conversation on the phone with his son as he waited for the tender. *There was no other way out*, she thought, rising from the chair, a sense of urgency in her stride as she left the hostel with new hope and determination.

◆

Mac checked his watch after his status call from Swan and Curry surveilling the condo; 8:00 pm. He had given a lot of thought about which operation to choose even if Typhon did attack the condo that morning. It was entirely possible that the Gunderson's and team would not participate. It was also true that the files would still be out at the ranch. In the end, they might be taking a hell of a lot of risk with no benefit at all, if they did the Auckland operation. Unfortunately, there was no way of knowing how it would go down until it went down. It was definitely a tough call, he thought.

He was mulling it all over when his mobile rang, caller ID unknown. He ignored it. Several minutes later, his phone buzzed again this time with a voice mail. Curious, he pulled up the VM to see what the number was, assuming just another solicitation. The number did not have a familiar area code, in fact, as he compared it to the other local calls he had made while in Auckland, it was the same local code. Strange, he thought no one else locally knew he was here. Well, he decided, only one way to find out, as he retrieved the voice message.

"Mac, this is Jasmine, we are both in trouble, please call back now!"

Mac listened to the message several more times. Each time he tried to ascertain the stress level, the volume, tone and any other nuances that might provide a clue to intent, subterfuge or truth. He didn't know if Typhon could trace his return call to voice mail to his location. It was unlikely that could be done on a VM call, but if he actually returned Snow's call, he could be jeopardizing everything. For all he knew, she was only blocks away with Typhon and the attack team and this call was to verify his location. The minute after he made the call, this location could be attacked even as he was down by two of his team. Not a good scenario, but he didn't want to put this decision to a vote. He needed to act now one way or the other. Either ignore it or follow up. Before he decided, he made another call on his comms.

Curry answered this time, "what's up boss?" he asked, concerned. "Pat, if I don't contact you at exactly 8:30 pm, fifteen minutes from now, beat feet it back here, but close on this location cautiously, because we may have company. Do you understand?" Mac asked.

"Copy," said the big Aussie as he rang off.

◆

Snow left the hostel and asked directions to the nearest Wal-Mart where she purchased a burn phone and by 8:00 pm was back in her room dialing Mac Sisco's mobile number from memory. Finally, after the fourth ring, the call went to voice mail and she left her urgent message. She knew this might happen. It wasn't good tradecraft to pick up random, unidentifiable voice messages while on a highly classified mission, especially one out of country. She also knew that her message had to be very carefully crafted in the event that he even retrieved it. It had to be natural and believable and be appropriate for the circumstances. If Mac found the message to be in any way contrived or manipulating, he would discount it and be even less trusting of any story she told. Five minutes went by and still nothing. She decided to give it another couple minutes and then she would call again and pull out all the stops.

Mac hung up the call with Curry and retrieved Snow's voice message, listening one more time and pushed recall. The phone didn't even complete the ring when Jasmine answered,

"Mac, thank God!"

"Jasmine," Mac responded, "where are you and what in the hell is going on?" Mac knew that Snow was not aware of the tracker that he planted and decided not to disclose that fact. In fact, as far as Snow was concerned, she didn't even know where he was, unless of course, she was back with Typhon and they had discovered it and informed her.

Snow responded, "look Mac, I know you have every reason not to trust me and have every reason to believe that I burnt you, and I get that, but I'm hoping that I can give you a reason to change that opinion."

"Well Jasmine, you would be correct in your assumption," Mac answered sternly, "and whatever you say, it will have to be over the top to convince me, let alone my team."

"I understand, so let me start from where we last saw each other and I'll do my best," she urged.

"Fire away," Mac answered.

She proceeded to describe every detail of her experience since their operation outside Paris, only leaving out overhearing Peter Gunderson's conversation at the ranch, her trip to the coast and Gunderson's yacht. That was her insurance and about the only bargaining chip she had left. She had to convince Mac and his teammates that, no matter what had happened, she was worth more alive than dead. She had substituted a scenario for her escape where she stole the Hummer and made her way to Te Hana where she ditched it, fearing that Typhon could trace it somehow, and from there took a bus to Auckland. As they say, the best way to lie is to tell the truth and every other part of her story was, in fact, true.

Mac listened to Jasmine's story closely and everything seemed plausible except her escape from the ranch. He just didn't see how she could have avoided capture by all the troops bivouacked on the property, especially when she didn't know where she was going. He asked her about that, and she had a ready response, her amazing Garmin watch with GPS and mapping showed her the way. *It was possible just not very feasible*, he thought. The real question was, what did she want from him, and her answer was troubling.

"Mac," she said, "I want to rejoin the team and prove to all of you that I am on your side and I have been since, we met in London. So where are you guys now," she asked, "and how do I hook up with you?"

The time had come for Mac to decide and he didn't hesitate. No matter what the truth, the old saying, "keep your friends close and your enemies closer," now rang true more than ever. Snow on the loose could be much more dangerous than Snow under observation.

"OK Jasmine, let's take this one step at a time," he answered. "You tell me where you are, and I'll come pick you up and we'll take it from there."

"OK Mac, and thanks. I won't let you and the team down, I promise." As Mac hung up the line, he thought to himself, *Boy Howdy, here we go again!*

Mac and Joe took a circuitous route to the Albert Street hostel, parked a block away and walked separately towards the building where Snow anxiously waited. Mac entered first and Franklin waited five minutes scanning the location for anything suspicious before following. Mac waited outside snow's door and listened carefully. A few minutes later Franklin joined him. Mac gave him the signal to hang back until he cleared the room of any surprises and then he knocked softly. The door unlocked with a click and Snow slowly pulled it all the way open, knowing Mac would want full visibility before entering.

She stood back a few feet from the entrance and said, "hello Mac, good to see you."

Mac took a minute to study the interior and then responded, "Jasmine," and stepped into the room leaving the door ajar.

As he moved into the room, she said, raising her voice somewhat, "I'll leave the door open, Joe, so you can wait until Mac clears the space before entering."

Standing, out of view, Joe quietly chuckled to himself and thought, *that Jasmine doesn't miss a trick.*

A minute later, Mac called out, "clear, Joe!" and Franklin entered the room closing the door behind him.

Mac turned to Jasmine and said, "OK Jasmine, this is how it's going to go. My team has been briefed on your miraculous escape and your request and has agreed to listen to your story. We will then decide what your future in the next few days looks like. I can tell you that you have an uphill climb, but you already know that. If we determine that you continue to be a risk in any way, at a minimum, we will neutralize you for the duration of the operation. After that, your outlook will depend upon which organization most wants to prosecute you for crimes against humanity."

Jasmine nodded gravely and said, "I understand."

"OK, Joe, search Ms. Snow for any weapons and then let's get back to the team." Mac led the way, again separating from Franklin and Snow and crossed to the other side of the street as he returned to the car. On his way, he went on comms to Pat Curry back at the stakeout to let him know all was OK and for Pat and Carrie to hustle on back to their apartment.

By the time Mac and Franklin returned with Snow, the whole team was already assembled in their chosen spots in the large living room.

Mac opened the discussion by saying, "before we get into Jasmine's issue, I have made a decision to abandon our secondary operation and focus on our original and primary one. I will elaborate more on my reasoning once we have all had a chance to interrogate Ms. Snow and determine if there is any new information that would require a different direction. Since you all have not yet heard any details about Jasmine's activities, I will ask her to review those again. I expect each of you to really drill into her story because our future and that of our mission may well depend upon Ms. Snow's credibility and information."

By 10:00 pm, Snow had repeated the same story she had related to Mac and Joe earlier with her imbedded fabrications. The questions had been many, very critical and insightful and she had answered them skillfully.

Mac turned and looked at each member of his team and asked, "are there any more questions you want to ask?" There was silence. He continued, "OK, well I still have a few. Jasmine. Why should we trust you and what value can you bring to the team to help us take down Typhon once and for all?"

Jasmine knew this was coming and she also was certain that she would never convince Mac to trust her or give her the opportunity to prove her innocence without answering both questions.

"Mac," she responded, "I will do my best to answer, but with a few caveats."

Mac's eyebrows raised just slightly as he fired back, "of course you do, please continue."

"Your first question about why you should trust me is easy to answer," she said, "you can't, or at least not yet. There is nothing I can say that could earn that trust," she went on. "I must earn it through action and that is why I want to be part of your active operation to take down Typhon. Unless I can achieve that, my life is forfeit. On the second question, about my value, I have two ways I can provide high value to Team Apogee. First, if I am allowed to participate in the op, I can be an active combatant. That is what I have been trained to do and I am damn good at it. The second value I can provide is additional intelligence regarding Typhon that I have not yet shared with you."

So there it was, Mac thought. The negotiations had begun.

Mac could hardly hide his sarcasm as he responded, "why Jasmine, you mean to say you are holding out on us, what a surprise." Then in a surprisingly sad voice he said, "Jasmine, you are building a wall of mistrust you might not be able to scale with this kind of tactic."

Jasmine, answered somberly, "yes I know and for that I sincerely apologize, but I really have no choice. To be honest, it is my only bargaining tool to convince you to take me on the operation, the only way I can prove my innocence. Without that opportunity, I have nothing."

Mac looked around the room and finally said, "ok team, any opinions or recommendations?"

Elaine answered, "as one Brit to another, that was a bloody good speech, Ms. Snow, but how do you propose we accommodate your request when we don't have a clue about the intel?"

The room grew silent and finally Jasmine answered, "well Elaine, I guess we'll have to start by trusting each other and I'll go first. I believe that what I know is valuable enough to be worthy of my accommodation, but I must trust that you will agree and keep your side of the bargain. So, here is my offer," Jasmine continued, "I will tell you what I know and if you agree that it is valuable enough, you will allow me to participate in an active way in the operation against Typhon." Mac looked around the room for reactions.

Peter said, "I certainly think Jasmine has handed us all the cards."

"And is taking all the risk," agreed Joe.

Carrie jumped in and said, "what the hell, I'm in," as the rest of the team nodded in agreement.

They all listened intently as Jasmine described Gunderson's heated conversation with his team before departing the ranch, her actual harrowing escape in the Hummer and Gunderson's call back to Ardyh Ranch about the ambush plan. She decided, however, to hold back with identifying Leon Fowler as the mole. She didn't know who he was and decided that a bird in the hand was worth two in the bush, at least for now. It was almost 11:00 pm, when Snow finally finished her tale and looked around the room expectantly. Mac again looked to his team for guidance. It was their asses as much as his, so they needed to chime in, and they did.

Joe said, "I have to say, if what Jasmine has said is true and I figure if she is on the operation with us, for her sake it better be, it is worth its weight in gold."

"I agree," said Elaine, "we now have confirmation on the Auckland attack, along with who, how many and even what time."

"We also know," added Peter, "that old man Gunderson is steaming out to sea on a yacht named Calamity."

Mac turned to Jasmine, "OK, Ms. Snow, you're in, but I warn you, once I have briefed you on the operation, you may wish you never asked.

Team Apogee, while I do that, let's suit up, we leave here for the airport in thirty-five minutes."

The De Havilland Twin Otter was one of the most popular platforms for sky diving on the planet. It could accommodate up to twenty-three jumpers and that extra room came in handy when you had as much high-tech gear as Team Apogee did. It also sported a huge side launch door and had short takeoff and landing capability, which made it highly flexible when uncertainty was almost guaranteed. The aircraft climbed quickly to their 25,000-foot altitude and cruised effortlessly to their jump coordinates. The sky was moonless and clear and bursting with stars. The conditions looked good and they could even make out the tiny lights of their target contrasted against the darkness of the unpopulated terrain surrounding it. They slid the big jump door open and lined up in their teams as planned.

The time had come, and Mac yelled, "GO," as Pat and Carrie leaped one after the other out into the darkness. "Go," and Peter and Elaine followed and finally, "Go," as Joe and Jasmine took their turn disappearing towards terminal velocity with Mac quickly behind.

The ground raced up to them at 120 miles per hour as the seven jumpers prepared to pull their chutes. Their free fall would last under two minutes but would seem like an eternity as they concentrated on the ever-growing glow of the lights illuminating the main residence below. Then on cue, one after another the dark canopies of their Para gliders burst from their bodies like wings as they fell into formation like geese migrating south. Swan took the point guiding them downward in steep spirals to their impossibly small landing spot. Spacing themselves with precision, acquired through hundreds of jumps, they stalled their chutes feet from the roof's surface and alighted softly in a silent cadence one after another.

The weather report had been accurate and only a light breeze wafted across them, but it was still strong enough to make collecting their chutes a challenge. Mac was the last in line and was on his final approach as he followed Snow down. He noticed that her trajectory was too high, and she was going to overshoot the roof.

"Jasmine," he warned on his comm unit, "you are going to overshoot unless you come in much steeper."

Her breathless voice came back, "copy."

Mac watched concerned as she adjusted her incline steeply and her speed increased dramatically. He knew immediately at that speed, she would have to give herself lots of room and flare the hell out of her rig to avoid serious injury. Jasmine was a little out of practice, but she knew what she had to do. Well before impact she flared her chute as hard as she dared.

The breaking force was hard and brutal, jerking her harness painfully and knocking the air from her lungs as she hit the deck. She went to her knees trying to catch her breath as the chute billowed up above her and began to drag her towards the roof's edge. Mac saw all this unfolding as if in slow motion and knew he had to get down there fast or she was going over the edge. He changed his trajectory, targeting further down the roof. He had to collapse her chute as he landed and stop her forward motion. If he screwed it up, they were both going over the edge. Snow was still struggling as Mac hurtled into her open canopy just above her head and jammed his feet down on the surface in front of her while stalling his own chute. Now only feet from the edge, planting his feet wide apart and leaning back up the roof's pitch he gathered both silks in his arms as she slid to a stop against his legs.

She lay there stunned, still short of breath, as he leaned down and gently helped her sit upright.

"Are you hurt, Jasmine?" he asked, a real note of concern in his voice.

"I don't think so," she stammered, "but that landing was a little rough."

"You think," he said with a wry smile as he helped her to her feet. They made their way back to the team who had congregated together, witnessing the near tragedy.

"Everyone ok," Mac asked. Thumbs up was the silent response from each member. "Pat and Carrie," Mac continued, "gear up with your night visions and check out each side of the house. Let's see how the guards are configured and make sure we're still stealth."

"Copy," they both answered and disappeared.

"Peter and Elaine take a look at the skylights and see if they pan out as our best entry point. Meet back here in ten minutes and we'll figure out our best way in."

Singe and Warsaw returned first.

Elaine reported, "Mac, as the house plans showed, there are six skylights. Three of them provide light to bedrooms and three larger ones cover common rooms. Obviously, we need to avoid the sleeping quarters and use the large ones. Two of them access rooms not far from the HVAC/ utility room."

"How's the glass look, can we cut it and lift it out," Mac asked.

"It's several inches thick, but I tested the laser and it will cut through it, but it will take some time," Singe answered.

"Define time," Mac shot back.

"I estimate fifteen minutes per skylight," Peter acknowledged.

As Peter finished his answer, Swan and Curry returned.

"What have we got," Mac turned and asked the two.

"It doesn't make sense," Curry said.

"What doesn't make sense?" Joe asked.

"We scoped the entire perimeter and saw only four guards," Swan answered for her teammate.

"That's it," Franklin asked, astonished.

"You're right," Mac agreed, "that makes no sense." Mac turned to Jasmine and asked, "didn't you say that Gunderson was planning on a 4:00 am assault?"

"Yes," Snow answered emphatically.

"Maybe they moved up their timetable," Franklin offered.

Mac turned back to Curry and Swan and asked, "did you see any other guards anywhere on the property?"

"Negative," answered Curry, "not one."

"Well, we still can't assume that there aren't more security personnel rotating in or even positioned inside the residence," Mac pointed out. "But this does offer us an opportunity to penetrate from both a skylight and the exterior wall. Peter, pick the skylight closest to the HVAC room and cut the glass. We can use that entry point to penetrate the interior. Joe, you, Peter and Elaine rappel down through the skylight. Cover Joe as he sets up in the utility room. Pat, you and Carrie scale down the north side from the roof and Jasmine and I will take the south side."

"Our outside teams will take out the four guards and then penetrate the house. Pat and Carrie will enter via the back entrance and Jasmine and I will hit the main entrance. Deadly force is authorized. Masks on when in the house until Joe gives us the all clear on comms. Outside teams will clear and secure any combatants and then move to contain the targets for extraction. Keep in mind that Gunderson, Krishinko and Von Stemp may be passing us in the night on their way to ambush us in Auckland."

"If we have no captives, let's hope that their files are here. Elaine, as soon as Joe starts the gas, you two find Gunderson's records and meet us back at the entrance foyer. If you need Carrie's help, comm her in. Peter, I'll confirm the entrance exterior clear so you can advance to the hanger and get the chopper staged for extrication." Now finished, Mac asked, "any questions? Good," he said as all gave him a thumbs up. "Comms on, let's move," he ordered as Team Apogee plus one fanned out across the roof.

CHAPTER NINE

COME HELL OR HIGH WATER

The outside teams spread out across the roof and grappled their lines at opposite corners. On Mac's signal they silently rappelled over the edge to the ground forty feet below. The guards were facing outward scanning the perimeter in a systematic pattern that brought them together periodically as a security precaution. But for most of their rotation they were out of sight of each other. There was no percentage in a forty-yard sniper shot with a suppressed 9 mm, but these guys needed to be neutralized and fast.

Mac once again whispered into his comms, "Go," and his ground team moved out of the shadows breaking into a full sprint with their weapons already on target. There was no cover, so they had to close half the distance before discovery to get a high probability kill shot off. Their advantage was surprise and having their weapons already positioned.

Both Swan and Snow were light on their feet and smaller in frame and were less than ten yards from their targets when they turned and raised the AK 47's. Both women fired two rounds, one center mass and the second higher as insurance, that neither needed, as the two guards dropped unmoving. Curry was very quick for his size, but his target was turning his way as he made his dash. He was still over twenty yards out when he saw the big guard site him in. He desperately zigzagged and pulled off four rounds, knowing his chances were slim and hoped that at least one round would find his target. With an anguished look on his face, the guard's rifle flew from his hands as his left arm went limp. Knowing he had to close on Curry to avoid another round, the big man unsheathed a large combat blade and rushed forward. And then they collided. Curry was a brute, but this guy was massive, and he was catapulted backward like a quarterback getting sacked by a big lineman. Before he could even regain his footing, he saw the big knife slash down at his chest with enormous force. All he could do was throw up his left arm as a deflection as he rolled away from the attack.

Pat felt the searing pain as the blade cut through his padded combat coat and sliced deep into his forearm, even as he rolled clear. But as he shakily began to rise, the guard rushed him again. The big man reached out with a slashing motion, but this time Pat was ready. He dove into a forward roll, the blade missing high and exposing his opponent's left side. Pat kicked his right foot up and into the man's useless dangling left arm and the result was immediate. The man roared and dropped the knife, grabbing his left side as the blood erupted from the newly opened wound. Curry's own arm was soaked with blood as he grabbed the combat knife lying only feet away. Whirling around 360 degrees, he launched himself at the guard, now within his reach. The ten-inch blade sank deep into the man's chest, severing ribs and arteries on its path of destruction. The guard crumbled without a sound; his eyes open wide in astonishment. Pat collapsed to the ground; his relief clouded by his knowledge that it wouldn't be long before he bled out.

Mac had taken no chances with his prey. But he had an advantage over his teammates; he was a trained and highly skilled sniper. And while most of his kills were using a specialized U.S. Barrett M82 sniper rifle, he was equally adept at taking out targets with handguns at significant distances. Unlike most shooters, snipers understood all the geometries of ballistics from velocity and drop to wind and humidity. It was a natural part of how they approached every shot and the good ones almost never missed, no matter what the weapon. And Mac Sisco was one of the best on the planet. Now still standing back in the shadows, he raised his favorite weapon, the Sig Sauer P226 Tacops with suppressor, and sited in on his quarry.

The guard had wandered further from the house and Mac was a good sixty yards away. At that distance his round would drop more than three inches, but its velocity would still have killing force at over 1,000 feet per second. There was a slight breeze and low humidity both of which would have only minor impact. All these factors were instantly correlated as Mac placed his hand lightly on the trigger and squeezed off a single round. The back of the guard's head showed only a small red entry point, but the front was wrecked by the round's exit as it rocketed into the night and the man collapsed, almost gracefully, to the ground.

As Mac began to move cautiously towards their rendezvous, he heard a cry from the west corner of the residence. That was Curry's position and he knew that meant trouble as he raced in that direction. By the time he rounded the corner he could see both Carrie and Jasmine kneeling beside their fallen comrade. Mac's heart sank, this didn't look good.

"What happened?" Mac asked urgently, as he approached his team.

"We heard the scream and came running and found him down and unconscious," said Jasmine.

"We're taking his vitals now chimed in Carrie, but the only wound we have seen is to his arm." Swan had pulled out her tactical knife and was already cutting away Curry's left coat sleeve, to get at the wound. She ripped the shredded cloth away and examined the red soaked gash.

"Well, now we know what happened here," she observed. "Pat must have gone hand to knife with this brute," pointing to the dead guard, "and disarmed him, then used his attacker's knife to take him out. I've got to stop this bleeding. Fortunately, the tightness of his combat jersey and coat have kept the blood loss to a minimum." Snow handed Swan the emergency med kit and they worked together to staunch the bleeding and wrap the wound.

"He'll make it, but the attack may have clipped an artery which is a hell of a lot better than it could have been," Carrie concluded.

Mac sighed with relief, but said, "we need to get him conscious and determine how mobile he is." Carrie grabbed some smelling salts and placed them under Curry's nose.

Almost immediately his eyes fluttered open and he looked up confused. "Pat," Mac asked, "how do you feel?"

"Like a Wallaby's ass coated with fire ants," he moaned. "Do I have any blood left?"

"Yep, probably more than you deserve," joked Carrie, relieved to see her big partner still had his Aussie sense of humor.

"Let's go guys, we need to get out of the open," Mac warned. Pat struggled to his feet, but even as Mac helped him, he seemed to regain some strength.

"I think I can make it on my own," he said as the group pushed open the big doors of the entrance to the main house.

"Carrie," Mac said, "take Pat to the HVAC room and meet the others while Jasmine and I start our search. If Pat is still marginalized, he can go with Peter directly to the chopper."

"Copy Mac," Carrie responded and headed into the house with her teammate.

Mac went on comms and said, "outside team has breached residence, masks on," followed by, "Peter, status?"

Singe came back immediately, "penetrated skylight, no issues, now on way to HVAC, should start gas in five minutes."

"Copy," Mac responded and quickly gave an update to the rest of the team on Curry and their new plan.

"Any hostiles?" he added back to Singe.

"We didn't hear or see any activity, but we only covered a small area, so I wouldn't count on our intel."

"OK, thanks and give us the heads up when Joe is done," Mac reminded.

Mac and Jasmine waited in the vacant lobby for the call from Singe and when it came, they delayed another five minutes to let the gas permeate the residence before making their way into the interior. Mac led the way with Snow a few meters behind as they worked their way down the hall to the suites where they hoped the Typhon boys would now be snoozing heavily. The master suite, where Peter Gunderson most likely resided proved to be empty, as they anticipated, but they did take the time to do a quick search in case the Typhon master had left any obvious evidence. Finding nothing, they moved on.

The next suite was also empty, and Mac began to worry that maybe Gunderson's son and his team were already in Auckland on their own mission. But the third time was a charm as they quietly entered suite #3, to the heavy breathing of a deeply drugged Jefferey Gunderson, dimly visible in the glow of a night light on the adjacent wall. Jasmine moved rapidly up to the figure and carefully rolled him over, repositioned his hands behind him and zipped tied him securely. She then pulled thick bungee cords from her pocket and secured his legs just tight enough that he could shuffle along if necessary.

Mac whispered to Jasmine, "check out the room for evidence while I move on to the next suite. Then advance to the next one and I'll join you. Hopefully, we can bag all these guys in this cluster of suites and beat feet it out of here without any interruptions."

"Copy Mac," she answered as he closed the door behind him.

Mac quickly advanced to the next room and tried the door. "Shit, locked," he said under his breath. Retrieving his pick set, he set about working the lock. The New Zealand locks were a little different and he bent down to get a better look at the mechanism as he manipulated the pics.

Just as he heard the satisfying click of the lock opening, a menacing voice rang out from just up the hall, "who the hell are you and what do you think you are doing?" Mac, startled, stood up and turned to see a guard in full camo pointing an AR-15 squarely at his head. *Not good,* he thought, as he struggled for some explanation that might save his ass. He had none and so he elected to stay mute. A guy in tactical gear, weaponized to the gills, picking a lock inside a private residence would have to be Houdini to get out of this one.

The guard now impatient, commanded, "OK you SOB, push your weapons this way slowly, then lay down on the floor face down, hands behind your back and legs spread. And my friend," the guard warned, "if you even twitch the wrong way, you are dead meat."

Even as Mac began to kneel down, he wondered, *how in hell is this bastard still standing?* "Now take your weapons out real easy and slow with the tips of your fingers, put them on the floor and slide them forward out of your reach," his captor directed. As Mac carefully began to open his OWB holster to retrieve the big Sig, he heard a familiar PSST sound and looking up watched in disbelief as the guard collapsed in a heap, blood already oozing from a wound just above his thick black eyebrows. He turned to see Jasmine Snow lowering her weapon and moving to him to help him up. *Timing is everything,* he thought.

He looked into her eyes and said, "thanks Jasmine, I owe you one."

She smiled back and said, "Indeed you do Cowboy."

They dragged the guard's body into Jefferey's room and searched for any useful accessories. Mac retrieved the guard's mobile radio that would no doubt be useful both offensively and defensively. Snow was tempted by his AR but passed it up because it lacked a suppressor. Then, they left the room and separated, each entering one of the next two suites in search of the last two Typhon henchmen. Now unlocked, Mac quietly opened the suite door and moved into the living room. It was clear that the suite was occupied from the personal items arrayed around the room and as he got a better view of the bedroom, he could make out a sleeping form was visible in the king-sized bed.

Approaching, he soon identified the man as Nicholi Krishinko, from his briefing photos. Mac repeated the same process Jasmine had used on Gunderson on the big Russian and did a quick search of the suite. There were several weapons and a mobile phone, which Mac stored, in his combat coat, but little else, so he retreated to the entrance and cautiously opened the door. The hallway remained clear, so he quickly advanced on the next suite and entered.

He was surprised to see Snow bending over a figure on the floor in the living room and asked, "Jasmine, did you have any trouble?" Startled, she whirled around, her 9 mm already out. For a brief moment Mac wondered if he had made the wrong call as he stared down the barrel.

Then, she quickly lowered the piece and said, "sorry Mac, you startled me, and my training kicked in."

"What happened here, was he awake?" Mac asked.

"No, I found him like this. It's Wart Von Stemp," she said knowingly. "My guess is, he couldn't sleep, maybe because of his injury, and got up to get something when the gas kicked in. But he is resting comfortably now," she quipped. "I was just about to do a quick search."

"We need to get a move on," Mac urged. "We lost some time with our little interruption and my guess is that more guards will be coming to check on their comrade soon. Check out the suite while I get some muscle down here to help us." She nodded and headed for the bedroom.

Mac went on comms and said, "Joe, can you and Peter get down here to the suites and give us a hand with the merchandise and use caution, we might have some guards who didn't get gassed, still on the prowl in the house."

"Copy," came back the immediate reply. "And Mac, the clock is ticking. We're at T minus twenty minutes," said Joe.

As Franklin and Singe were leaving for the living quarters, Swan said, "guys, I have got to find those files. I will leave Pat here with Elaine for now and while you guys are helping Mac and Jasmine, I 'll get on with that search. Hopefully, before you get back, I'll get lucky."

"OK," responded Franklin, "but heads up Carrie, it sounds like not everyone went sleepy time." The two men hustled down the hallway, weapons out and as they were about to turn down the last hall, they heard voices coming their way.

"Where the hell is that son of a bitch Brewer?" one guard exclaimed in frustration.

"Probably out for a smoke break, while the big boys are snoozing," another man responded.

The voices were almost upon them as Franklin and Singe fanned out and pressed themselves against the wall in shooting stances and patiently waited for the two guards to come around their corner.

The guards were still complaining about their missing comrade when one said, "hold up, let me see if I can raise him now on his mobile so we don't have to search all over the place." The guards stopped and were still not visible as Joe and Peter anxiously waited out of view. "Brewer, this is Jake, where the hell are you, over," radioed the guard. There was a pause and then he repeated the request and waited again for a response.

"Well?" asked the other man.

"Nothing," said the first guard.

"Now that is not like Brewer. He might be screwing around, but he doesn't go dark unless there is a real good reason. I don't like this at all, I'm checking in with HQ and we'll see if he came back already."

The two Apogee agents had heard all this and knew that any alert could jeopardize the whole mission and endanger the rest of the team.

Joe whispered, "now," as the two men bolted around the corner. One guard was moving his radio up to his ear as Franklin fired his first round point blank into the guard's chest and followed with another to his head. Singe fired a single round into the second guard's temple as he began to turn toward them in surprise. It was over in less than five seconds.

Joe immediately went on comms to the entire team and said, "we just took down two hostiles in the hallway leading to the suites. They were about to report to HQ, whatever that is, but for sure there are more where these two came from, so we need to move up our timeframe. Their comrades will be wondering why these two haven't checked in soon enough."

"Yeh, and then come looking," interrupted Mac. He continued, "we'll drag these suckers into the hall and meet you there."

"Copy," yelled Joe as he and Peter sprinted down the hall.

By the time the two men rounded the last corner, thirty feet away, Mac and Jasmine had just dragged the last Typhon operative out and Mac was already hoisting Gunderson onto his shoulders. Franklin grabbed the big Russian and copied his boss as Singe and Snow slung Von Stemp between them, avoiding his injury, so that he didn't wake from added pain. They went straight to the entrance foyer and lowered their captives to the floor. Mac checked his watch, less than fifteen minutes before the gas would wear off.

"Joe," he commanded, "get Pat and Elaine and bring them here. Peter, get out to the hanger and get that chopper as ready as you can without alerting everyone. Jasmine, stay with these guys and knock them out if they come to. I have to find Carrie stat," he said and took off.

Mac bolted down the hallway not sure which room to look in. As he ran, he called Carrie on comms, "Carrie, where are you? We need to go, and I mean now." There was no reply. He repeated his urgent request as he threw open one door. It led into the library and was empty. Still no response. He lurched out into the hall and rushed to another door throwing it open in a panic, a dining room, and nada. Down the hall, he saw a door slightly ajar and heard muffled voices. He slowed his pace and carefully peered into the opening.

He could see Swan, her back to him, standing in front of a large ornate desk, completely absorbed as she stared into the eyes of Peter Gunderson's image on a large flat panel display that she had swiveled to face her.

"Carrie, what the hell is going on? I've been calling you and we've got to boogie," he said. Carrie looked up in surprise.

"Oh shit, I'm sorry Mac. I discovered this file and was trying to see if it is part of Chaos, so I had to mute my comm for a minute to hear it."

"Is it," asked Mac.

"It sure looks that way from the thirty seconds I heard, and it sounds very bad."

"OK, pull the file quickly or just grab the whole drive."

She said, "no time to try to copy any of this. I'll just pull the whole processor and any attached drives."

"Let's go," Mac urged, start handing me the gear." Within five minutes Swan had disconnected every possible component that might store any data. *Thank God for tech miniaturization,* she thought. Between the two of them they managed to carry two processors and five hard drives.

As they were rushing out the door, Mac asked, "did you see any safes or vaults of any kind in the office?"

"Not specifically," she answered, "but there was a locked door off the room that I couldn't access, so who knows what might be in that room."

"OK, well it can't be helped," Mac, responded, as they raced down the hall to the residence's entrance.

The entrance foyer looked like a wartime med unit during a bio attack, with the bodies of the drugged Typhon agents sprawled out on the tile floor, surrounded by mask-clad personnel on every side.

"Joe, are we safe now without the masks?" Mac asked.

"Should be," answered the Seal.

"How's Pat doing?"

Elaine answered, "I had a bloody tough time keeping him from bolting after you guys when you called in."

Mac stooped down to his friend and said, "OK Pat, no bullshit, how are you doing?"

"I feel like shit, but I'm good to go. I think Elaine managed to keep my blood inside my body for a change," Pat answered with a smile that looked more like a grimace.

"Hang in there buddy, we're blowing this joint now."

"Peter, status," Mac barked into his comm.

Peter came back, "I've done all the pre-flight check I can without firing her up. I need some help with moving her out of the hanger manually."

Joe, who was already staked out at the door scanning for hostiles, yelled back, "I'm on it," and bolted out the front door headed for the hanger.

"Hey Mac, I think these guys are about to come out of their beauty sleep," Jasmine warned. Mac looked over at the bodies spread out on the floor and did notice some movement.

"OK, Jasmine. Carrie, you and Elaine assist Pat over to the hanger and get him into the chopper. Elaine, stay with him and Carrie get Joe and come on back to help us get these boys loaded up."

Pat, with Swan on one arm and Warsaw on the other moved slowly out the door leaving Mac and Jasmine guarding their precious cargo. As the trio disappeared, Mac heard static from the Typhon comm unit he had taken off the dead guard and then a voice.

"To all units, check in starting with interior sentries." There was static. "Repeat, to all units check in."

Then a response came over the air, "this is unit seven, interior north station, checking in." This response was followed by acknowledgments from several other interior sentries occupying different areas of the large house.

HQ repeated its request several times to some units that did not respond. Finally, HQ came back on and commanded, "Search party, check in now." There was static. "Repeat, this is HQ, search party check in." Again, no answer. "This is HQ, perimeter sentries check in." Again, no response. "This is HQ, general alert is in effect. We may have a breach in several locations. All units secure the principals in the living quarters, then fan out and clear the residence. Report status and confirmation as areas are cleared." *Damn, this is about to get very nasty,* thought Mac.

Just then, Joe and Peter burst into the foyer.

"Hey Cap," Franklin yelled, "lights are going on everywhere inside the house and outside. I think we've been made."

Mac looked around him and knew what he had to do. All the treasure was still here, the computers and hard drives and the captives with all the knowledge of Typhon. He had to get them out or the mission would fail and maybe the world with it.

He turned to his teammates, "OK, slap these suckers awake so that they can at least stagger out of here and you don't have to carry them. Joe, take Gunderson and Krishinko. Peter, you and Jasmine grab all the tech stuff and lead Von Stemp. Get those bastards and the gear into the chopper and be ready to lift off. I will position myself just outside by the pillars to cover both the inside and the outside."

"What about you?" asked Jasmine. "If you're under fire, how are you going to get to the chopper?"

"I'll figure that out when the time comes, but if they get here without opposition, they'll blow you guys out of the sky before you can get clear. Now go," Mac yelled, as he started to help Franklin resuscitate their captives. One at a time the three men's eyes began to open. The drug would keep them woozy for at least another five to ten minutes, but they were able to be pulled to their feet and the team began to guide them staggering out of the building.

The static on the Typhon mobile unit was muted again as a frantic voice came over the speaker. "Unit 3 and 4 to HQ, we have just completed a search of the suites. Brewer is dead in Von Stemp's suite and all three principals are missing."

HQ immediately came back, "were there signs of a struggle in any of the suites?"

"No sir," came the immediate reply. "All looks normal."

"Maybe they left earlier than planned for Auckland," came one guard's reply.

"Not likely," responded HQ. "What about Brewer? What's the cause of death?"

"A single round through the forehead, Sir," the guard responded.

"No, too much shit is wrong, and several stations have not checked in. Get to the chopper and secure it and send some guys to check out the rest of the interior fast," came the command. Mac looked across to the hanger. The doors were open, and the chopper was positioned for takeoff, but the rotors were not turning. His team was loading up the merchandise, but several still had to board.

"Peter," Mac yelled into his comm. "fire the bird up now, we have company coming." Immediately, Mac heard the ignition fire and the big engines kicked and smoothed out as the huge rotors began to spin.

And then the shit hit the fan! He didn't need a radio to hear his enemy approaching, because a slug hit the pillar next to his head, the concrete exploding in all directions. He pulled behind it as he saw several guards positioned in the foyer with AK 47s raised. Mac grabbed one of the AKs that Franklin and Singe had lifted off their hallway kills and returned a brutal barrage of automatic fire into the entrance. Glass and wood shattered as the big rounds hammered the exterior. One guard screamed and went down, but there were more arriving to join the fray. Mac glanced back down the driveway and could see several guards running toward him and the chopper. *No more time*, he thought.

"Peter, get the hell out of here now," he yelled into his comm.

"No can-do Mac, we're not leaving you. We can lay down some fire, so you can make a break."

"Won't work, Peter. There are too many of them with too much firepower from inside and outside the house. You have to go now, that's an order. Now do it!"

The roar of the accelerating rotors was deafening as the big bird lifted into the air, turning quickly away from the oncoming attack, its nose dipping dangerously close to the ground as it disappeared into the night. Mac had alternated between the oncoming street assault and the interior attack, as he ripped through the thirty round magazines in each borrowed AK. His suicidal defense forced his assailants to scramble for cover; heads down and weapons silent just long enough for his team to survive to live another day. As the last rounds were exhausted, the air went suddenly deathly quiet. Mac had known that for a few seconds after his last rounds were gone he could do some open field running while his adversaries questioned what would come next.

He actually began his sprint while pulling off his last ten rounds and was already halfway to the large building next to the hanger when his ammo ran out. Jerking the door open he escaped inside before the first shooter lifted his eyes to track his movements. Quickly scanning the interior, he realized he was in a very large garage housing every mode of transportation. There were exotic cars, dirt and road bikes, tractors and trucks and all-terrain vehicles. He turned back to the small glass window in the steel door through which he had just fled and peered out. Over two dozen guards were gathering by the hanger with one large man obviously making search assignments. He had already disbursed one group towards the hanger and a second was being given instructions as he pointed at Mac's building. Mac locked the door to slow them down and then quickly retreated into the dark interior looking for some way out. At the far end of the building was a second large equipment exit door that could be electrically raised from a control panel on the wall. At least he had a way out if he could just find the right vehicle and get it running and navigate it through this maze of iron and rubber.

It wasn't long before he could hear the search approaching the locked door and curses as its condition was discovered.

"Get that channel lock over here," yelled a voice. "We don't have time to get the key." Time to exit with or without wheels, he thought as he raced to the back. The prospect of escaping on foot with Typhon militants combing the grounds was anything but appealing and then he heard the dogs in the distance. He was as good as anyone at avoiding search parties even with poor odds, but dogs, forget it. You couldn't hide from them. They could hear and smell you from miles away. And a healthy German shepherd would mow down even Usain Bolt running all-out at twenty-seven mph.

Mac found himself struggling with a rare situation, he didn't see a way out. He pulled his big Sig out and prepared for the final confrontation, knowing the odds were not in his favor. Suddenly, the big rear door began to open, its well-greased motor and draw chains humming softly. This was it, he thought as he pulled the slide back and racked a live round into the chamber.

And then a familiar voice rang out only feet away in the dim light, "hey cowboy, let's roll before these Typhon morons try to ruin our day," said Jasmine Snow, as she stepped out of the shadows smiling.

"Jasmine, what the hell in high water are you doing here? I gave you and the team an order."

"Now don't be so stuffy," Jasmine reprimanded, "they obeyed your command, even if they were fuming, but then you are their commander."

"So why aren't you with them?" Mac asked, genuinely concerned that this woman had just forfeited her life for him.

"Well, it's really quite simple even for a Yank," she quipped. "I don't officially work for you or them, which I reminded them when they tried to stop me from jumping out of the chopper on lift off. But we can discuss my alleged insubordination over a pint at the first pub we find once we have extricated ourselves from this predicament."

"And how do you propose we do that?" Mac asked.

"On two wheels," she responded, as she pulled him around the corner of a large truck where two 250 cc Kawasaki dirt bikes were leaning on their kick stands ready to roll.

"Well I'll be," he exclaimed incredulously. "How in the world did you pull this off," he asked.

"I've been here before, remember," she answered.

"Well Jasmine, if we get out of this it looks like I owe you again."

"Indeed," she said, "and as you know two times are a charm."

The chorus of barking was growing ever closer as the two roared out of the garage heading away from the pack with Jasmine in the lead. With no moon, just keeping the bikes upright was a challenge, but as their eyes adjusted the canopy of stars provided some help. Mac had no clue how Snow was navigating or where they were going, but it didn't feel like they were headed for Auckland. On several occasions they could see searchlights in the distance that detoured them to higher ground as they wove their way into the mountains. Finally, after a grueling hour of treacherous off road running where even a switch back or two would have been a gift, she pulled to a stop under some large pines and shut her bike down. Mac followed suit and joined her as they both sat, backs propped against a thick tree trunk to recover.

There was a chill in the air that seemed to come with the altitude as Mac turned to Jasmine and asked, "do you know where we are?"

"I think so," she said. "I did have a plan to start into the mountains because logic told me, Typhon wouldn't put a lot of resources into guarding such harsh terrain."

"That appears to have been solid," said Mac.

"Then, I was going to work south once we were far enough clear of their perimeter and finally pick up the highway into Auckland to re-join your team. Unfortunately, we've been pushed higher into the mountains than I planned, so it's going to take us a lot longer to get back to the city."

"But, how do you even know which way that is, Mac asked. Jasmine smiled and stuck out her wrist with her Garmin GPS watch.

Mac laughed, "you know Jasmine, you remind me of a Boy Scout."

"What does that mean?" she asked, offended.

"It's their motto," he explained. "*Be Prepared*, and you always are."

"Somebody has to be," she chided him gently.

"OK," Mac replied, "what's the plan Ms. Snow?"

"Here's my thinking, given that we are seriously off course. We have maybe two more hours of darkness. While these bikes are fuel efficient, they gobble up fuel off-road, and they only had a half tank when we left. So, we will need petrol and water before long. I say, let's put a little more distance between us and those clowns and then shut down until daylight when we can see better. We're actually damn fortunate that one of us hasn't crash-landed yet. My mapping software shows a lake about eight miles further up the range. These are freshwater lakes and are pristine, so we can hydrate there and get some rest before we head for Auckland."

"Sounds like a plan," Mac said impressed.

The lake was large and ripple free as the two slowly pulled to a clearing fifty feet from its shore.

"Oh my," Jasmine said in wonderment, "how can a world so ugly produce so much beauty?" Mac had to admit, it was breathtaking. The smooth dark surface reflected every star perfectly in a mirror image as if one viewed two heavens simultaneously. They almost felt apologetic as they knelt down on the bank cupping their hands to gather the clear fresh liquid that sent ripples cascading across the perfect surface, temporarily disrupting the magical effect. The air was even colder at this altitude and the two felt the chill as their bodies cooled down from their intense activity. They had removed their heavy halo gear once on the ground during the assault, and their light camo coats were not insulated, and they couldn't chance a fire.

"Jasmine, have you checked the bike's rear storage for any camping gear? We sure could use something to deal with the cold."

"Sorry, didn't really have time for that," she said. "But no time like the present, cause it's getting seriously chilly. I am not optimistic," she continued. "Those bags don't look big enough to carry a thermos, let alone a blanket."

Both bikes had small leather storage bags strapped just behind the seat that they both unzipped. Jasmine discovered a black plastic bag that took up half the storage area and a couple of energy bars.

"I don't know what's in this bag, but at least we have dinner," she said, raising the food in the air.

Mac said, "I got the same treatment, so I guess we can each have seconds."

As Jasmine unzipped the zip lock on the bag, she said, "what the hell," and pulled out a thick square of light fabric.

Mac stepped over to examine her find and exclaimed, "another break for the good guys."

Jasmine looked up and said, "this looks like a place mat."

"Shake it out Jasmine," Mac directed. She did as she was told, and the small square billowed out into a five by seven-foot piece of fabric.

"OK, it's not a place mat," she admitted.

"No it's not," said Mac. "It's a silk thermal blanket and it's just what we need."

After their double helpings of dinner the two agents settled down on a bed of pine needles generously deposited below several of the towering conifers. The silks were amazing insulators, but the dropping temperatures soon drew them closer together until they ended up sharing the two silk thermals draped over them.

A warming sun broke through the pines as it rose towards its zenith. As the bright rays played on his face, Mac awoke with Jasmine's arms splayed across his chest and her head nestled against his side. As she breathed softly, a gentle purring sound whispered from her lips and a look of calm contentment caressed her lovely features. He gazed at her unmoving, not wanting to break the moment. *She was beautiful,* he thought, but not in the conventional sense. It was the combination of her features and expressions that took your breath away. But beyond that, she was basically brilliant with an extraordinary British sense of humor and almost fearless and unflappable under pressure. He had to admit, he had never met anyone quite like her. *Whoa, cowboy,* he thought. You're getting way ahead of yourself. *Good advice,* he thought as he closed his eyes dozing off. Feeling her move, he woke again, only minutes later, his last thought still lingering as he opened his eyes and stared up into her gorgeous face as she gently pressed her parted lips onto his.

◆

While steaming out to open sea, Peter Gunderson spent several hours on the final trappings of Chaos' launch. Then, following a light dinner served under the stars of the aft deck, he retired. At 5:30 am Gunderson was jolted out of a deep sleep by the ring tone of his secure line. Expecting a glorious story from his son about their brutal destruction of Team Apogee and the capture and interrogation of Sisco, he anxiously reached for the phone.

"Gunderson," he responded automatically as he put the mobile to his ear.

"Sir," came the reply, "I have some bad news."

"Who the hell is this?"

"This is Security HQ Squadron Commander Frey," the man responded. "I am in charge of the security at Ardyh Ranch." Gunderson remembered the man now.

"Yes Commander, what is the meaning of this call?"

Over the next thirty minutes, Gunderson was briefed in excruciating detail about the early morning raid, the kidnapping of his son, Krishinko and Von Stemp, the theft of the computers and drives and the escape of the assailants using his own helicopter. To add insult to injury, the ambush of Team Apogee in Auckland had never materialized, because their targets had never showed up and Typhon's team had just now returned to the ranch missing all the action. It now seemed irrefutable that NSA's team was responsible for the ranch attack even though there had not been any specific identification. It was also reported that one of the Apogee members had never boarded the chopper and a full search was underway, with no results so far.

"What about the woman," Gunderson asked, clearly irritated and hardly able to contain himself.

"Sir, she is also missing and disappeared earlier in the evening before the raid. We also have a search underway for her," the Commander said, ending his comments and signing off.

Gunderson was apoplectic with rage at the sheer incompetence of his entire organization. But as he gripped the side of his bed, his hands reddening from the strain, he realized that he had to calm down and maintain control. Gunderson had a temper, but he also had an enormous ego that provided an unusual capacity to control his bouts of anger. Even as he finished the call, his mind was already assessing the damage and finding solutions. Actually, he was not overly concerned about losing his lieutenants. Even his son Jefferey was expendable as far as he was concerned. Of course, the Agency would break them all, so it was important that he move up his timetable on Chaos and begin activating the triggers earlier to avoid any complications. He also had the foresight to take steps to mitigate most of this scenario.

His compartmentalization and security measures and the false information he had been feeding to Jefferey and his boys was part of his natural paranoia and would protect Chaos' implementation. The work they had done together to develop the details of many of the Chaos fractals, although valid, were not all the ones he would trigger or in the same priority. If NSA acquired this Intel, it would serve more to confuse them than provide actionable information. The computer and disk drives, however, were a different matter. Those systems had serious intelligence that NSA could use to damage Typhon and maybe even Chaos, but it was very tightly secured and while he had no doubt they would eventually break that security, it would take NSA a lot of time to crack. And the Agency had very little time left.

Gunderson picked up the yacht's intercom phone next to his bed. Immediately the captain came on the line. Gunderson asked,

"Captain, what is our current position?"

The captain answered, "well Sir, we are currently in international waters, as you instructed, about thirty miles north of Auckland."

"Good," Gunderson said, "set a course to Ponui Island. When we arrive set anchor in the most secluded cove with access to the island. That would be the last one we visited a year or so ago, when I first acquired your services."

"Yes Sir, very good Sir," replied the captain respectfully. With over 600 outer islands surrounding New Zealand, it was among the most secure locations on earth if one desired to disappear. That had been one of the critical criteria for selecting Typhon's HQ-2.

Years before, when Gunderson purchased that property, he had also negotiated a perpetual lease for another property, the privately owned island called Ponui. It was located in the Hauraki Gulf to the east of Auckland in the eastern end of the Tamaki Strait. A tiny island, with only seven square miles of farmland, but it offered the anonymity that Gunderson needed to carry out the final steps in his quest for world domination, come Hell or high water. His final task before breakfast was to contact Leon Fowler via Martin Stabler's secure connection and find out what the situation was with his boys and what leverage he might have to free them.

CHAPTER TEN

THE LIST

By mid-day they pulled into the town of Wellsford, riding on fumes and relieved to quickly find a petrol station. The bikes had held up fine, but not so much their derrières. The final cross-country run out of the mountains had been treacherous, even in broad daylight. They wasted no time grabbing bottled waters and energy bars and got back on the road for the final seventy-seven kilometers down Route 16 into Auckland. They had decided early that morning not to try to contact their team, because they had no idea what their status was. They could have been shot down, captured or worse and Mac and Jasmine figured they might need the element of surprise in any skirmish they might encounter. They parked the bikes two blocks away from the team's apartment and approached on foot. It was midafternoon and the sun was beginning to cast long shadows as the day moved towards dusk. They saw no movement and all the curtains were drawn. Mac signaled for Jasmine to hold back as he worked his way around to the rear entrance and peered into a first-floor window but saw no one. He tried the door, but it was locked. He motioned for Jasmine to stay back as he raised his fist and boldly knocked on the back door.

A minute later he heard heavy footsteps approaching the door and then it opened rapidly. He stared into the welcoming eyes of Joe Franklin whose look of surprise and relief was truly heartwarming.

"Well I'll be damned if it isn't Mac Sisco back from saving all our asses. We thought you might still be kicking and have been spending the last twelve hours planning on a replay to get you out."

Mac smiled and said, "I can't wait to see what that plan looks like" and gave his friend a fist bump.

"But Mac, I have some bad news," the big man said frowning.

"What happened Joe," Mac asked concerned.

"We lost Jasmine. She jumped out of the chopper just as we lifted off and we couldn't stop her. We've got to mount a plan to go find her stat," the big Seal said miserably. Before Mac could say a word to console his distraught teammate, a voice boomed behind him, as Jasmine stepped out of the shadows.

"I would say that is downright insubordinate," she laughed. Joe looked up to see her and grinned ear-to-ear as he rushed up and lifted her into the air in a crushing bear hug.

"Take it easy big guy," Jasmine complained, "I didn't come all this way just to be crushed by a muscle-bound Seal."

The reunion was a fitting end to a mission that was now successfully in the books. The bleary-eyed team had been up all night, since escaping from the ranch, searching for an angle to save Mac and Jasmine, but had not made a lot of progress. Their captives were still gagged and bound in separate rooms and had been sedated since they had returned. Carrie had alerted Admiral Clausen to the situation and their status. The Admiral had praised the team for their incredible feat even as he somberly dealt with Mac's predicament.

Swan had already made copies of all drives and backed up the processor to another computer, so that they had redundancy. Using an agency encryption key and cipher, she had transmitted the terabytes of data directly to NSA for immediate analysis. Clausen had directed her to continue with her own efforts to evaluate the devices and their contents, knowing her extraordinary talents. They had agreed that tomorrow, barring any attempt to save Mac; they would begin interrogating their captives. Clausen, in a rare moment of empathy had agreed that once they were certain that Jefferey Gunderson had no more informational value, they could use him as a bargaining chip with his father to free Mac, if he had been captured. Every member of Team Apogee would forever appreciate that gesture from the old warrior.

Mac sighed as the reverie of his return subsided and watched as each member of his team warmly greeted Jasmine. It looked like she had earned their trust and that they now saw her as part of the team. He had to admit that he was of the same opinion, while admitting his obvious growing bias. Her performance had been truly outstanding. She had made a significant contribution to the success of the mission and that would be in his report to Admiral Clausen in the morning. He would also request that she be permitted to continue working with them and gauge the Admiral's appetite for her exoneration if their mission was successful.

But Mac's exhilaration was short lived as he considered what still had to be done. For all their efforts, they still had not really impacted Typhon's primary activities, nor did they understand what and how it meant to carry them out. In fact, their successes may have only served to accelerate Peter Gunderson's timetable as the increasing pressure imposed even greater urgency on the global terrorist. Feeling worn out from the day's journey and a bit stymied by the current situation, Mac wandered into the office where Swan and Warsaw were working.

Mac said, "sorry guys for interrupting, but Carrie, back in Gunderson's ranch you said that the video you were watching was very disturbing. Did you finish it, and can you tell me what it said?"

Carrie and Elaine had turned to him as he spoke and now Carrie answered, "no worries Mac and yes I did finish it and it's the kind of thing you should see for yourself. Hold on, I'll tee it up." She pulled up some files on the system and then clicked on one link which started the video. Suddenly, Mac was looking into the eyes of the most dangerous man on the planet, Peter Gunderson as he began to speak.

"I have recorded this video under Typhon's Command Protocol for Jefferey Gunderson's eyes only. Once viewed, that protocol calls for its immediate destruction. I will be departing tomorrow to board Calamity to avoid the risk of discovery. My destination will not be determined until I am at sea and will not be disclosed. The Chaos planning fractals we jointly developed will be incorporated in the final plan while I am in transit. The priorities for the LIST will be finalized and triggers set within the week. I anticipate the first fractals will launch no later than one week from today. Others will continue to detonate over time. Some may be manually triggered if situations require alternative actions, but the vast majority of catalysts will engage without any intervention on Typhon's part. Typhon will continue to develop and add additional fractals so long as management control can be maintained, and stimuli are required. You and your team will receive instructions remotely until our venues can be safely integrated once again. Typhon will succeed!"

The video went dark and the two agents looked at Mac anxiously.

"The clock is ticking," said Elaine, "and I'd say, to put a fine point on it, Mr. Gunderson's soliloquy is indeed very disturbing!"

"Has the Admiral seen this video?" Mac asked.

"Yep," said Carrie, "it was the first thing I sent him. He has already shared it with POTUS and some members of the NSC. They have been in meetings on it and I believe are going to engage the NATCOG."

"I don't blame them," said Mac, "but if this leaks, we could easily have a worldwide panic. No matter what happens, we have got to have a ground plan. We just can't sit here and wait while this thing goes down."

"I totally agree," said Elaine, "but I have to say, I am at a loss as to what that plan looks like."

"There's really only one way we can deal with Chaos now and that is surgically," Mac reasoned.

"What do you mean," asked Swan.

Mac continued, "consider, this maniac set in motion Armageddon on auto pilot. There is no single action that will shut it all down. That's his failsafe. We must get this list. If we can't decipher it with the technology, then we must find him. If we get the list, we can use our resources and NATCOG's to surgically deactivate the fractals according to their priorities and timetables. I believe it's the only shot we've got," Mac exclaimed. "Carrie, get back to the Agency and see if they have made any progress. I need to run all this by the Admiral, so we're synched up. Let's get the team together in one hour and see what we can collectively come up with."

An hour later Team Apogee sat mesmerized as they reviewed the Gunderson Video. As the screen went black Mac provided an update.

"I just got off the horn with the Admiral a few minutes ago and he agrees with our assessment. POTUS has convened an emergency meeting with NATCOG members tomorrow EST, sometime in the late afternoon. The problem is that without any definitive specifics all he can do is provide a general warning. Everyone has already tightened up their security, so this is more about going on alert. We need a breakthrough and it's either going to come from one of those guys in the other rooms, the tech here or in Ft. Meade or finding Peter Gunderson and it's a very big ocean." Mac turned to Swan, "what's the update from NSA on the decryption work?"

"Still a work in progress," she said. "They gave me a few ideas and I gave them some, but nothing earth shattering yet. I do have a couple ideas; I'd like to try tonight and then maybe one of those thugs will slip up tomorrow and give us a hint."

"OK," Mac said, "any recommendations?"

Franklin said, "well tomorrow, you, Peter and I will be running these interrogations so I think we should spend a couple hours brainstorming techniques and role playing."

"I agree," chimed in Singe, "and I have a few ideas that might loosen their tongues."

Swan added, "Elaine and I have been working the computers and Pat said he is feeling much better and is a whiz with numbers, so we'll recruit him."

Jasmine almost sheepishly asked, "what about me?"

Everyone turned to her and Joe said, "I figured we'd offer you the best job of all, Jasmine."

"And that is," Jasmine asked suspiciously.

"You get to be on whichever team you want, because we all now know that you are really good at everything," he laughed. "Also, you are the team mascot, who takes no orders and takes no prisoners,"

Curry piped in grinning, "and no one here has the cojones to piss you off."

The whole table laughed as Jasmine thanked them appreciatively and said in that case, "I accept and would like to work on a separate area that has not yet been assigned."

"Really?" asked Mac curious, "what is that?"

Jasmine snarled and said, "I want to find Calamity and that bloody bastard Peter Gunderson!"

♦

What a roller coaster ride this Typhon catastrophe had become, thought the Director of NSA. And yet, there might be a silver lining if the world could recalibrate and Typhon could be defeated. Clausen was a bit of a Sci-Fi zealot and couldn't ignore the parallels of today's world with the movie The Matrix, where the world was divided into those who took the red pill and the ones that preferred the blue pill. The red pill represented those who accepted harsh realities, no matter how unpleasant, and wouldn't be deterred by false narratives or sacrifice their personal rights. And then there were the blue pill advocates, who preferred a world of blissful ignorance in exchange for a total capitulation of free will. Typhon was exploiting the vast blue pill believers who couldn't recognize their own false sense of reality. Typhon was dedicated to filling the void for dissatisfied false victims who blamed everyone for their perceived misfortunes and promised equality of outcomes and a state of utopia for all. It was a powerful potion built on decades of false education and warped ideologies, evolved from the roots of Engels, Lenin, Stalin and Alinsky. But the blue pill had stuttered and faltered over the ages as its promises failed to materialize again and again and its future appeared precarious until Typhon had reared its ugly head.

Tomorrow would be a seminal moment in history, as leaders of the free world began their defense against the greatest existential threat humanity had ever faced and Clausen was worried. They had made great progress in a short time, but he still felt they were losing. Gunderson had developed a model that appeared unstoppable. The sheer inertia and global reach of Typhon's disruptions might already be past undoing. If Typhon could add even more hysteria to an already unstable world, governments would topple, wars would break out, anarchy would explode across the world and humanity would devolve into a very dark place. *But why,* he mused, and knew the answer. It was so Typhon could come in and pick up the pieces, creating their new world order. It would be perceived as a white knight and embraced by a frightened and desperate populace far and wide.

Of course, in the beginning, it would appear benign, but as its tentacles reached out and solidified its control, its authoritarian rule would enslave the world. Clausen knew this to be true because it had been tried many times before, just on a smaller scale. Sometimes it had been defeated before it could take hold. But other times it had metastasized too quickly, and the suffering lasted for generations until finally the human spirit revolted and started over. They had to find the list and decrypt it, but that was like finding a needle in a million haystacks.

It would take divine intervention and right now he really needed that miracle. He could almost feel the darkness closing in, when his secure line suddenly rang.

"Admiral, this is Robert Worthington, I think we might have caught a break."

Clausen sat up in his chair gripping the grey phone and said, "yes Bob, what have you got?"

"Sir," Worthington continued, "one of my cryptology teams was on the line with Carrie Swan from Team Apogee and she suggested we analyze Gunderson's Video for clues. She said it was a long shot, but she and Elaine Warsaw had a hunch that it might be important. After analyzing Gunderson's video to see if there were any clues, we think we may have an angle."

"Yes?" Clausen urged, standing up as if it might help him hear better.

"Right now it's just a theory, but the video makes no sense," Worthington explained.

"What do you mean?" asked Clausen, confused.

"Well Sir, there is no reason for Gunderson to have sent this message to his son, because everything in it, Jefferey Gunderson already knew. Furthermore," Worthington continued, "why video the message when he could have simply sent it via a secure email or text?"

"OK, Bob, I agree that is strange, but hardly conclusive. Even so, what would be the point?" asked Clausen.

"We believe that the video is a onetime pad," Worthington explained. "As you know, OTPs are an archaic method of substitution encryption, but very inexpensive and virtually unbreakable unless you have the key, because it's entirely random. Also, the message it encrypts can only be as long as the pad itself, so it is used for shorter communications and is never re-used."

"But why the video?" Clausen pressed.

"Only one reason we could think of," said Worthington, "paranoia."

"I don't follow you," the Admiral shot back.

"Admiral, it's a good bet that no one would think to look in a video for a one-time pad key. In fact, in my thirty years in the business, I've never seen that done before and neither has any of my team." Clausen paused and thought about what he had just heard, his mind racing. *Could this be true, was this his miracle,* he wondered.

"Admiral," Worthington asked, "are you still there?"

"Yes, Bob, I am, and I was just thinking, what kind of message would you go to so much trouble to secure that was so short?"

"There is only one I can think of," answered Worthington.

"Me too Bob, me too," said the Admiral.

◆

Leon Fowler was not at all happy with the way Gunderson was treating him. He had assumed that his services would be limited and strategic, but the most recent demand was almost frivolous and very risky. He could care less about Gunderson's boys. They had gone and gotten themselves captured and their incompetence was not his concern. Actually, if they were that dumb, they shouldn't be in charge of anything. Not to mention that with them out of the picture, his stock with Typhon just took a big leap. That said, he would follow up on the request and tip toe around, but he sure as hell wasn't going to stick his neck out on this one. Tomorrow was the big NATCOG meeting with the President and Admiral Clausen would be there to provide an update for the group. Leon would also be there as one of the representatives from the NSC. He'd see what Clausen reported and maybe there would be something there. If not, Gunderson would just have to live with it. At this point Leon was in the catbird seat with all his options open and he intended to keep it that way.

♦

It had been a long night for the whole team and despite a five-hour interlude of sleep, they were all up early and back at their appointed tasks. The plan had been to meet again at 10:00 am for a readout from each team and go from there. Franklin circled the big dinner table topping off everyone's coffee mugs as the team assembled for their update. As Mac surveyed the group, surprisingly, they looked no worse for the wear, but then coffee and adrenaline will do that, he figured.

"OK, folks," he began, "today is a big day for us because tomorrow U.S. EST is a big day for the world. As you know, POTUS will be conducting a NATCOG meeting then and my hope is that we can help him out with some good news, so let's get started. Let's start with Carrie and Elaine."

Swan said, "sure, well Elaine and I threw a lot of decryption routines against the few files we could actually open without any results. That means that either my software is not sophisticated enough, or those files are simply clear text."

"Was there anything useful on the files you opened?" Singe asked.

"Not really, most of it was operational information about the ranch," Elaine responded.

"What about the files you couldn't open?" asked Franklin.

"Not much to say about them either, other than we couldn't break them. We're still running decryption routines against them, even as we speak, but I'm not optimistic."

"Have you spoken with the agency teams to see what they have so far," Mac asked.

"Yes, in fact I spoke to them earlier this morning and discussed an angle of investigation Elaine and I thought might be fruitful. They said they would check it out and get back to me. I actually expect them to call back any time now and if they do, I'll take the call and brief all of you," Swan promised."

"Well, let's keep our fingers crossed, we sure need a break," Mac responded.

"OK, how about our interrogations?" asked Mac.

"I'll begin," said Franklin. "Peter and I decided that I should handle Krishinko, at least in the first run. We figured that Von Stemp would be too lathered up if I took him. Frankly, there isn't much to report. Krishinko was mum throughout the entire interview. I shouldn't even call it that. Every question I asked he refused to answer, not even name, rank or serial number. We need an angle or some leverage to crack his armor or we may need to use some other more convincing techniques."

"With Von Stemp, it was similar," interjected Singe, "but I did manage to get some profanity out of him along with some interesting threats to my family and friends."

"That is disappointing, especially since we went to so much trouble to capture and drag them back here," Mac complained. "Well, regarding Jefferey Gunderson," Mac said, "Joe, Peter and I agreed to leave him until last and use whatever we learned from the first two as leverage with him, but it looks like that strategy may be out the window. I will have a go at it after this meeting. Worst case, they may have some value as bargaining chips with the old man," Mac concluded.

"I wouldn't count on it," said Elaine. "Peter Gunderson's profile suggests that he would sacrifice his own mother for Typhon and his vision."

Jasmine suddenly interrupted, and in her inimitable manner said, "I see you left the best for last."

Mac answered mimicking her playfully, "indeed we bloody well did."

Jasmine smiled and said, "don't worry my report is short, unless you beat me up with dumb questions. I contacted the maritime authorities here in New Zealand for any information on a boat registered here under Gunderson's name or any other logical pseudonym, without success. Then it occurred to me to research the original documentation about the ranch he owns. Ironically, the first place I looked was the architectural drawings you guys already acquired to plan the raid on his ranch. Those plans identified a Gilbert Schroeder as the owner. Low and behold," she continued, "there is an unnamed 250-foot yacht registered out of Auckland under that same name. Further research using that registration and Calamity as the boat's name identified that the yacht is slipped right here in Auckland Harbor."

"You're not going to tell us that Peter Gunderson is sitting right here under our noses are you?" Curry asked astonished.

"Unfortunately no," Jasmine answered, "but based on where he was picked up when I escaped and the data on the yacht's performance capabilities, I have already determined search parameters that narrow down where he might be. My guess is that he had a predetermined escape contingency and has moored under the cover of one of the outer islands."

"You don't think he would head for open seas to make the search more difficult?" asked Mac.

"No I don't," responded Jasmine.

"Why not?" Swan asked.

"Because he knows that we could muster significant aerial reconnaissance and he hasn't had enough time to escape our range."

"OK, so he's hiding behind some island; how many are there?" Mac asked.

"Well, that's the rub," Snow responded, "there are somewhere around 600, give our take."

"Well, bloody hell," said Warsaw, "that doesn't narrow it down much! That kind of search could take forever."

"Maybe not," Jasmine said. "As soon as this meeting is over, I will plot Calamity's possible target islands based on her probable speed under the current cruising conditions. She just can't go full throttle if the seas are high or wind conditions are severe. That will narrow the field significantly. I will also see if I can get maritime data on craft locations via our friends here in Auckland. If we do narrow it down, say to a couple islands, Mac, with your help, maybe we can get some satellite images to validate it is Calamity."

"Good work Jasmine. I will be checking with Admiral Clausen after our meeting. I'll make the request to get the ball rolling. Let's all get back on task and if anything breaks no matter how insignificant, get me immediately."

As the room cleared and everyone got back to work, Mac checked his watch. He and the Admiral had agreed, Mac would call him with an update by noon NZ time and it was close to that now, so he dialed Clausen's secure private number. The call went straight to the Admiral's special mobile phone that could not be intercepted, even by Martin Stabler.

Clausen answered immediately, "hold on Mac, I'm finishing a meeting."

Mac heard the Admiral say, "thank you gentlemen, I'll speak with you later and we'll see what else you come up with." Then Clausen was back on the line, "thanks for holding Mac, what have you got?" Mac detailed his morning meeting for the Admiral and concluded by saying that he was personally going to interview Jefferey Gunderson after their call, but he wasn't optimistic that he could break him.

After he had finished, Clausen said, "Mac, your team has done really outstanding work and I know it has been very frustrating. I know this because we have struggled as well, but I finally believe we may have something that you and your team can really get your teeth into." Mac could feel the excitement stirring as he wondered what the Admiral was about to disclose.

"Mac," Clausen said excitedly, "we have the list!"

Mac was aghast, "what, how he stammered?"

"Well, first let me give credit where it's due," answered the Admiral.

"We actually have Carrie and Elaine to thank for this breakthrough," he said. "They put us on to Gunderson's video."

"They did mention this morning that they had an idea, but it was a long shot," replied Mac.

"They were certainly right about that and one that we never would have found, but for them," explained Clausen. "But they hit the trifecta, that's for sure. Essentially, the video turned out to be a one-time-pad. It took us a while to open the files, but those big parallel processors we have eventually broke them open and then we could run the OTP from the video against them. We don't know if we have the whole Chaos Fractal List, but we believe we have the current top priorities, based on the severity of the disruptions." Mac was excited, a real break and maybe a chance to finally strike a blow to Typhon, save lives and even unravel more of their plans.

"How many actions are on the list?" Mac asked anxiously.

"Thirty-seven," answered Clausen.

"Damn Admiral, that is a shit load of trouble to undo."

"Yes, it is Mac, but we have already begun developing counter actions for many of them. Fortunately, Gunderson has assigned dates to each one, and they are sequenced, so we have a chance to target them selectively. In some cases there are multiples at the same time, so we will have to coordinate a lot of resources in parallel all over the world. I'll send you the list as soon as we finish our call. I need you and your team to deal with the highest priority fractals that are due to initiate the soonest. The first of those will begin in seven days. There are two fractals plus one other mission objective that we must accomplish, and I only trust you and your team to take them on. The extra mission objective is to find and neutralize Peter Gunderson and must be done first before we act on any of the others."

"Why is that?" Mac asked.

"Once your team begins to shut these fractals down, Gunderson will immediately know what is happening and simply trigger new ones. If that happens, we won't have the benefit of a list or the ability to forecast future catastrophic actions. Under no circumstances can we let that happen," stressed the Admiral seriously.

"Yes Sir, I understand," Mac responded. "If we cannot locate him and we run out of time, what then?" he continued.

"That leaves us with only two options, depending upon the nature of the disruption," answered the Admiral. "Where possible, we put out fake news that the fractal succeeded. If that can't be done plausibly, we have to let it happen. It is the only way we can have any chance of defending the world from future chaos! Mac, one final thing, we must keep Gunderson from knowing that we have the list. Obviously, your team must know, but you need to consider carefully bringing Ms. Snow in on this information until we have handled Gunderson. That means you have a choice, either we take her into custody now or you figure out a way to run these operations without her knowing about the list. Let me know later today how you want to proceed so we can coordinate accordingly," Clausen concluded.

"Yes Sir, I will," Mac committed. As he signed off, his head was spinning. Things had gotten very complicated all of a sudden.

CHAPTER ELEVEN

SUBTERFUGE

Mac sat quietly after his call with the Admiral. *One week and counting*, he thought, not much time to save the world. He wanted nothing more than to pull the team together and announce this new breakthrough and begin the planning as a team, but could he do that with Snow present? The Admiral had shown enormous confidence in Mac by allowing him to make that decision. In a prior call, he had reported on Jasmine's engagement since her escape and Clausen had been amenable to Mac allowing her to continue on the mission, but he had left that decision up to Mac. Clausen was an enormously experienced and skillful field officer and he knew that one had to trust their ground operations leaders to call the shots. But this one had global implications and Mac almost wished the Admiral had made this call.

He personally felt good about Jasmine and he did recognize that her choices had largely been driven by circumstance. Typhon was going to terminate her, so she aligned with Team Apogee. And then there was her behavior in Paris, which was curious. It was almost as if she was waiting to see who would win before picking sides. It was also true that she had volunteered to hire on with Typhon against her own country in the first place and that decision was very disturbing. In spite of it all, he had to admit that he did not want to sideline her by arresting her and taking her into custody. Part of that was his gut impression that she was basically trustworthy and even though he could replace her with one of his team on the work she was doing to find Gunderson, she was a valuable asset and very good at her job. Also, there was a lot of ground to cover with very little time and he could certainly use her help. He also felt she had earned a chance to legitimize herself and he didn't want to eliminate that opportunity.

This was a real conundrum, he thought, so let's break it down and come to a solution. It appeared there were four options. He could trust her and tell her about the list along with his whole team. He could inform each of his core team about the list and exclude Snow and operate their missions without her knowledge of the list. He could delay disclosing the list to anyone and launch the Gunderson initiative immediately and only release the intel until after they had neutralized Gunderson. Or he could arrest Jasmine and have her held while he and the team executed their missions against Typhon.

His big problem was, if he didn't disclose the list to his team, he couldn't initiate their counter Chaos activities and that wouldn't work. They needed to get moving now. There was also another minor wrinkle. If he excluded Snow from the information and she became aware of his deception, it could create mistrust and jeopardize their mission. Not to mention the outrage his team might have after she had done so much to support them, even at the risk of her own life. On the other hand, if they were wrong about her and she somehow communicated with Gunderson about the list, the impact would be catastrophic and largely irreversible. Could they take that chance? *There are times in one's life when one experiences the loneliness at the top of the pyramid and this was one of those days,* he thought.

He continued to consider his options and thought about his call back to Clausen, when an idea came to him. The team knew he was speaking with Clausen and that he would update them with new orders. And therein lay the solution. *As disdainful as it was,* he thought, it was time for a little subterfuge to get the ball rolling. Mac pulled out his mobile and sent a secure text to Clausen that read, "don't disclose the discovery of the list to any of my team yet, working the issue, Mac." He then pulled up the list and examined the first two fractals that Clausen had assigned to his team. He was astounded by the ambition of them and the immediate damage they could have on destabilizing whole countries and even regions of the world.

The first one was short; assassinate the Prime Minister of Israel. The second was even more outlandish; assassinate at least one of the royals, preferably the King of England. *My God,* Mac thought, just these two operations, if successful, would throw the world into a state of turmoil. Israel was in the midst of major peace negotiations with its Arab neighbors, a truly historic initiative. Britain had set a course of independence via Brexit from the EU and was working its way through that transition.

He walked out into the hall as Joe approached him and asked, "Mac, are you ready to have a go at Jefferey?"

"Not right now, Joe, we need to have a team meeting. I have a new set of directives from Ft. Meade."

"OK, listen up everyone," Mac announced, as they all assembled once again. "We have a new set of orders. Unfortunately, the agency is still striking out on finding or decrypting the list, but they have new intel that has come in from some of the NATCOG members. We don't know how valid these leads are, but we simply can't risk inaction and Admiral Clausen believes our team is the best to take on these critical operations." Mac described the first two operations to the horror of everyone.

Snow jumped in and said, "I want to volunteer for the British op. It is my homeland and I obviously know the terrain."

"Me too," Warsaw demanded, "for the same reasons."

"OK, slow down guys," Mac said. "We'll sort the assignments out, but we also have an additional objective which frankly trumps the rest."

"What in hell could ever trump assassinating world leaders?" demanded Curry.

Mac answered, "we have got to find and take out Gunderson and get the list while we're at it. We need to know where future hits will come from and we need to stop him from adding any more. That said," Mac continued, "we believe the timing is critical, so we need to operate in parallel as we did in Set 3."

"I'll let you guys weigh in, but here's my thinking," Mac elaborated. "Peter and Elaine, you set up operations in London and connect with MI-6. Pat, how are you doing?"

"I'm a little sore, but good to go," the big Aussie responded.

"OK, you and Carrie head to Tel Aviv and hook up with Mossad. Joe, you and Jasmine and I need to find and neutralize Gunderson and get that damn list."

"What about our little kitties in the other rooms," asked Swan.

"I'll call our intel boys here in Auckland and have them escorted to a local lock up under strict security until we return," Mac said. "They may still come in handy, but right now our priorities have to be on stopping these immediate threats and getting Peter Gunderson and the list out of play."

"I am all in to take down Gunderson, but I still want to be in the British operation, even if MI-6 arrests me after it's over," demanded Jasmine.

"I get it," Mac responded, "that's why, what I just described is phase 1. Phase 2 is that each team will rejoin the other operations, if they complete their missions in a timeframe that allows it. These are clearly serious gigs and we all can use the support of Team Apogee if possible. No one is on the sidelines. I'll call those audibles as they occur. Everyone ok, with your assignments?" Mac asked.

"Copy," came the unanimous reply.

"I'll let the Admiral know the plan and he will run the traps for you. Look for details from him in the next few hours. Jasmine, you, Joe and I will sit down and see what you've got that's actionable, so we can get our butts moving. The rest of you should pack up and get ready to deploy today."

CHAPTER TWELVE

CALAMITY

As the others got up to leave, Mac turned to Franklin and Snow and said, "Jasmine, make me proud and give us a lead on this asshole." Jasmine was more than happy to take the floor.

She began, "I completed my investigation into the whereabouts of Calamity, and this is what I found. I began with tracking maritime activity during the twenty-four hours after my escape, using transponder data for ships in the immediate search perimeter. There were fifty-seven ships cruising in those waters. Five of them fit the general characteristics of Calamity. Further scrutiny eliminated all but two. After researching their registration data, I concluded that neither could be our target."

"So where does that leave us?" asked Franklin.

"Patience, big man," Jasmine chided. "I knew that it would be unlikely that Calamity would have their transponder on if they were trying to go dark, but I had to eliminate that first, just in case they screwed up. Once I did that, I mapped the islands within our search grid to see if there were any obvious refuges. There are twelve islands in the grid. Half of them are too small to qualify. Three have very shallow shorelines making them useless for cover. The remaining three would make reasonable sanctuaries for Calamity."

"How wide a range are we talking about here?" Mac asked.

"The three islands are within a thirty-mile circumference," she answered. "My approach would be to do a quick drone overfly and get aerials of all three islands. Odds are we'll see her hiding in a cove of one of them."

Mac responded, "I will make the call. I know we have a couple drones still on station here in New Zealand after our operation on Gunderson's ranch. We may be able to get confirmation within a couple hours and move on the yacht either tonight or tomorrow."

By 2:00 pm that afternoon Mac's two teams were ready for departure. Clausen had arranged for a military transport to depart at 3:00 pm for London and then on to Tel Aviv. The teams had spent the prior hour reviewing communications protocols and contingencies so they could effectively integrate their activities. Timing would be critical, and execution had to be precise, not an easy accomplishment when you were operating on the fly. They exchanged their typical thumbs up and fist bumps as the four agents left for the full day flight to their target cities.

On the optimistic assumption that they would get favorable photos in their search for Calamity, Mac and his team had already planned their operation and packed up their gear. He had used the dead time to connect with the military on picking up his prisoners. Clausen again had greased the skids by calling the commanding general and explaining the sensitive nature of the situation and the crucial need to lock up the three terrorists in very secure, separate cells with absolutely no communications with anyone. Those arrangements made; Mac expected a pickup by 5:00 pm that afternoon.

Thirty minutes later, he got the digital images of the drone overfly. They were on pins and needles as they all grouped around the big flat panel examining each frame. Each of the islands offered excellent moorings for large private crafts close to their shorelines. And as one would expect, all three had crafts moored nearby. Two of the islands had several large yachts hugging their coasts in separate navigable coves and one island had a single craft off its coast. As they scrutinized each island, Snow pulled up its name, characteristics and ownership details. The first two islands were owned by New Zealand and operated as national parks. The last island, Ponui was privately leased by an LLC. She did another quick search as Mac began to pull up the aerials of Ponui's coastline.

As the LLC details appeared on her iPad, she smiled and exclaimed, "got you, you son of a bitch!"

Joe jerked around from the screen and joked, "are you referring to Mac or Me?"

"Neither," she answered, "my remarks are directed to Mr. Peter Gunderson."

As Mac focused in on a small cove on the northern side of the small island, he asked, "what have you got Jasmine?"

"The name of the LLC that leases Ponui is GS Enterprises LLC."

"OK," said Joe, "why is that an aha moment?" he asked innocently.

"Initials are why, she responded excitedly. "GS Enterprises is short for Gilbert Schroeder Enterprises, the pseudonym Gunderson used to buy Calamity." Mac enlarged the aerial and zoomed in. The drone had taken several images from directly over the deck, port and starboard views and a shot from the bow and one aft of the stern of the craft.

Mac said, "well I am no yacht expert so I hope we can positively ID this one, having never actually seen it."

"Well if there is one thing I know, its ships," exclaimed Franklin. "Pull up the aft image," he said, "and zoom in all the way."

As the image sharpened up, Mac said with a smile, "well I guess that's a wrap," as the three stared at the scripted letters, *Calamity*.

Promptly at 5:00 pm, two Army MPs arrived to pick up their charges. To avoid undo observation, they escorted each prisoner individually from the rear entrance of the building to their waiting unmarked van. It was a moment that Mac and his team relished with a few parting gestures. Joe couldn't help smiling at each one as they shuffled out, especially his nemesis, Wart Von Stemp.

Mac simply commented, "this isn't over Gunderson," as Jefferey was directed out, and Snow, one hand raised in defiance, delighted in making a silent one finger sign at all three as they passed by.

"Karma is a bitch," laughed Franklin as they closed the door behind them.

They spent the next several hours going over their assault and extrication plan. They would go in by chopper around the side of the cove, flying at a low level for an amphibious drop into the sea, about a mile off the coast. They would navigate on the surface, propelled by sea scooters until they approached the cove and then submerge, making the rest of the way undetected below the surface. Ditching the scooters, when they approached the yacht, they would board the craft with most of the crew asleep and capture Gunderson and the rest by surprise.

"OK, gentleman and ladies, let's get this show on the road," Mac said. The three strapped on their back packs, picked up their gear and headed out the door on their way back to the Army hanger they used before. It was time to cut off the head of the snake. By the time they got there, it was close to midnight. The flight would take less than thirty minutes and they planned to board the boat no later than 3:00 am. The general had been very supportive of their mission and had provided a Bell UH-1Y Venom, utility chopper and his best pilot to ferry them to the site. Thirty minutes later they were cruising at 160 mph at 10,000 feet to eliminate any chance of detection.

There was a slight cloud cover and they approached the cove from the opposite side of the island, which also helped conceal their approach. Two miles out they began their decent dropping vertically down to 500 feet, above a choppy sea. They slowly cruised toward the low hills in the distance until they reached their drop zone, well outside the cove, and a mile out from the shoreline. Mac signaled to the pilot to take them down as they slid open the big exit door. Unlike their last aerial assault from 25,000 feet, this drop was more like twenty-five feet above the rolling waves, but it was still a challenge. They were going in with a shit load of amphibious gear. Aside from the scooters, they were fitted out in wetsuits, bubble free re-breathers, regulators, buoyancy compensators, fins, waterproof comm units and wet bags with their weapons. Jumping from the chopper with all this bulk was tricky. The scooters were tethered to them with fifty feet of nylon line, which went out first. Once it hit the water, they would jump away from it to avoid injury and then retrieve it.

It was a surgical jump, with feet first, hands on the mask and a slight backward lean breaking the water to avoid equipment issues. Franklin went first, followed by Snow and then Mac. The pilot hovered in place for a few minutes to ensure that his passengers were good to go and seeing Mac's raised arm, slowly gained altitude before turning back the way they had come and disappeared into the night sky.

Mac retrieved his scooter, stowed the rope in a hatch and went on comms, "everyone is cleared to proceed."

"Copy," came the reply from both agents.

"I'll take the lead. Jasmine, take second position aft of me by twenty feet and Joe, you follow Jasmine. When we get just outside the cove, I'll hold up and we'll move in on my command." The state-of-the-art Seabobs were the fastest underwater scooters on the market capable of speeds up to fourteen mph on the surface and only a little less under water, but the cove was almost four miles away, so it would be a twenty- to thirty-minute run in the unruly sea.

They arrived at the edge of the entrance to the cove without incident and Mac slowed to a stop. They huddled a few feet apart as Mac, pulled out his night vision binoculars and peered into the darkness. He could make out the silhouette of the large craft against the lighter colored shorefront. It looked to be moored about 100 yards off the shore. Its anchor lights were not illuminated in violation of maritime code, but then again, Typhon certainly didn't want to advertise its whereabouts. There were a couple cabin lights on, but they were barely discernible because their shades were drawn.

"OK, guys," Mac came over on the comms, "she is about a half a mile in and 100 yards out from shore. Let's dive to about forty feet and maintain that depth as far as we can. As we close on the yacht, stay just off the seafloor, the rest of the way in. I'll navigate on the compass heading but will surface when I need to verify our progress. Stay down while I do that. When we get to the hull, we'll regroup at the anchor line off the bow. I anticipate we'll be at about a twenty-foot depth. We'll secure our scooters, tanks and BC's there and free dive unencumbered to the surface and make our way along the hull to the stern for boarding. When we get on board, we'll spread out and neutralize any sentries and then we'll hit the crew quarters. Jasmine's data listed a limited crew for short hauls of a captain and six hands, but there may be a couple more personal guards on board. They will most likely be quartered in the guest staterooms. Deadly force is authorized, if necessary. Your tasers may be more effective in close quarters, but maintaining a surprise is our primary advantage. Let's try to synchronize and stay close to each other for back up. Most important is to take Gunderson alive and keep the boat intact so that we can search for intel once we have it secure. Everyone good?" he asked finally. Franklin and Snow nodded as Mac turned his scooter towards the yacht and began a gradual dive toward the bottom.

Navigating underwater is tricky under the best conditions, but at night without the benefit of lights, it's almost a crapshoot. Mac followed his bearings carefully, but halfway in, he surfaced to verify and correct his trajectory. Fortunately, he was only slightly offline and soon had the team back on course. Their depth was shallowing gradually as they closed on the island and soon without another correction, they could make out the dark form of the large yacht's bottom hanging above them no more than thirty feet away. They had come in broad side and followed the long hull seventy-five feet to the bow where the huge Danforth anchor was solidly entrenched in the sand.

Carefully untangling themselves from their amphibious gear and taking a final breath from their rebreathers, they followed the anchor line up to the surface under the long bow of the yacht. Keeping tight against the boats water line, they quietly moved to the stern that boasted a large swimming platform with a ladder to the aft deck. Mac signaled for the team to stay back and advanced to the rear of the platform where he could get a better vantage point and raised his head just slightly above the surface. One guard was sitting in a deck chair leaning up against the superstructure, scanning the back section of the deck.

Mac quickly submerged and returned to his team and huddling close said, "we've got one visible sentry on the aft deck. There may be more patrolling the main cabin, side decks and bow, so we're going to have to move fast and quiet. Follow me to the rear of the swim platform and stay low. I'm going to take out the aft guard and then board. As soon as I signal you, board quickly and we'll clear the deck."

The two nodded in unison and Mac returned to the platform with the two close behind. Again, Mac slowly raised his head enough to observe the aft deck. The guard had not left his seat. Mac retrieved his waterproof belly pack and gently pulled out the Sig. He would have only one shot at this and it had to be a precise headshot. The 9 mm was already charged as he aimed just over the stern gunwale and squeezed the trigger. Soundlessly the round hit its mark, a small red entry point immediately appearing squarely in the center of the man's forehead as it slumped forward onto his chest. Mac kipped himself up onto the platform and in three strides was up the stern ladder to the main deck. He moved across the large aft space to the main cabin and staying low below the cabin windows, crossed to the starboard side deck and peered down it toward the bow. He repeated the same exercise, crossing the boat's expansive forty-five-foot beam to the port side and surveyed its side deck as Franklin and Snow watched intently. Finally, he turned and signaled the two to advance to his position.

Mac signaled for Franklin to take the starboard side and he took the port, with Snow backing him up. It was a long way to the bow and with no illumination along the 175 feet, the side deck was largely obscured. Franklin made it all the way to the end of the forward cabin and risked a look out to the bow section. Toward the front of the yacht was a large circle painted on the deck with the letter "H" at its center on top of which rested a sleek executive helicopter. Another section of the forward deck sported a large hot tub surrounded by deck chairs and lounges. He could just make out three figures sitting in that section and hear a low murmur of conversation. Suddenly, one stood up and began walking in his direction. He quickly retreated into the shadows of the cabin, looking for some cover, but saw none. Moving further down the deck, he came upon a large storage locker and crouched down behind it.

The guard appeared around the corner and continued his way. Joe had to let him get far enough so that his fall would not alert the others. When the guard was only fifteen feet from Joe's position, the big Seal stood up and fired two rounds in rapid succession, one to the chest and a second to the guard's head. The man crumpled towards the railing and hung precariously over. Joe rushed to the body, grabbing it in a desperate attempt to prevent it splashing loudly into the black water below. He reached it just as it was about to go over the side and caught one arm and the man's belt and manhandled the body back onto the deck. His heart and lungs pumping from the exertion, he dragged the corpse back to the large locker, dropping it onto the shore lines resting neatly at its bottom, and closed the lid.

Like Franklin, Mac and Jasmine encountered no opposition as they progressed towards the bow, but just before reaching the end of the main cabin, they heard a door open behind them. Both spun around instantly to see a large man stepping through a mid-cabin doorway and turning in their direction as he closed the door. Snow immediately couched down into a shooting position allowing Mac a direct shooting angle as well. Both of them fired simultaneously and the man's open mouth never emitted a sound as he collapsed to the deck in a muffled thump. Concerned about discovery, they moved quickly back to the bow where they saw the three sentries, still oblivious to their encroachment. Mac made several hand signals to Jasmine indicating that they should fan out as they sneaked onto the deck and fire when ready. Two of the guards were facing the bow and the one opposite had a clear view of the main cabin looking aft

They stayed very low using the two other guards as cover to block the third's view as they moved into position. Just as the guard perceived movement, his eyes wide open in surprise, Jasmine fired a single round. The guard went down as his two stunned comrades lurched up in bewilderment and turned to face them. Mac pulled off two rapid shots felling both before they could begin to grab the AK's leaning against the table next to them. *So much for tasers,* Mac mused. Oh, well, you have to use the right tool for the right job. Just then Franklin, came around the cabin, sweat glistening on his face and neck and rushed up to them.

"Joe," Mac asked softly, "you OK?"

"Peachy," he answered, "just had to catch one before he went seaside with my round."

Mac said, "good, I think we're clear here. Three decks to go."

CHAPTER THIRTEEN

WRINKLES

To say that Jefferey Gunderson was out of sorts was the understatement of the century. Hands and ankles zipped tied and mouth ducked taped shut, he felt like a pig going to slaughter. Looking across at his two lieutenants, it was obvious that they were of the same mind. But that description would be accurate unless they could quickly escape before they reached the Army's lock up. And that was exactly what he was going to do right now. They were just pulling away from the house after being tossed into the prisoner compartment of the Army van by the two MPs and Gunderson figured they had about twenty minutes. Their guards had separated them and bound their feet with large zip ties to metal U rings welded to the body of the van. They could stand or sit facing the van's sides but couldn't assist each other in anyway.

He was surprised that no steel cuffs had been used, but convenience and a short ride had apparently overridden caution. It had been years since his early training and he had never actually had to deal with his own capture before, so he hoped he had been a good student. He got to his feet and facing the side of the van raised his arms behind him as high up as his joints would allow and then came down hard with all his strength. The pain shot into his wrists and he could feel the blood trickling from a new wound. Shit, he thought as he raised them again for another try. *This should work,* he thought. The ties were tight and that was important, they needed to be for him to break them. With the knowledge that he might not have the will to try again, his arms came down again even harder this time and with an almost magical snap, the zip tie broke and his hands were free.

Krishinko smiled knowingly, as he stood to follow his boss' lead and soon was rubbing his wrists and removing the duct tape from his mouth. Von Stemp's injury had saved him from the behind the back treatment. He had not recovered enough to execute the maneuver and waited patiently for help.

Krishinko whispered at Gunderson and asked, "what about the feet?" Jefferey raised his finger to his lips to silence his partner and indicated for him to be patient. He reached down and undid a Para cord shoelace from his boot and knotted each end with a loop. Then he fed the Para cord under the zip tie holding his feet and gripping each loop in his hands began sawing the cord back and forth against the tight tie. In less than a minute the tie separated freeing his legs.

Krishinko mouthed the words "son of a bitch," as he smiled broadly. Gunderson made short work of Krishinko's bonds and then went work on Von Stemp.

They crowded near the back of the van and waited. They had only been traveling about ten minutes and felt certain the van would have to slow at some point for a stop sign or red light, but if it didn't soon, they would risk a jump. Moments later their assumption proved correct as the van began to slow and then stopped. Krishinko carefully opened the rear twin doors and jumped out, followed by Gunderson and Von Stemp. As the light changed, he gently closed the doors to avoid any vibration that might be felt up in the front cabin. Their luck held as they quickly ducked down behind a row of parked cars next to the van, as it began to pull away in the heavy traffic. They were free and it was payback time. Gunderson spied a Starbucks on the corner and as soon as the van was out of site, walked quickly to it and entered.

Approaching the counter, he politely asked the cashier, "would you mind if I used your land line, my car broke down and I left my mobile at home and I need to call for help."

The clerk smiled and said, "of course sir, as long as it's a local call, just step over here and I'll hand it to you."

Jefferey dialed the number for Security at Ardyh Ranch and after two rings a deep voice came on the line, "this is Frey, who am I speaking to?"

"Commander, this is Jefferey Gunderson, I need you to get down here to Auckland immediately, we have escaped and bring some extra muscle. We have some shit to clean up."

An hour later, Frey and four of his men met Gunderson, Krishinko and Von Stemp at the Starbucks and they all piled into a big SUV.

"I need a detailed update Commander," Gunderson declared, "but first we have some cleaning up to do. I know where Apogee has been hiding out and we need to go there now and take care of business." Frey nodded and turned the big car into traffic and headed back toward Mac's rental. They parked around the block and then approached the residence from the rear where Gunderson had exited less than an hour before. They observed no activity and saw nothing through the back windows as they approached. Krishinko made short work of the back door with a powerful kick to the lock and they rushed in weapons raised and spread out through the house. One by one they cleared the rooms and re-grouped in the living room.

"Damn," exclaimed Jefferey, "at least three of them were still here when we left. It looks like they may have gone for good, but let's do a complete search and see what we find."

Ten minutes later, they again convened and Gunderson, asked, "well, what's the verdict?"

Frey answered, "there are still some clothes and toiletries here, but nothing of consequence. I would say there is a fifty-fifty chance they are out temporarily and will return."

"Well, if there is even a ten percent chance they are coming back, we want to be here to greet them," Gunderson said angrily.

"Yes Sir," answered Frey. "We'll leave three of our boys here to give them a proper home coming."

An hour and half later, Frey and the rest arrived back at the ranch and sat down with the Commander for an update on the Apogee assault and their kidnapping. The three Typhon leaders were astonished as Frey described the assault, Typhon's casualties and Team Apogee's escape from the ranch.

When Frey had finished and Jefferey had filled in the blanks of their kidnapping, as much as he could remember, he asked, "what about the woman and Sisco, how did they get off the ranch?"

"Sir, we found two of our dirt bikes gone from the garage and have to assume that's how they got back to Auckland," Frey responded.

"Well, shit, first they steal our chopper and then our bikes. Commander, how the hell can we explain this bullshit to my father?"

Frey stammered, "there is no excuse, Mr. Gunderson. This was a monumental screw up all around. What are your orders?" he asked meekly.

"By now, the Army knows we escaped and will figure that we might come back here. We need to lock this place down and get the hell out now. Disburse all your men to holding quarters throughout New Zealand. The three of us will head out now cross-country and head for the private hanger. From there we'll get to a Typhon safe house, either in Australia or elsewhere." Jefferey looked at his watch, 11:00 pm. "Right now, I need to call my father and bring him up to speed. I have a feeling, once he gets over ripping me a new asshole, he'll have a contingency plan."

Peter Gunderson was reading in his study as Calamity gently rocked in the calm waters of the cove off Punai Island when his mobile phone rang. He saw the caller ID and cautiously lifted the phone assuming it would be his son's captors making some silly demand and waited without replying.

"Dad," came the urgent voice, "its Jefferey."

Peter Gunderson replied, "if you are alone, cough."

Jefferey coughed, and his father replied. "Status?" Jefferey was not surprised at his father's response. This was all business and there was no time for niceties.

He brought the old man up to speed and was rewarded with an atypical compliment, "that was a good job escaping, you didn't forget your training."

"Dad, we have to shut down Ardyh and are withdrawing our men. The Army will more than likely be on their way here to look for us. We need to get into the wind and figured on taking the jet out of the country."

"Not a good plan Jefferey," replied Peter Gunderson. Jefferey knew to wait for it and remained silent. "They will have traced the jet to us and are likely heading there as well. Contact our flight crew and tell them to register for a flight to Sidney and depart immediately. That will throw them off the hunt and when our jet arrives, there will be no passengers on it, and they'll have to start their search over."

"OK, sounds good," Jefferey agreed. "How do you want us to proceed?"

"Take the Hummer and drive to the coast where I was picked up to board Calamity. It should take you about three to four hours. I'll have the captain pick you three up there. We should be able to meet you about 6:00 am. If anything changes, I'll call you and you can disappear temporarily either in Auckland or in one of the rural town's outside the city," finished Gunderson.

"Got it, we'll leave here in fifteen minutes," Jefferey answered back.

The boat's layout had shown the crews quarters to be on a lower deck accessible from both forward and aft entrances from the main level. They agreed to split up the same way and enter those cabins from both ends in a pincher movement. Franklin would take the forward end and Mac and Snow the aft. Since the yacht called for a full crew of eighteen plus a captain, who had a separate stateroom, and was operating with a minimal compliment, it was likely they were not doubled up. That would make the job a lot less risky. These take downs would be in very tight quarters so the tasers would be the best weapon. They made their way into the main cabin, knowing that they were likely to meet more sentries on this deck.

Franklin crept down a starboard hallway by a kitchen area to the stairway, without any opposition. Mac and Snow followed a port hallway aft and soon found themselves about to enter a large living room with leather chairs and bar. Halfway down the lounge, a guard sat comfortably with his back to them, watching a movie on a large flat screen against the far wall, the volume muted as he listened through blue tooth headphones. *Boy, do I love technology*, Mac thought as he moved forward closing on the unsuspecting guard, his taser outstretched. The man jerked uncontrollably and fell unconscious and then went slack, as the voltage surged through his big frame. Snow was already on him with zip ties and duct tape for insurance.

They continued down the hallway and found the stairs to the lower deck as they exited the lounge and started downward. Now came the challenge. There were ten doors off this hall. They had no idea how many crewmembers were on board or in which rooms they were, so stealth was crucial. Franklin was dimly visible in the floor and ceiling lighting at the forward stairway and he signaled he was going in. Mac also began to turn the brass handle on the first starboard door and enter while Snow held her position in the hall for back up. Less than a minute passed, and Joe emerged and gave a silent thumbs down.

Mac also exited his room and whispered, "nobody home." They continued to the next two doors. Joe opened and then closed his door without entering and signaled a thumb down again as Mac disappeared again. Mac soon returned and signaled a negative as well.

The next two rooms they checked were also empty. Mac was becoming concerned. Where the hell was the crew. One of the remaining doors was separated from the others and was likely the Captain's stateroom and Mac moved to it. As he opened it, he could see a desk light on across the large and well-appointed living area and two other adjoining rooms. Both doors were slightly ajar. One was obviously a head and the other a dimly lit bedroom. Both were empty. *Uh oh,* he thought, that explains it. The Captain and at least some of the crew were somewhere else on the ship, probably the bridge. But why? Without entering, he closed the door and saw Franklin exiting another of the quarters without success. They cleared the last couple rooms without finding any occupants and huddled in the corridor to plan their next move.

"Most likely they are all on the upper deck where the bridge and navigation equipment are," Mac whispered.

"Why would they be up there at 3:30 in the morning?" Jasmine asked.

"No clue," answered Mac, "but this is not good, something is going on."

"Only one reason for them to be on duty this early," Joe said, "they're preparing to get underway!"

And then they felt it; a slight vibration suddenly began to throb through the corridor.

Joe exclaimed, "holy crap, they're raising the anchor."

"OK, screw the stealth," Mac yelled. "Joe, you and Jasmine get up to the bridge and try to neutralize them. I have got to find Gunderson now!" Mac turned and raced aft as his two agents sprinted up the forward stairs toward the bow on their way to the bridge. Mac took the steps three at a time to the main deck and then quickly found another stairway to the upper decks, beside an elevator, which he avoided.

Like most super yachts, Calamity sported six or more decks, but the guest cabins were usually clustered on one deck while the owner's suite was frequently on its own separate deck. At each landing he quickly identified the deck's function and finally reached the guest's deck four floors up from the main deck. He cautiously scanned the corridors for activity and seeing no one stepped out to find the next stairway up. Only an elevator was visible on the landing and that would be a dead giveaway. *There had to be another set of stairs to access the next deck, but where?* he thought. He searched his memory for the details of the ship's plans they had reviewed before leaving Auckland and vaguely remembered a forward stairway but couldn't recall which decks it accessed. *Oh well,* he thought, he had a fifty percent chance and it was logical that it would be nearer to the bridge and access to the heliport at the bow. Turning, he moved rapidly down the corridor in that direction.

Peter Gunderson felt the vibration before he opened his eyes and knew immediately what it was. After his call from his son, he had contacted the Captain and ordered him to lay in a course back to the north New Zealand shoreline where they had picked him up and plan their arrival at 5:00 am. The wall clock glowed faintly, 3:45 am. In a few minutes he would hear the low rumble of the big diesels kick in six decks below and they would slowly move out of the cove into open sea. He closed his eyes to relax a few more minutes before rising to get his thoughts in order. He only needed to evade Clausen's witch-hunt for six more days and then the world would be way too busy to worry about Typhon or Peter Gunderson. He also knew that U.S. intelligence wouldn't hesitate to violate maritime protections even if he could find a friendly country to provide his cover. Oh, he had several dictatorships across the globe with whom he had protection agreements, but he couldn't get there quickly enough on Calamity. He had to get his team and fly to his closest ally for sanctuary.

He rose from the big king bed and walked over to turn on a coffee maker, when his mobile vibrated on his nightstand.

Returning to the bedside, he picked up the phone and said, "Gunderson."

Captain Reynolds responded, his voice quick and breathless, "Sir, we have an attack underway on Calamity."

"What?" gasped Gunderson, incredulously. "I didn't sound general quarters because I didn't want to let our assailants know we are aware of their presence," the Captain continued.

"Where are they and how many?" gasped Gunderson.

"Sir, we don't know how many, or where they are now, but I do know that our guards on the bow are down."

"OK, arm up and get my pilot to fire up the chopper. Do a radio check with all our security personnel and contact me right back with their locations."

"Yes Sir," said the Captain as he closed the call. Gunderson quickly dressed in his field gear, an ammo belt and leather gloves and pulled on hiking boots. He threw some additional clothes into a backpack with several forty-five cal mags for his STI 1911, which he shoved into a holster on the belt. His mobile rang again, and he connected waiting for the Captain to give him a read out.

"Sir," Reynolds said gravely, "we lost the aft sentry, both side deck sentries and our four bow guards. Our mid deck men and our upper deck sentries have checked in."

"So in addition to you and your five crew and my pilot, we have four guards still available, is that correct?" Gunderson barked.

"Yes sir," the Captain replied.

"Order three of the guards to muster to the bow and take cover and protect my exit to the chopper. Send our most senior man to my suite immediately to escort me to the bow. Direct all our people to defend my exit and then use your crew and our men to engage and destroy these interlopers. Is that all clear?" demanded Gunderson.

"Yes Mr. Gunderson, crystal clear."

"If you take care of these SOB's, you and everyone involved will be able to retire, verstehen zie?"

"Absolutely," brightened the Captain. "We'll get it done!"

Mac reached the end of the corridor and entered a rotunda with several doors and three additional hallways. He checked each door and on the second try found one that entered a landing to another stairway leading upward. *This had to be it,* he thought as he began the climb. He exited to a short hall that opened up to a foyer with a large teak double doorway that had to be the entrance to the owner's suite. He tried to turn the large brass doorknob, but it was locked. Both the locks and the door looked as if they would stop a tank without breaking a sweat. He had his picks, but there was no keyhole or lock on the knob. The lock had to be a high-tech electronic system. Above the door and in several locations around the foyer were a set of cameras and on the wall beside the door was an intercom panel.

He retreated to the stairway out of the camera's view and went on comms to Franklin and said, "Joe, what's your status?"

"We're just behind the bridge on the starboard side deck behind some cover, but we have a problem," Joe answered. "I think we've been made, because four armed crew members are guarding the entrances and one is on the forward deck going towards the chopper."

"Well I'm in no better shape," Mac retorted. "I'm stymied outside the owner's suite, but I think I have an idea. It looks like Gunderson is going to make a run for the chopper and that a crew member is going to fire the bird up so as soon as he boards, they lift off. Unless he has already left the suite and is on his way, he will have to open up his door sooner than later and I'll be waiting. Get down to the main deck and position yourselves near to the bow deck as close to the helipad as you can get. And Joe, under no circumstances let that chopper lift off with Gunderson on it even if it means taking him out."

"Copy," Joe said.

Mac moved down the stairs to the landing below the Owner's deck and looked for somewhere to conceal himself as he waited for Gunderson. There were cameras here as well, but not as many. He checked each of the doors off the rotunda and two entered into large functional rooms with access to the outside decks, but one was a large utility room with cleaning supplies and other tools. *Perfect*, he thought, no one could ambush him in here. He entered and closed the door leaving just a small gap and waited. Five minutes passed and then he heard footsteps. Curiously, they didn't seem to be coming from Gunderson's suite, but from one of the corridors in the opposite direction. Peering through the tiny slit, he got just a glimpse of a big man in camouflage gear moving down the hall toward him. He quickly closed the closet door and waited, listening intently, his ear against its surface.

The footsteps began to recede and then he could hear the sound as they climbed the steps. *This might be more challenging, but could offer an even better opportunity,* he thought, as he left the closet and silently ascended the steps.

At the top, he saw the big man approach the intercom and announce, "Mr. Gunderson, its Jack Freeman here to escort you out."

Gunderson's metallic response was immediate, "OK Freeman, I'll unlock the door for you." There was a click and the door swung open soundlessly.

Gunderson stood in the inner foyer of the big suite and stepped back to retrieve his backpack and a briefcase as the guard stepped across the entrance. Mac knew that there would be no better chance to surprise both men and launched himself up to the landing, his Sig coming up to sight in the big man. Then something totally unexpected happened. As Gunderson turned to retrieve his luggage, he glanced at the security video screen on the wall and seeing Sisco rushing towards them, he lurched left to find cover. His accomplice, seeing his boss' gyration, dove to the right of the big door just as Mac was squeezing off his first round, which missed the big man by inches.

Mac's forward momentum drove him through the suite's entrance, catapulting him into the big guard's side and spinning him around as he careened into the partially open door. But even as he fell, the man kicked out his foot that crashed into Mac's arm, his Sig flying across the teak floor. The guard leaped to his feet and rushed Mac, trying to catch him before he could defend himself. Rather than try to avoid the attack or get to his feet, Mac flipped onto his side as he spun, both his feet catching his attacker's legs like a scythe, just above the ankles. The force of the guard's leg movement coupled with Mac's leveraged kick snapped the first ankle explosively and severely sprained the other. With a scream of pain, the guard went down, clutching at his legs as he thunderously hit the hard deck. This time, Mac was on his feet in an instant and turning back to the guard, brought his booted foot down hard on the guard's temple crushing his head against the teak.

The whole episode had only lasted a minute, but when Mac looked up Gunderson had disappeared. *Damn*, he thought, as he rushed over and picked up the 9mm! Mac checked the pulse on the guard to verify what he already knew. This guy was out of play for good. Glancing back, he saw the backpack laying where Gunderson had left it, but the briefcase was gone. He quickly ripped open the pack and rifled through it. Clothes and ammo. This was good news. The terrorist had no extra ammo and carrying the briefcase would slow him down. But most importantly, if he had gone to the trouble of taking the case, it must be very important.

As he turned to follow Gunderson, Mac went on comms and said, "Joe, he's coming your way and I'm on his tail."

Gunderson had been tempted to enter the fray, but decided the risk wasn't worth the reward, besides his guard had things under control, as he sprinted out of the suite. By now Sisco was likely dead and his odds of escape had therefore improved. As he headed towards the bow, he hit the speed dial for Reynolds who picked up immediately.

"Captain, get those guards down by the chopper and make sure I have a clear path to board and lift off," Gunderson yelled breathlessly.

"Yes Sir," replied the Captain, as he directed two of his crew to get down to the bow to help secure Gunderson's escape.

Franklin and Snow remained in hiding on the main deck. They had positioned themselves in the forward most salon which served as a fitness facility filled with free weights, strength machines, stationary bikes and ellipticals among the myriad of fitness equipment. The room had large windows on both sides and across the forward section providing a perfect view of the bow and helipad. The two knelt behind a large juice bar in the rear of the room and waited. It wasn't long before three guards took positions up on the side decks as if expecting action.

Periodically, they risked a peek to check activity, but everything seemed static. Then, Mac came on the comms and minutes later two more men joined the three guards, who re-positioned themselves out on the bow around the chopper. As Franklin peered over the bar reporting the changes, Snow called Mac and gave him an update.

"Jasmine, do you think you can take out the two guards closest to you without alerting the rest?" Mac asked.

"Not sure, but if we can lure them back out of view somehow, it's possible," she answered.

"OK, do it now," Mac said. "Gunderson should be down there any minute and I'd like to even up the odds a bit."

Jasmine relayed the orders to Joe and asked, "how do you want to play it?"

"We'll have to split up. You take the starboard guard and I'll take the port one," Franklin replied.

"Make some noise or do something to pull them out of view, then take them out."

Jasmine nodded and suggested, "we should hold that position in case Gunderson shows."

Joe said, "good idea. I'm not sure what other access there is to the bow deck, but I sure hope he comes our way."

Jasmine hugged the exterior cabin wall as she moved forward toward the unsuspecting guard and stopped just before a final curve that blocked her view of the forward deck. She didn't know how far up the side deck he would be, so she carefully inched forward to risk a view and came face to face with a surprised crewmember. Even before she could grab a weapon, he dove forward driving both in a heap onto the deck surface. They hit hard and the man landed on top of her as her head collided with the teak decking and her vision blurred. He was not a big man, but lanky and surprisingly strong and in the tangle of their bodies managed to get his hands around her throat. She desperately thrashed out in practiced defense but could not break his grip. Even as her vision began to clear from the crushing collision, the light began to fade as her gasps for air were deprived. And then without warning, only darkness was left as her body went slack.

Mac erupted onto the main deck and raced up the port side toward the bow. As he rounded a curve in the cabin superstructure, he saw a figure stooped over something on the deck his back to him. *Oh shit*, he thought anxiously, maybe Gunderson had surprised Joe or Jasmine. As he crept closer, the Sig poised in his outstretched hand, the individual's features became clearer and he recognized who it was. The man spun around suddenly, an AK leveled on Mac's body.

The two men let out audible gasps of relief as Joe said, "damn boss, you scared the shit out of me."

"Likewise," said Mac, "who's that?"

"Not Gunderson," answered his friend. "Just one of the crew guarding the bow deck, while Gunderson's guards are out by the chopper."

"Where's Jasmine?" Mac asked.

"I just left her to take care of the guy on the starboard side."

"I better check on her, in case she needs a hand," replied Mac.

"Gunderson has to get to the helicopter some way. Hang tight here until I call you." Mac took off back to the gym entrance and crossed over to the opposite exit on the starboard side of the yacht. Turning to the left, he could see a vicious struggle was going on and Jasmine was on the deck. He raced forward pulling the Sig from the holster yet again. At fifteen feet, he could see that she was losing the battle and had stopped moving. Mac hesitated only long enough to make sure he had a really clean shot as he differentiated all the body parts and fired. The man flopped over, falling next to Jasmine in a pool of blood emerging from an enormous exit wound in the right temple. And then he was beside her, cradling her head in his hands as he felt for a pulse. It was faint, but there and he said a silent prayer of thanks.

In another minute, now no longer deprived of life-giving oxygen, her eyes fluttered open and she lifted her head and with a weak smile said, "hello cowboy, I guess now I owe you one."

Gunderson knew the outside decks might be the fastest route to the bow, but not the safest, so he wound his way through a myriad of connecting corridors and stairways on his way forward. Finally, he came to the maintenance and crew deck just below the main deck. Moving forward through the crew's quarters, he continued past the forward stairway that Franklin had used earlier and ascended another set of stairs under the bow. The stairway ended at a large hatch that accessed the bow deck mid-way between the heliport and the lounge area. Gunderson spun the big round handle to unlatch the waterproof door and pushed it up onto the deck. The loud grumble of the helicopter close by assaulted his ears as he lifted his head gingerly to look around the deck. A quick 360 told him that his men were in position and no one else was visible. This looked like as good a time as any for him to make his escape. He only had to make a thirty-foot sprint to get to the helicopter. It would take only seconds and the chopper's blades were already spinning up in anticipation of his arrival. His three guards were hunched down, AK's directed aft, ready to provide cover fire. His left hand grabbed the railing just outside the open hatch as he held the briefcase firmly for his final step up to the deck. He focused on the chopper and made his move. There was no sound as the man guarding the chopper's doorway suddenly crumbled to the deck. Gunderson knew instinctively what had just happened and dropped prone onto the deck lying still in the dim light that would soon be dawn. The two remaining guards retreated behind the chopper for cover and began to return fire. Rounds whizzed over his head from both directions forcing him to remain glued to the deck.

Snow had recovered quickly, but she and Mac had only just reached the bow deck when they saw the hatch thrown open.

Mac called Franklin and said, "we need to take out the guards Joe, but we can't afford to hit the chopper, or it is likely to go up in smoke and incinerate us all. You have an AK with the best accuracy so you get sniper duty and Jasmine and I will keep Gunderson pinned down on the deck."

"Copy," Joe yelled back over the deafening cacophony all around them. Mac could just make out Gunderson's form stretched out on the deck in front of the opened hatch and fired a round splintering the deck near him. The result was the rapid reports of an unsuppressed AK 47 and a big chunk of Calamity's superstructure exploded just above his head from the high velocity 7.62x39mm slugs.

Mac pulled back and said to Jasmine, "shit, this is a standoff and we are definitely at a disadvantage. I have got to change the equation and force their hand."

"I get it Mac, but how?" she fired back.

"I have to make Gunderson panic before we go on the attack."

"OK," she said hesitantly, "what's the play?"

"Just cover me," he answered as he called Franklin.

"Joe, I'm going to make a run for the furniture cluster out on the bow and see if that will spook Gunderson or his men. When I do, if they even peak out nail them."

He turned back to Jasmine and said, "you have a clear shot at Gunderson's position. If he moves. put some rounds out there to keep him pinned down, but don't hit him. I want him alive."

It wasn't far, but it almost seemed as if he was running in slow motion, as Mac flew across the deck and launched into the air careening into the base of the heavy teak couch between him and the helicopter and mere feet from Gunderson's prone form. The thick top frame of the couch exploded as more AK rounds plowed into the heavy wood, a large fragment splintering off to lodge itself painfully into Mac's left thigh. He grimaced with pain as a red ring surrounded the shard. Knowing it might be a mistake; he ripped the piece from his leg and quickly examined the wound. *A lot of blood, but no artery,* he thought, so on with the show.

Franklin came on the comms, "one down, one to go." Mac risked a glance around the end of the couch and with the increasing dawn light, he could clearly make out the evil glare of Peter Gunderson staring straight at him. He was clutching the brief case in his right hand and a large handgun in his left. It was almost as if in that moment of confrontation, Gunderson made his mind up that he would take control. He quickly moved his weapon into his right hand and swiveled around to stabilize his aim as he pulled off a round at Mac. The bullet went wide but pushed Mac back behind the couch for cover and Gunderson leaped to his feet grabbing the case as he rose. Mac saw the motion and trusting in Joe, he rose and raced after the fleeing man. Gunderson was only feet from the chopper's door as his final guard stepped from cover to get an angle on Mac.

There was nowhere to hide, but Mac knew he had to get out of the line of fire and improve his odds, so he dove forward feet first, as if he were sliding into home plate for the winning run. Wincing with pain, he made a last desperate attempt at slowing his quarry, as he kicked out his right leg in a judo move at Gunderson. Suddenly, the big guard was driven backwards as several of Franklin's rounds found their mark and he collapsed, partially blocking Gunderson's path to the chopper's door, and slowing his advance. That hesitation was just enough for Mac's outstretched foot to catch the case and drive it from Gunderson hand, the rotor blast pushing it further out of reach. Gunderson stared in horror as the case came to a halt fifteen feet away, an irretrievable relic of his lifelong plan. And then, as Joe continued to dig up the deck with the AK, Gunderson resolutely turned and dove into the chopper, already lifting off Calamity's deck.

Mac gave Joe a thumbs up as he scurried over and grabbed the briefcase. The helicopter was fast disappearing, but it was still way too risky to take a shot. The big bird would likely come hurtling back down in a fiery ball on top of the yacht, if it was disabled. But Mac knew it was getting harder and harder for Gunderson to disappear into the wind and he was counting on some real answers from the briefcase. He turned to look back at the main cabin and his gaze went up to the bridge. Suddenly, the interior lights flared on and he saw the captain and three crew men standing strangely erect with their hands placed forward on the big, slanted window above the ship's instrumentation panel. Standing just behind them stood Jasmine Snow, her small frame silhouetted in the glare holding court with her large 9mm. *Hooyah*, he thought, she is one tough lady!

CHAPTER FOURTEEN

THE BELLY OF THE BEAST

Peter Gunderson's anger was so palpable; he was almost unable to bark out his orders to his pilot as the chopper soared high into the morning sky.

"Head for the pickup point on the north coast of NZ," he commanded. Gunderson then dialed the number of his ground team at his private hanger in Auckland and gave them new instructions to refuel his jet in Sydney and then immediately return to New Zealand for a quick turnaround out of the country. He would call them with the destination before the flight. Finally, glancing at his watch, he texted Jefferey and typed in, *Change of plans, we'll pick you up in Calamity's chopper. Be ready, ETA 6:30 am, PG.*

◆

The NATCOG meeting was scheduled for 6:00 pm and although it would have over seventy-five countries participating, most would be streaming in on secure video channels from around the world. Nonetheless, there were numerous members who opted to attend in person. Mexico, Canada, many of the South American democracies, numerous Eastern European and EU allies and several of the Mideast countries, including Israel, had elected to attend in person. The meeting was scheduled in the Situation Room, officially known as the John F. Kennedy Conference Room. It was a 5,525-square-foot highly secure conference room and intelligence management center in the basement of the west wing of the White House managed by the National Security Council for POTUS.

At 5:00 pm, Admiral James Clausen met in the Oval Office for a pre-briefing with President Steven Holbrook.

The President opened the conversation, saying, "well Jim today's the day. The world is in real turmoil and even though our NATCOG work is being done in secret, as always, everyone is looking to America for the answers. So, do we have the answers?" the President asked earnestly.

"Candidly, Sir," answered Clausen, "not to be cute, but it depends on the questions. We now know there is a real global conspiracy, called Typhon, which has been largely responsible for driving the societal disruptions across the world for the last fifty years and is fast approaching the achievement of its objectives. We have identified the principals behind this abominable operation, and we are currently in pursuit of all of them. But, as you know, probably the best news is that we have acquired their blueprint for accelerating their specific disruptions, called Chaos."

"Speaking of which, what is the latest on our progress combatting Chaos?" asked Holbrook.

Clausen quickly summarized his last report from Mac that he had just received before the meeting, including the episode on Calamity and the recovery of the mystery briefcase.

Holbrook sighed and said, "that is quite a story, Jim and I want to hear more, but I've run out of time. The meeting begins in fifteen minutes and I have got to speak with the PM of the UK in five minutes and the Prime Minister of Israel right after that to explain their immediate risks as, you outlined earlier. I think it would be helpful if you would join me in those conversations. Given the threats both face, I think you should be here to provide whatever detail they want."

"Absolutely," answered Clausen. "Are we on the secure link from here?"

"For the UK, yes, but the PM of Israel called me yesterday to let me know he would be attending the meeting in person."

"I had heard that from your chief of staff earlier," said Clausen. "That's quite a commitment."

"Well, I let him know that his personal security might be at risk and it would be important that he participate in some additional briefings," answered the President. "He agreed and said he could use the opportunity to visit with some good friends while he's here in the states."

In the two subsequent meetings, Holbrook laid out the high-level details of the impending assassination attempts to each of the PM's and Clausen outlined Team Apogee's assignments and connections with the UK's MI-6 and Israel's Mossad intelligence agencies. Clausen explained that both agencies would be thoroughly briefed by the NSA and the NSC in the next twenty-four hours and that additional security would be provided to NATCOG members while stateside. The briefings concluded and the three men in the Oval Office made their way down to the Situation Room where many leaders of the free world waited anxiously.

After working through the room with personal greetings and acknowledgements, Holbrook moved to the head of the long oval conference table and tapped his glass firmly. The room went silent, all eyes on the President.

"Thank you all for being here and welcome. As you all know this is not our first meeting, but it may be our most important one. The objective of today's meeting is to review the progress each of us has made in our countries to mitigate disruptions and weed out those responsible. We will also review the strategies you are employing to reverse the common societal shifts that are undermining your cultural values and norms. Before we address that part of our agenda, I have asked Admiral James Clausen, Director, National Security Agency, to update everyone on the status of our special Apogee Counter Terrorist Operation."

Clausen stood up, thanked the President and began a detailed description of NSA's work and Team Apogee's activities to date. As he neared the end of his report, Clausen described the most recent interactions between Sisco's team and Typhon including their discovery of the Ardyh Ranch files and his agency's deciphering of the Chaos List. In the back of the room, Leon Fowler sat appearing quietly composed even as small beads of perspiration began inching down his forehead in the air-conditioned room. Finally, Clausen wrapped up with his final bombshell as he shared the details of the Calamity operation and the acquisition of the mysterious briefcase that was currently airborne at 30,000 feet in a C5 Galaxy on its way to Andrews AFB, arriving by midday tomorrow. Following his report, the Admiral entertained questions for the next twenty minutes and then the group took a fifteen-minute break before proceeding. Leon rose quickly and began making his way from the room. He dutifully glad handed several diplomats and heads of state as he hurried towards the exit.

As he approached the door, he found himself beside the Admiral who smiled and said, "hello Leon, how is it going?"

Leon, wiping his brow with a handkerchief from his inside coat pocket, replied, "not bad Admiral, but certainly not as well as you. This List is a great break. Will you be sharing its contents with the members?" he asked innocently.

"Not collectively, at this point, but we will inform every member of any relevant activities that would affect their nation," replied the Admiral.

"I see," said Leon, "that makes sense. I certainly hope the members are willing and able to address their risks competently, since failure could negatively affect others," Leon continued.

"Very true, that is why I have Team Apogee engaging with the earliest target countries," said Clausen. "I am confident that with our team and the member's intelligence agencies working together, we will prevail."

"How about this briefcase, Admiral, what do think that is all about," Leon asked, as nonchalantly as he could.

"Not sure yet, Leon, but according to Sisco, Gunderson was loath to lose it, so my guess is it could be a real game changer. We know it contains a bunch of digital files and some custom tech hardware, so it's coming to the right place and my team is the best in the world. Whatever it is, we'll crack it Leon and put an end to this nightmare, of that you can be certain," the Admiral stated emphatically.

Leon smiled and nodded saying, "I would never bet against you Admiral. Good luck and let me know how I can help." Fowler continued up the stairs to the main floor and exited out of a back entrance. Passing a security guard, he nodded and pulled a cigarette out of a pack from his pocket and stuck it in his mouth but didn't light it. Sauntering casually down the walkway, he stopped by a well-pruned maple, pulled out his burn phone and keyed in Peter Gunderson's secure line.

Several rings later, he was about to end the call and try a text, when a gruff voice answered, "Gunderson."

"Mr. Gunderson, this is Leon Fowler, I have that information you wanted."

"Go ahead," said Gunderson. Leon described the Admiral's briefing, holding back on Clausen's final remarks about Team Apogee's deployments. Why give away everything unless he had to. When he finished Gunderson came back on the line and said,

"Mr. Fowler, most of your information is a day late and a dollar short."

Leon asked, "what do you mean, this is fresh off the press. I'm taking a big risk even calling you. I'm standing right outside the White House, for God's sake!"

"That is your problem, Mr. Fowler. The only information of value that you have provided is the fact that my list has been compromised. So, if you have nothing more of real value, you are wasting my time."

In a panic now, Leon stammered, "well I might have something more."

"I'm listening," Gunderson responded dryly.

"What's in it for me, Mr. Gunderson? I'm the one taking all the risks here," Leon whined.

"You are growing tiresome, Mr. Fowler," growled Gunderson. "But let me provide you with an incentive. If you don't stop screwing with me, you will either be exposed to the dear Admiral and your career ended with an orange suit or no longer be breathing before your first cup of coffee tomorrow morning, and I am currently leaning towards the latter. Now, unless I have confused your small mind, make your decision so we can get on with this debacle."

Leon had been around the block and was no push over. He'd dealt with some very nasty folks, but this guy was certified, and his decision was immediate.

"OK, ok, can't blame a guy for trying," he quipped, trying to make light of his miscue, but failing miserably. "Well, I heard two other tidbits that you might find useful," he went on. "Clausen spoke about the briefcase you lost in the scuffle with Sisco. It's being jetted back here to Ft. Meade for analysis and will be here by tomorrow mid-day. Clausen seems confident they'll figure out its contents. The second item is that Clausen is sending Team Apogee to help protect the high priority targets on the list." After several seconds with no reply, Leon said, "Mr. Gunderson are you there? Is any of that important?"

"Important is a very relative term, Mr. Fowler, but it is concerning," responded Gunderson gravely. "I'll put off your untimely demise for the time being," he warned, "but keep your ears to the ground and update me regularly."

"Yes Sir, I will," answered Fowler, humbly.

"Oh and by the way," Gunderson asked, "was the Prime Minister of Israel on the secure video live stream from Tel Aviv?"

"He was scheduled to be, but actually he showed up in person at the last minute," Leon answered.

"That is indeed a strange alteration to his busy schedule," Gunderson observed.

"Find out why and get me the details on his plans while he's in the U.S. Get me that information tomorrow and you just might redeem yourself Mr. Fowler."

Mac, Joe and Jasmine were bone tired as they lay in the military style berths on the huge C-5, as it thundered towards the CONUS. Clausen had discussed next steps with Mac while the three waited for an Army chopper to pick them up from the yacht and drop off some MP's to take the crew into custody and Calamity back to Auckland. When Clausen reported that the Israeli PM would be at the NATCOG meeting in person, Mac winced visibly and asked the Admiral why he had changed his plans. Clausen said he didn't know, but was sure it had to do with getting more detail about the U.S./Israeli joint op. He had added that the PM was an ex-Mossad officer, so you would expect that reaction. With this change and the need to safeguard Gunderson's briefcase on its way to the Agency, it made sense for Mac to cover the Prime Minister, while in the U.S. and his team in Israel could pick up his security detail and protection when he returned home.

After a brief delay at the Army base in New Zealand, while the team got some chow, hot showers and clean army fatigues and Mac got a dozen stitches and antibiotics, they had climbed aboard the enormous plane for the eighteen-hour flight to Maryland. As soon as they got into the air, Mac borrowed the crew's sat phone and dialed a number from memory.

After several rings, a voice came on the line, "Joe Sisco, may I help you?"

"Hi Dad," Mac replied, keeping his voice calm.

"Mac, great to hear from you. Your mother and I were a little worried, since we haven't heard from you for a while, but I told her that's typical when you're on an operation. Is everything ok, son?" the ex-US Ambassador to Israel asked, concerned.

"Yes Dad, everything's fine. Tell me," Mac continued, "are you planning on a visit from your old buddy, Aaron Cohen, the Prime Minister of Israel any time soon?"

"Funny you should ask," said Joe Sisco. "He called me, out of the blue just yesterday, and said he'd be in Washington this week and would love to see Winnie and me, so I invited him down to the ranch for a couple days."

◆

Peter Gunderson and his team sat comfortably on the big Typhon jet as it headed on the long northeastern haul from NZ to America. They had made the chopper pick up without incident and flown straight to their hanger where they waited for their ride to return from Sydney. As the plane was being refueled, Peter asked his pilot about his greeting in Sydney and as he expected, agents had questioned the crew and searched the plane, but finding nothing had left. The captain had explained that the plane was being checked for a malfunction that could only be done in Sydney and would then await further flight instructions from its owners or lessors. The crew had refueled, waited an hour and then returned as instructed. Once Gunderson's backup crew had arrived, they boarded and began their journey back to the US. Their flight plan was currently registered for the destination of Louisville, Kentucky, but Gunderson expected that to change mid-flight. He just needed Fowler to come through. Six hours in, Gunderson was awakened from a fitful sleep when his mobile buzzed with a text message. It read, *PM in DC two days, then in Wimberley, Texas visiting Ex U.S. Ambassador to Israel, Joe Sisco. LF.* Gunderson picked up the intercom from his private cabin and called his pilot.

"Captain, register a new flight plan and change course for Austin, Texas," he ordered. Gunderson then called the main cabin up front.

"Jefferey, get a cold bottle of that Dom Perignon and four glasses and bring the boys back to my cabin, I have some good news," he exclaimed.

They all raised their glasses in a toast and waited for Gunderson senior to speak.

A rare smile creased his face as he proclaimed, "to Mac Sisco and his merry men, Typhon's first victims."

"Here, here," said Jefferey, as they all downed their flutes in unison. "Care to share?" asked Krishinko taking advantage of his boss' temporary good humor.

"OK boys, listen up," Gunderson began. "With all the screw ups and bad luck, we still have a chance to pull a rabbit out of the hat."

"As you know, Chaos is scheduled to commence in a few more days. That will be an automatic occurrence by design, but for Chaos to be ignited, the first trigger must be achieved according to a defined schedule. That trigger is the first fractal on the Chaos list, which is the assassination of the Prime Minister of Israel. That assassination must occur within a twelve-hour interval from 12:00 am to 12:00 pm, three days from now. If we miss that window, Chaos will shut down until it can be reprogrammed. NSA has the List and has somehow decoded it. They have most certainly informed the Israeli PM of this Chaos action and are taking every precaution. They don't know that the PM's death will trigger Chaos, but they have my briefcase and in it are encrypted files on Typhon's entire structure, contacts and every detail of our organization, including a hardware device that can literally shut down our entire network. But once Chaos begins, all that will be moot, because the sequence will continue to its completion and we will be home free."

"Dad, I'm not sure why the toast. This sounds like very bad news," Jefferey said.

"Except for the fact that we know exactly where the PM will be during that twelve-hour period and when we terminate him, we will also take out Sisco, his cronies and his family all in one delicious operation and that's why they say revenge is sweet," exclaimed Peter Gunderson enthusiastically.

CHAPTER FIFTEEN

CRUNCH TIME

The C-5 Galaxy's wheels touched the tarmac at Andrews with hardly a bounce after its 8,500-mile journey and taxied slowly up to the military terminal. The three Apogee agents were escorted to a waiting NSA van and driven straight to the NSA HQ for a meeting with the Director. Once in the Admiral's conference room, they sat quietly discussing the details of the last forty-eight hours and what they might expect in the next few days. Clausen's secret door opened, and the Admiral entered, greeting them all.

"Great to see you all and welcome to the NSA, Ms. Snow. For the record, you have been granted a temporary limited access Top Secret clearance for Apogee/FACET code word information based on a Need-to-Know basis. Do you understand what that means?" Clausen asked.

"Yes Sir, I do," Jasmine answered. "I have previously worked on MI-6 Five Eyes Operations, so I am familiar with your security protocols," she explained.

"Excellent," replied the Admiral.

"Good to see you again, Joe, as well."

"Thank you, Admiral, I am very happy to be back," Joe responded.

"Mac, how is the leg?" Clausen asked, concerned.

"Well Sir, I probably won't be running a sub seven-minute mile for a few weeks, but I'm healing up nicely and it certainly won't impact operational performance."

"That's the spirit," laughed the Admiral. "OK, first things first," continued Clausen. "The NATCOG meeting ran into the early morning hours, but it was enormously productive. Today, all the members will be meeting with our support infrastructure teams from across the NSC membership depending upon their specific situations and the impact of the LIST on them or their neighbors. That activity will be coordinated by Leon Fowler, Deputy Director, National Security Council."

Jasmine's mind suddenly went into high gear as she tried to grasp the immensity of what she had just heard. This was the name she had overheard Gunderson reference in his conversation with his son in the Hummer. It was also the name she had neglected to share with Mac in case she needed additional leverage back in Auckland. *What a mistake that had been*, she thought admonishing herself. Now she was in a real box. She would lose everyone's trust if she admitted that now, but this guy Fowler was a real threat. He was a mole at the highest level and could even be undermining NATCOG's efforts across the world.

As the Admiral continued his summary, Mac glanced over at Jasmine. Something was wrong. She had been listening intently only a moment ago and now seemed strangely disconnected. The color seemed to have gone out of her face and her expression was very introspective as if she was struggling with some perplexing thought.

The Admiral seemed to be wrapping up as he explained, "our objective is to complete those meetings by the end of the day so that the members can get back to their countries and go to work."

Mac broke in, turning to Snow and asked, "Jasmine, you seem to have had heard something in the Admiral's update that might concern you. Do you have any ideas or observations that we might have missed that could help us?"

Well there it was, she thought. Now is the time to come clean or take your chances. She knew she couldn't live with the consequences of withholding her information now that she understood the stakes. But she did have two options, spin it and hope she was convincing, or lay it all out and take the heat.

"Jasmine," repeated Mac, "have you got something for us?"

"Sorry Mac, so much has happened over the last week and I was trying to remember some details that I now realize are very relevant to our mission." The three men all leaned forward and stared at her intently.

"And what are those details, Ms. Snow?" the Admiral asked skeptically.

Jasmine cleared her throat unconsciously and dove in.

"When I was hidden in Gunderson's Hummer at the rendezvous with Calamity, I overheard a conversation he had with his son Jefferey. During that conversation, he referred to a name. It was very difficult to hear from where I was hiding, but I am certain that the first name was Leon and I believe the last was Fowler. Gunderson referred to him as 'his man in Washington' and he had received information from this man about setting up an ambush for your Apogee Team in Auckland." Mac's face had darkened, and Joe looked dumbstruck as Jasmine prepared for what she knew was the next question.

"Jasmine, for God's sake, why didn't you tell us about this before now?" Mac asked incredulously.

"Mac, I could try to explain that away by saying that it didn't seem important at the time, but that would be a lie. When I escaped from Gunderson, I was running for my life. I knew you would not trust me, and I felt I might need a bargaining chip if things went south and I couldn't convince you of my loyalty. I realize now what a terrible mistake that was and now that I understand who this Fowler is and the threat he is to Apogee and NATCOG, I couldn't withhold this information. I am so very sorry, and I accept full responsibility for my actions," she said sincerely.

"Ms. Snow, would you please step outside into my sitting area," requested the Admiral. "This is an extraordinarily serious breach and I would like to discuss this with my colleagues."

"Of course, Sir," said Jasmine, who then rose and exited the room, closing the door quietly behind her.

"Well Gentleman," Clausen said with a sigh, "this is very disappointing and presents us with a bit of a dilemma."

"Yes it does," responded Mac. "This is one more instance where Jasmine has not been entirely forthright, and it concerns me greatly."

"What about you Joe?" asked the Admiral. "What are your views on the matter?"

"Well, you know me, Admiral, I am a non-conformist at heart, but I do agree absolutely with your observations and concerns."

"Well then, we all seem to be on the same page," said the Admiral.

"Sir, I'm not so sure about that," interrupted the retired Navy Seal.

"Oh," the Admiral looked up, "why is that Joe?"

"Well Sir, because I have spent a lot of time in the field with this lady and she has been absolutely solid. She has been fearless, covered our asses numerous times and I would not hesitate to go into the toughest operation with her. She has earned my trust not through what she says, but what she does and that is how I judge people."

"Well that's quite a testimonial Joe," said the Admiral, turning to Mac. "What's your opinion and recommendation, Mac?" he asked.

"Admiral, everything that Joe said is true and very important. Back in Auckland, our whole team weighed in positively on Jasmine and since then we have been through even more action in which she has proven herself and her loyalty. She has actually saved my life more than once in less than a week and I do agree with Joe that actions speak louder than words. I would also add that given her predicament when she contacted me, her rationale, while not what we would like to hear, was understandable."

Admiral Clausen leaned back in his chair and seemed to come to a conclusion.

"You both know my leadership style and how I trust my people. Mac, I am going to leave this decision up to you, but I would caution you about one thing. Jasmine's actions most certainly had a deleterious impact on our mission. We have no idea how much Fowler leaked to Gunderson or what damage that may have caused. In fact, I have no doubt that Fowler has already provided him with a very detailed description of everything that happened in yesterday's NATCOG meeting. That alone has put many people at great risk including those targeted by Chaos on the List."

Mac said, "thank you Sir, I understand. I would like to keep Ms. Snow on the team, and I will make it a point to reinforce strongly what she already knows."

"And what is that?" Clausen asked, like a teacher mentoring a student.

"That trust is hard to gain and easy to lose," Mac answered resolutely.

Mac excused himself and promised to return in fifteen minutes with Jasmine so they could continue with the briefing. He found her gazing out of the large picture window looking out on the enormous NSA complex, her back to him. She heard his steps and turned to him, her face emotional.

"Mac," she said, "I am so sorry. I let the whole team down and most of all I let you down," she sobbed. Mac didn't respond but directed her into a small conference room off the lobby and closed the door.

"Jasmine," he said, "we have been through a lot together and despite your deceptions, I have trusted you. The Admiral has allowed me to decide how to proceed and frankly I am very torn. You have been a great team player and performed wonderfully under every condition, but trust trumps all else for me and my teammates. You have achieved that trust in a very short time, but you have also squandered it without regard for its value. Do you understand what I am telling you?" he asked.

"I do now Mac," she replied. "I have to admit, I have always been on my own and had to look out for my own ass. I guess, it's become my default. But since I have been on your team, I have learned the power of a great team and the trust that binds it together."

Mac nodded his agreement and said, "Jasmine, if I agree to keep you on Team Apogee, I need your solemn word that you will never violate our trust again!"

Jasmine looked straight into Mac's eyes and said, "Mac, I promise to keep that trust."

The two returned to the conference room to join Franklin and the Admiral.

Clausen looked at Snow and asked, "Jasmine, I hope we are all on the same page?"

"Absolutely, Admiral," she answered. Glancing around he looked at Joe and he winked approvingly with a wry smile on his face.

Mac jumped in and asked, "Admiral, your assumption about Fowler's leaks concerns me a lot. Is every NATCOG member still here?"

"No Mac," the Admiral answered, "quite a few of them have already left by now."

"What about Prime Minister Cohen," Mac inquired.

"Mac, that is one of my greatest concerns," answered the Admiral. "He left on an NSA jet for Texas right after midnight with his security detail. By now he is probably already at your Mom and Dad's ranch."

Mac's heart sank, "Sir, I need to get down there now!"

"Yes you do," Clausen responded, "and I have a jet waiting at Andrews to take you three down there as soon as you leave here."

"Thank you, sir," Mac said gratefully.

"But before you bolt," the Admiral continued, "I'll get Gunderson's briefcase down to Worthington in Ciphers and begin to dig into that and get back to you with any positive findings."

"What are you going to do about Fowler?" Joe asked the Admiral.

"I'm going to pick him up immediately and bring him in for interrogation. I will also arrest Martin Stabler and put him in holding here and play the two of them against each other. They will both try to lawyer up, but I have a feeling that they will turn pretty quickly once they feel the real heat. POTUS will have to do some fancy footwork with the NSC, but we'll figure that out. Once I get anything helpful from either of them, I'll contact you."

Mac, impatient to leave, rose and said, "thank you Admiral, you have really had our back."

"And you have had ours, Mac," the Admiral said, as he too rose to say goodbye.

"Oh and Mac, I'll call your father and the Prime Minister and alert them to this new risk and get my team on both sigint intel and flight and travel data to see if we can locate Gunderson and his boys."

Once in the air, the three began to discuss their plan to intercept Typhon. They knew from the General in Auckland that their three captives had escaped, and it was likely rejoined Peter Gunderson. What they didn't know was where Gunderson would go now and what he would do. Mac's concern was that however the PM's termination was planned, since his change of venue to the U.S., it was hard to predict how Typhon would respond. One likely scenario was that Gunderson would send Jefferey and his team to make the hit, to stay with the original schedule. In any case, they had to get down to Wimberley and fast. The clock was ticking, and Gunderson had a head start.

◆

Aaron Cohen had known Joe and Winnie Sisco for over thirty years and was really looking forward to spending some quality time with them in the beautiful Hill Country outside Wimberley, Texas. He also had been to their ranch several times in the past and it always provided him a sort of peace and tranquility from the frenetic chaos that monopolized most of his life. He was concerned about the List and his personal security, but as an ex-Mossad agent, this was by no means his first rodeo. Furthermore, his personal security team accompanying him was handpicked and were the best in the world. Both Victoria Bakman and Alan Belks were under his direct command at one time and were now senior Mossad anti-terrorist agents and he trusted them with his life. They arrived early in the morning at Austin-Bergstrom International Airport just south of Austin, Texas where Clausen arranged a limo for their trip south to the Sisco's spread.

An hour later they slowly drove down the three-mile-long, winding crushed granite drive and pulled up to the large ranch. As was their custom, Joe and Winnie Sisco stood on the long porch and greeted their guests, warmly hugging their old friend and graciously greeting his two Mossad agents. Winnie had already set out a lavish brunch buffet that they all happily set upon as soon as they had deposited their luggage in their private guest rooms and the agents had made a thorough sweep of the residence. The weather report was pleasant, and it looked like it was going to be a glorious day at Agave Ranch.

CHAPTER SIXTEEN

FULL CIRCLE

It was late afternoon when the Typhon jet parked inside the private hanger, adjacent to Austin's airport, before its passengers descended the gangway to step onto the glistening concrete floor. The four men piled into a big SUV parked near an exit and drove out of the facility and onto a feeder road on its way to Rt. 183 south. Twenty minutes later, the car merged onto Rt. 35 toward San Antonio. They continued south past Buda and Kyle and eventually exited onto Rt. 12 just south of San Marcos, continuing west towards the iconic artist community of Wimberley in the heart of the Texas Hill Country. They checked into a small bed and breakfast with individual cabins near the Main Street of the quaint tourist destination.

At 7:00 pm, they met at Peter Gunderson's cabin to review their plan of destruction. They crowded around a laptop computer, while zooming in on the Sisco's ranch on Google Earth. The aerial views were extremely clear and detailed. The house was large at 10,000 square feet and it had numerous outbuildings scattered close by. There were stables, a large equipment pole barn, run ins inside cross-fenced pastures and a well house. A two-story guesthouse and a separate five-car garage also were positioned on the large circular drive that fronted the main residence's entrance. The whole compound sat on a gentle hill with manicured lawns, a large limestone patio, with sunken hot tub and a large swimming pool surrounded by neatly trimmed boxwood hedges. Dark stained board fencing separating its perimeter from the expansive pastures and towering Live Oaks protected the immediate acreage.

The visuals identified an obvious approach route from the south. Heavy trees and changes in elevation provided excellent cover and ran almost to the equipment barn. The route was ideal for their assault and provided great cover and excellent access to the residence and guest house. It was a big property at 500 acres with gated access, so their only practical way in was on foot. They had their weapons already, provided by Typhon partners from San Antonio. A couple AK 47's, two 12 gauges, two Kimber 1911 45's, four Glock 9mm semi auto's and extra ammo. They still needed to pick up some other essentials tomorrow in Wimberley and San Marcos. The operational Chaos time sequence began the day after tomorrow at midnight and ran through noon, so they planned to hit the property at 1:00 am with the real action scheduled for approximately 2:30 am. The terminations wouldn't take long and while they expected security personnel, they were confident in their capabilities and had built in significant contingencies. They were amped up about their mission and their pay back. Their day of reckoning couldn't come soon enough.

◆

Joe had suggested they fly into San Antonio so he could pick up some extra gear at his place since their destination was only an hour's drive north. Mac had called ahead and explained to his father their plan to provide additional security to Prime Minister Cohen and his parents during their visit. Joe Sisco, being an ex-CIA intelligence officer, could read between the lines and understood his son's concerns and didn't argue. Mac said they should be there about 10:00 am, but if there were any signs of Typhon activity contact him immediately. At 8:00 am, the three agents pulled into Franklin's driveway and joined Joe in collecting his 'essentials.' After three trips apiece, they had loaded the Suburban rental with six boxes of goodies from flash bombs to sniper rifles. Satisfied they had what they needed, they headed north on Rt. 281 to Agave Ranch, where destiny awaited them.

Their arrival at the ranch was like Old Home Week. Hugs, handshakes and intros all around made everyone feel welcome and part of the team. Mac hadn't seen Aaron Cohen in years, but it was like yesterday as they greeted each other warmly. Joe Franklin knew Mac's father and Winnie Sisco well and they had always been close. And Jasmine was overwhelmed as Winnie took her by the arm to check her into the guesthouse. Belks and Bakman, the Prime Minister's Security team, stood to the side watching vigilantly as the group engaged in their reunion. Mac disengaged from his father and Cohen and walked over to the two Mossad agents and introduced himself. They agreed to meet in the main house in thirty minutes with Mac and his team to work out assignments and coordination.

It was soon apparent, as the two teams met, that they were well matched. Alan Belks and Victoria Bakman had been on some serious assignments and their insights on protective service were wide and deep. Their tactical skills, close quarter engagement and weapons skills were also exemplary. An added bonus was that Victoria was a trained long-range sniper and had her equipment with her. By the time they had finished their session, everyone felt confident in their ability to protect and defend their charges. The assignments were soon parsed and agreed upon. Bakman would position herself out on the property and provide early warning and long-range cover fire. Belks would stay close to the Prime Minister. Snow would provide close in surveillance and cover Winnie. Franklin would provide perimeter security and back up where needed and Mac would provide backup and cover for his father. And then there was their secret weapon, every one of those they protected was accomplished in their own right in self-defense and weapons use. The PM was ex-Mossad, Joe Sisco was ex-CIA and Winnie Sisco was a tactical field weapons instructor with a black belt in Taekwondo. They spent the rest of the day scoping out the property, looking for vulnerabilities, determining optimal angles of site and defensive positioning.

They knew when the List had originally designated the hit, but with all the unplanned issues Typhon had endured, they had no idea if that timing was still valid. Typhon could have moved it up, delayed it or cancelled it all together. So they went on alert that night. Worst case, it would be a good trial run. The next morning came without incident, so they went on shifts to catch some sleep before the full court press that evening. That was Chaos' originally scheduled date for the assassination of the Prime Minister of Israel. During the day both teams met with their charges and reviewed the details, assignments and contingencies. Each one was given a comm unit, body armor and night vision glasses, the same as their agents and briefed on their operation. As evening approached, Agave Ranch had been hardened and they were ready.

◆

Peter Gunderson paced around the small cabin in anticipation of their upcoming operation. He hoped that he would be the one to take down Sisco. The man had been a singular thorn in the side of Typhon and generations of his family's work. He deserved to die, and Gunderson wanted desperately to be the one to pull the trigger. He felt good about the operation but would have liked more intel about what he was up against. He had heard nothing from Fowler or Stabler and strangely could not reach them. While he was not overly concerned, he had a growing sense of unease. He couldn't but his finger on it. It certainly wasn't about Fowler or Stabler. They were of no consequence. Finally, his discipline kicked in and he willed himself to dismiss his stress. Besides, he had insurance on this mission that was bought and paid for. By 12:01 pm tomorrow Chaos would be underway and Gunderson's plan for Typhon to dictate the new world order would be virtually inevitable.

They went in under a star filled Texas sky with a full moon. *It wasn't ideal for a stealth operation,* thought Gunderson, but it had its advantages. They were able to move quickly without donning their night vision gear and soon could see the outlines of the compound. Their plan was to go in fast, but in sequence, so that they would always have a backup in reserve. Since they didn't know who was where or how many combatants they faced, they just assigned areas to hit. Krishinko would go first penetrating the main house, then Von Stemp would hit the rear, Jefferey would follow, focusing on the guesthouse and Peter would handle any stragglers. All their weapons were suppressed except for the backup shotguns that Peter and Jefferey had slung over their backs. They were weaponed up and fitted with high-tech earpieces, and each was very proficient with tactical blades in close quarters that Wart, now in fighting form, actually preferred. They followed their planned approach and began to fan out at 300 yards. The first barn was only fifty yards away down the slope as Krishinko crept forward into the open field, his shadow following him in the full moon's glow. He was exposed and he knew it but only a few more yards and he would be at the pole barn.

Five hundred yards away, perched in the fork of a huge Live Oak, Bakman scanned her night vision binoculars slowly over the terrain. *What was that?* she thought, her adrenalin kicking in, as she glimpsed something move near the pole barn. There it was again. But what the hell was it? She increased her magnification and held the eyepiece still. *Ah got you,* she thought, as the horns of the big buck lifted out of the tall grass. *Damn, that's at least a 10 pointer, but not the quarry I'm looking for tonight.* Five yards to the right, Krishinko finally reached the cover of the barn.

Wart had one thing on his mind, finding Joe Franklin and gutting him. It had become an obsession and he knew it and he was enjoying it immensely. As he began his approach to the rear of the property, he saw movement by the corner of the house. He was too far away to get a clear view but could see it was a big man. Von Stemp dropped down to the ground and began a slow leopard crawl toward the figure. The high pasture grass made him virtually invisible as he slithered forward. The figure hadn't moved as Wart reached the fence bordering the stretch of lawn running to the large patio.

In the greenish glow of the night vision glasses he could see his next cover, a large wet bar twenty feet away on the edge of the limestone deck.

He turned back to check on the guard by the house but he had disappeared. Wart spent a full minute searching the rear of the residence for any signs of the man but saw no one. Finally, deciding it was clear; he quickly hopped over the board fencing and made a low run to the wet bar, crouching down behind it. His next move would take him up to the large back porch, which extended almost the length of the house. It was adorned with several wrought iron tables and chairs, matching lounges and a full outdoor kitchen facility with an outside gas grill, refrigerator and serving counter.

But what really caught Von Stemp's attention were several sets of French doors spaced along the rear of the house providing access from different rooms directly to the deck and pool area. He assumed the central set of doors exited from the great room, not only because that was a typical arrangement, but also because of the large, rattlesnake limestone chimney that thrust up from inside that room. That left the other double doors as exits from bedrooms or living areas. One more sprint put him onto the porch between two of the French doors and hugging the heavy rock wall of the main residence.

A quick glance into the room on his right confirmed his suspicion about the living room. Glowing ashes smoldered in the large fireplace and several night-lights spaced about the room provided a modicum of guidance through the dimness. Wart moved to his left and once again risked a quick peek into the next room. It was a large room with heavy leather and cowhide chairs looking out on the patio and toward the back he could just make out a large king-sized bed with a mammoth headboard of stripped Texas Mesquite. This must be the master suite, and the two sleeping bodies would have to be Sisco's parents. *What a great place to start his revenge,* he thought as he retrieved the pick set that would make short work of the brass lock.

Jefferey's tack was the least exposed as the guesthouse was nearer to the compound's out buildings and garage. He simply began working his way in from one to the other until he reached the back of the stone structure. He put his back to the wall and strapped on his night vision goggles to get a better view of the details around him. Turning his head from side to side 180 degrees, he saw no signs of movement. No lights were on in the guest house, so he approached the rear entrance. He had no information on the layout of the house but assumed that the first floor would house a living room, kitchen and bathroom while the upper floor would include a couple bedrooms and bathrooms. That meant the risk of arousing anyone by breaching the first floor was small. He delicately attempted to turn the knob on the back door, assuming it would be locked, but to his surprise it was not. *Well, typical naiveté of rural Americans thinking that being out in the country automatically made you secure,* he thought as he cracked the door and moved inside.

Finding himself in a kitchen, he navigated silently through an archway into the larger living room. On his right was a stone fireplace with a raised hearth surrounded by comfortable southwest furniture. Across the room, a dining area with a rustic rectangular table looked out of the front, onto a small grassy area bordering the main circular drive. In the corner near the paneled Texas redwood door was what he was looking for. Protected by a heavy mesquite banister were the stairs leading up to the sleeping quarters above and the opportunity of satisfying a vendetta that had been smoldering for some time.

Peter Gunderson watched through his night vision binoculars with growing unrest as each member of his team successfully closed on the compound. While he had hoped for a smooth operation, this was going far too well. He didn't like it at all. The plan had been to terminate each target silently without alerting the rest of the compound, but he had been realistic in his view that this would be unlikely. That was why he had staggered the assaults. But things were eerily quiet. Where were the guards, the defenses and the precautions? There were only two possibilities. Either Sisco had vacated the property to hole up in a safe house or this whole thing was a trap. Actually, both could be true.

His panic rising, Gunderson went on comms to his team, he needed a status now!

Gunderson whispered, "everyone stop where you are now and give me an update, we may have a problem." The readouts came in, starting with Jefferey, Nicholi and finally Wart.

After Von Stemp reported in, Gunderson asked, "Wart, you say you saw a guard?"

Wart answered, "affirmative."

Gunderson continued, "and you say you can see two people asleep in the master suite?"

"Affirmative," came back Von Stemp's reply.

"Wart, can you absolutely identify them?"

"No Sir," Wart whispered, "too far away."

"Any movement?" Gunderson pressed.

"Negative," Von Stemp answered. *Shit, that iced it*, Gunderson thought in alarm. This had to be a set up, but retreat was not an option. They were past the point of no return. But if their targets might not even be there, what was the point, and what were they up against? *This was the classic, damned if you do and damned if you don't scenario*, he thought. But they had discussed this contingency.

Gunderson came back on the comm, "Jefferey, you and Nicholi find secure cover away from the structures and stand by. Wart, you are closest to a visible target, so proceed, verify and make the kill."

The response was immediate, "going in," Wart answered.

CHAPTER SEVENTEEN

TAKEDOWN

Joe Franklin hadn't observed Von Stemp hiding beyond the perimeter, but Mac had picked him up when he spied the tall grass waving slightly in a breathless evening, and quickly updated everyone on the comms. So as not to be an easy target, Franklin had moved around the corner of the residence as Mac continued to give him updates on Von Stemp's progress. When the Typhon agent had hidden behind the outside bar, Franklin also moved into a position behind the built-in gas grill on the porch. After Wart made his final move to the porch, Mac instructed Joe to move on his command. The idea was to take down the big German once he penetrated the house, so that none of his team could see the attack and be aware that their operation was made. Joe waited anxiously for the command; his tactical field blade unsheathed.

"He's going in, go Joe!" came the urgent command from Sisco. Franklin jumped from behind the counter, moving silently towards the slightly ajar French doors. He could see Von Stemp's outline midway to the bed and crossed the distance in two strides, launching himself at the figure.

Von Stemp sensed the danger even before Franklin had made his rush and spun around to see the big Seal only feet away, his ten-inch blade glistening in the reflected moonlight. Von Stemp already had his tactical knife out, poised for his sleeping victims, and parried Joe's first thrust off to the side with an ease that stunned Franklin. He knew this guy was a real killer and he sure wasn't going to underestimate him this time. Von Stemp was crouched down; his blade positioned forward, his eyes glued on the Seal, his lips curling into a cruel smile. The two men circled each other in the space between the sitting area and the master bed, each looking for an opening, a vulnerability or a mistake. Joe head faked a move to the left and Wart responded instantly, turning slightly and thrusting his big knife out, but Franklin hadn't moved his body and Von Stemp's knife sliced harmlessly in the air. Joe slashed his blade out and down in one sweeping motion and felt it make solid contact with the grip on the German's knife and deflect backward to his hand. Von Stemp cried out as a large gash appeared from his knuckles to his wrist as he pulled his arm back to his body. But the Typhon agent didn't slow down. He adeptly switched the blade to his left hand and went on the attack.

Joe back peddled several steps to lure his opponent into making another careless attack and Wart seemed to take the bait, but then pulled back quickly. Franklin, expecting him to lunge forward, stepped back again and tripped on an unseen ottoman behind him, careening backwards onto the hardwood floor, his legs still dangling over the furniture. Von Stemp wasted no time, as he dove forward, his knife aimed directly at Joe's chest. Franklin desperately tried to roll to the side while kicking his left leg out as he spun and connected with Wart's head, throwing off his aim. The momentum of his blade, however, caught Franklin's upper back, the blade ripping through the tissue above his shoulder blade.

Both men were down, only feet from each other. The German had twisted onto his back on one side of the ottoman and Franklin landed on his knees on the other side. Once again, Von Stemp seemed almost superhuman as he raised both legs and kipped to his feet turning to finish the job, as Franklin desperately scrambled to face him. He was off balance and out of position as Von Stemp charged. He knew he couldn't stop him or avoid the thrust so he did the only thing he could do. He threw his big blade like a spear; tip first, as hard as he could at the German's left shoulder where his 9 mm had found its mark a lifetime before. The evil grin on Von Stemp's face was quickly replaced by one of sheer agony as the ten-inch blade buried itself almost to the hilt, the tip penetrating through his shoulder and out his back. His arm lost all strength and his knife clattered to the floor as he collided into the still kneeling Apogee agent and both men tumbled together to the floor. Von Stemp was still moving, but without any purpose as Joe pushed him away. His fall had driven Joe's knife even deeper into his flesh and only the grip was now visible. Franklin rolled the man on to his back, and for a second Wart's eyes peered up at him, the hatred and loathing visceral, and then they rolled back as the arterial blood drained out of his body.

Mac was providing a running commentary to the rest of the team, but once Joe disappeared into the rear doorway, he asked for a quick status. Jasmine was the first to respond.

"All clear here," she said. "I just checked on your father and mother and they're fine. I assume you want them to stay put in the second bedroom, here in the guest house," she said.

"Affirmative," Mac said, "and you need to stay there in the upper hallway until we've mopped this thing up."

"Copy," said Jasmine. "Victoria, how about you?"

"Mac, I'm roving at this point. I'm headed towards Typhon's probable approach point in the Live Oaks to see if I can pick them up from there."

"Good," came back Mac. "Alan, you there?" Mac asked.

"All clear here, Mac," replied the second Mossad agent.

"Is the PM OK?"

"Yes, we were a little concerned when we got your call about Von Stemp penetrating the main residence, even though we're all the way on the other side of the house. We considered moving to the Guest House, but figured we'd better wait for Joe to handle it."

"That's an affirmative," Mac said. "I'll get back to you as soon as I hear from him. I imagine he's a little busy at the moment."

Almost on cue, Franklin's voice came on the comms.

"Mac, Von Stemp is down and out. He took the bait, but not without some collateral damage."

"Joe, are you alright?" Mac asked urgently.

"Yeah, I'll live, but I could sure use some of Jasmine's magic to make me more useful."

"How bad is it?" Mac asked concerned, knowing Joe always downplayed his injuries.

"He got lucky with one of his thrusts and took a pretty good chunk out of my back. Problem is I can't really see it to assess the damage."

"Hold tight there Joe, I'll cover the guest house from here and send her over to patch you up."

"Thanks Boss," said the big man with a groan.

"Hey Jas, did you copy that?" Mac asked.

"Got it Mac, do you want me to wait for you to relieve me or go now?"

"Tell my parents to be heads up, but get over to Joe now. I don't know how bad off he is. I'm already on my way to your location. Jasmine, be careful, we still have bad guys out there."

Mac flew up the steps of the guest house and lightly tapped on the bedroom door, "Dad, Mom, it's Mac, everything OK?" The door opened and Joe Sisco appeared, his wife by his side.

"We're fine son," his father answered. "How are we doing?" he asked.

"One down so far, but Joe needs some medical attention."

"Oh my, is he alright," Winnie asked, a worried look on her face.

"I think so, but you know Joe, he always gives you an optimistic outlook, so I'm not taking any chances," Mac answered.

"Mac, if you need to go and help Jasmine, do it. Your mother and I can take care of us," Joe Sisco said.

"Thanks Dad, but I'll hang here unless we have a serious issue." His parents nodded appreciatively and closed the door and Mac took up his position just down the hall.

Peter Gunderson was not a patient man and Von Stemp's continued silence was not a good sign.

Finally, he went on comms and said, "Wart, status." There was no answer. Gunderson repeated his command without success. Well, his gambit had worked more or less. He might be down one man, but now he knew someone was out there and there was still a reasonable chance it would be his target. "Jefferey, Nicholi, I need your locations," he broadcast.

"I'm hidden behind some large crepe myrtles at the end of the residence," answered Nicholi.

"I'm back out by the fence line behind the guest house in the high grass," answered Jefferey. "Dad, I just saw Jasmine Snow leave and head for the residence and then Mac Sisco went into the guesthouse rear entrance."

"Yeah and I saw Snow run around the back of the house a minute ago too," chimed in Krishinko.

Peter replied, "good news, it looks like the whole gang is here, so let's get this done! Both of you head for the guest house and take down Sisco and whoever else is there. They just might all be together, and we could score a hole in one! And guys, if they put up a serious defense and you can't get to them, torch the place," Gunderson commanded.

Joe was lightheaded by the time Jasmine rushed into the master suite and knelt down beside him. He was slumped down beside the very dead corpse of Wart Von Stemp, the big knife protruding from his upper chest like a monument.

She hardly glanced at the body as she turned her attention on Joe and said, "good technique big guy, now lean forward so that I can see how badly you screwed yourself up."

In spite of the pain, he chuckled, "boy am I glad I asked for you!" Snow had already pulled a towel from her med kit and wiped the blood away to examine the wound. It was long but didn't appear too deep and wasn't bleeding arterially.

"Joe," she said, "can you slowly raise your arm?"

"Don't know," he said, "since I used up all my superpowers on that SOB, I haven't really moved anything." With a groan, he slowly raised his arm and then lowered it to his side.

"Great," Jasmine replied, "no arteries and no major muscles impaired, so let's get this patched up and you can rejoin the party at least as an observer."

"Oh, just wonderful," Franklin retorted sarcastically.

"Well, look at the positive side, Joe."

"And that is?" he asked. "You're lucky it was a knife, if it had been a gun, we would be pulling a round out of your body."

"Touché," came his pained reply.

Snow had just given Mac a status on Franklin's condition when his mobile vibrated silently in his fatigue's pocket. He lifted it out and saw an urgent voice mail had just come in from Admiral Clausen. *Timing is everything*, he thought. This couldn't be good. He anxiously opened the VM and listened,

"Mac, we just broke through on some of the briefcase data. There was more description on the fractals that included the sources and methods for each action. The mission to assassinate Israel's PM is to be carried out by one of his personal Mossad security agents. Unfortunately, the file didn't specifically identify which one. If you can't absolutely determine same, you must terminate them both ASAP!" *Oh crap*, he thought, this was bad. Both agents were in a position to kill Prime Minister Cohen. Bakman could take him out from long range and Belks could shoot him from five feet away right now. Taking them both out was also an unpleasant challenge. He was not in the habit of killing innocent people. He thought back to the conversations he had with both agents, focusing on any clue to identify which was the traitor. *Had either insisted on guarding the PM? Not really, that he could recall. What about their normal pattern of protection? Nothing seemed out of the ordinary. Damn,* he thought, *there must be something and he needed to figure it out fast.*

Peter Gunderson didn't know for sure where the PM was and he wouldn't know until after the fact, but one thing he did know, no matter what happened the PM had to die, or Chaos would. It was time to cash in on his insurance plan. He pulled out his mobile and brought up the Typhon application and accessed the imbedded Chaos sub-application. The Fractal List displayed down the screen with the execute date and timing sequence next to each action. The first action on the list, highlighted in green, was "Assassinate PM, Israel" and next to it was an unchecked box. The rest of the items were not highlighted because their dates had not yet arrived. Checking the box would send a code to the "actor" to execute the fractal. Gunderson tapped gently on the box and it turned to yellow. When the deed was done, it would receive an affirmative reply that would turn its color to red. Smiling to himself, he thought, now that was easy. No matter what happened, Chaos was now underway!

Mac had no choice; he had to decide. He pushed on the comm unit in his ear isolating his call only to Jasmine

"Jasmine, we have a problem, but before I get into it, how's Joe?"

"He's lost some blood and one arm is screwed up, but he'll be OK. However, he's not highly operational," she responded.

"OK, what about that problem?" she asked.

"Bloody hell," she exclaimed, after he had described their dilemma.

"Do you have any insights on these two agents that might identify which one is the traitor?" Mac asked. Jasmine scoured her brain, recalling her conversations with the agents during their meetings, but nothing obvious jumped out.

"Damn Mac, I got nothing," she finally answered exasperated. "Where is Victoria now?" she asked.

"She said she was moving on up to the approach point, but hell, she could just as easily have hiked back and be headed to the residence. Of course if Belks is Chaos, he may have already killed the PM," he concluded. "We can't let on we know any of this or the PM is toast," Mac said.

"You could bring Victoria into the guest house and I can take Joe over to join Alan with the PM and complicate matters. If either makes a move, hopefully we can prevent it and take them out," Jasmine suggested.

"It's risky, but it's about all we got, so let's go with it," Mac agreed.

Mac selected Bakman on comms and said, "Victoria, we took down Von Stemp. I need you to get down here to the guesthouse. I think this thing is going down soon and we need all the firepower we can get near the residence."

Victoria answered, "copy Mac, on my way." Jasmine updated Joe on the situation and helped support him as they made their way to the guest suite at the other end of the big house.

She knocked on the door and said, "Alan, its Jasmine and Joe, we need to come in." There was silence. "Prime Minister, this is Jasmine, is everything OK, can we come in," she asked again. The door unlatched and slowly opened.

Aaron Cohen stood back and seeing Joe, said, "oh my God, what happened," as Jasmine helped Joe in and got him to a casual chair by a coffee table in the sitting room.

"Long story, Sir," answered Jasmine. "Where is Alan?"

"Oh, he had to use the rest room, he'll be right back," Cohen said. Just then Alan Belks appeared, a 45-caliber handgun outstretched pointing directly at them.

Snow raised her eyebrows and staring directly at Belks asked, "Alan is there a problem?"

"Fortunately not, he smiled as he lowered the weapon to his side but didn't holster it. "I heard voices from the bathroom, but wasn't sure who it was so, better safe than sorry, right?" he said.

Jefferey and Nicholi had joined up by the fence line and were beginning their approach to the guesthouse when they saw movement further out in the fields. They both dropped to the ground and lay still as they waited. It might be Peter Gunderson joining the fun, they thought, but he had not said he was coming in yet. There it was again and suddenly they saw a tall figure breaking out of the big Live Oaks and heading their way. Without a positive ID, they didn't dare fire, but they positioned their AKs for a shot. The figure suddenly disappeared into a low area and was lost from sight.

Bakman was almost to the guesthouse when she saw the area in front of her suddenly light up just as if she had flipped on the infrared enhancement on her night vision goggles. The problem was that her infrared was not on, but someone else's was. There was a low area coming up and she raced to gain its cover and then began moving laterally along it. After moving twenty yards, she dropped down and crawled to the top of the rise and peered over it. She could see two men 100 yards away lying prone with assault weapons aimed at her last position.

She set her comms for Mac and said, "Mac, I'm 150 yards out from you and am observing two bad actors that made me. I may be able to take one out but could use some back up. They should be directly out from your rear entrance near the fence line and possibly visible from that angle," she finished. Mac listened to Bakman's call with a deep sense of unease. She was out there with a sniper rifle and the skill to take down a target from 1000 plus yards. If he did what she suggested, he could be walking into a trap and he would never see it coming. On the other hand, if he didn't help, and she was legit, both of them could be pinned down and in deep shit.

"Mom and Dad, we've got company and I need to get downstairs and deal with it. Stay alert, stay put and I'll stay in touch," Mac said through the door as he hustled down the hall and took the stairs two at a time. He donned his night vision gear, opened the back door a crack and looked out where the Mossad sniper had designated. He could just make out something beyond the fence whose dark color contrasted against the blond stalks of waving grass. OK, it looked like that part of Bakman's story was kosher. He scanned the area where she described her position and wasn't surprised to see no movement. Snipers were really good at camouflaging themselves.

"Victoria, I'm in position, what's the play?" he asked over his comm unit.

"I don't have a legitimate shot," she said, "but I can spice up their lives. I'll remove my suppressor to add some drama and maybe it will flush them out."

"OK, since they're focused on you, I may get a clear angle on at least one of them," Mac responded.

"Copy," she answered.

The report from the big sniper rifle was massive in the quiet of the Texas night and the result was equally violent as the two Typhon agents saw the muzzle flash and began strafing the ground where the Israeli's shot had originated. The sight was surreal as the dirt kicked up silently into the air, clouding the ridgeline for ten yards. As they pivoted to sight in on the new location, both figures had become more visible and Mac stepped out of the doorway, took up his shooter's stance and found a target. He didn't have much of a shot and was fifty yards out, but all he needed was a hit to change the game. He pulled off five rounds, re-aiming rapidly between each pull and then retreated back inside the door behind the cover of the rock frame. There was no immediate response, but nor was there any obvious evidence of a hit.

Suddenly, large shards of rock and wood began exploding into the space around him as he dove further into the cover of the wall. Now prone on the hard tile floor of the mudroom and off angle from the shooters, Mac quickly took an inventory for injuries. It was not uncommon immediately after a hit to be unaware of your condition, but fortunately, aside from some bruises, he was unscathed. He cautiously crawled back to the doorframe and risked a look and saw nothing.

"Victoria, are you OK?" he transmitted.

"Affirmative," she said. "I knew that taking my suppressor off would create a flash, so as soon as I fired, I dropped down behind the ridge and waited for your rounds before taking another look."

"Did I get lucky?" Mac asked.

"I'm not sure, but I think you might have winged one of them, but it didn't stop them both from unloading on you. After that barrage, they scattered and I think they spread out to reduce their vulnerability and probably to flank us," she answered.

Peter Gunderson held his position and waited for the call from his team. The report of a single round was confounding. His boys may have taken the shooter out. He hoped that was the case or things were going south. He didn't have to wait long as Jefferey came on comms.

"Dad, we cornered a sniper outside of the guest house and before we could take him out, he changed position and got a shot off."

"Anyone hit?" asked his father.

"No, but right after that, someone opened up on our position from the guest house and we were caught in the crossfire."

Gunderson flatly repeated his question, "anyone hit?"

"Nicholi took a round to his left calf, but it's just a flesh wound, Jefferey replied."

"Is he still mobile?" Gunderson asked.

"Yes, but not 100%," was his son's response. "We have already spread out to flank the sniper and attack the guest house from a different angle."

"Good, but don't try to breach the house," Peter Gunderson said.

"Any surprise advantage is gone, so just torch the place and then we'll deal with the main residence. But Jefferey, kill that damn sniper, we can't afford to have a loose predator out here screwing everything up."

Mac didn't want to leave his parents unprotected, but he had to get out on the grounds to help Bakman and take control of the situation. This was not the time for a defensive play. As far as Bakman was concerned, he was just going to have to take his chances. It had not gone unnoticed that she had not managed a kill shot on the Typhon boys. He decided his safest approach was not to telescope his movements unless he had no choice. He moved out of the doorway in a low run towards her last position figuring that one of the terrorists would be trying to get behind her. He knew that the other operative would probably be going the other way to attack the front of the house and that would give him a little time.

He had made it to the tree line when he heard twigs snapping loudly off to his right and ducked behind a big Spanish Oak. Peering around the trunk, he caught a glimpse of a man limping slightly down the slope and taking up a position overlooking the northern end of the guesthouse. Mac needed to get closer. He crept forward delicately, each step precise, avoiding dry leaves and brush, moving from tree to tree, silently closing the distance. At twenty-five yards, he halted and viewed the figure again. It was Krishinko. He was leaning heavily against a big Oak, his AK raised, his eye on the scope in a shooting stance. Mac shifted his focus to where Krishinko was aiming and gasped. Just out of range, but fast approaching, Victoria Bakman, loyal Mossad agent or despicable traitor, was unaware of the hidden terrorist.

Mac's mind was racing, if Krishinko didn't kill Bakman, that would prove she was part of Chaos and Mac could eliminate both of them right here and right now. But if Nicholi did take out the Mossad agent would that prove she was innocent? Not if Krishinko didn't know she was the assassin. Of course, he could take Bakman out first and then Krishinko would be easy pickings at this range. No more time, he thought as she came into range. Krishinko's hand moved slightly, as he positioned himself for the shot. Mac had made his decision and was already sighted in. He pulled off two quick shots at his target, who collapsed from the deadly head shot. The only noise was the dry twigs breaking as the body hit the ground. Re-orienting his eyes to her last position, Mac saw that Victoria Bakman had disappeared.

Jefferey Gunderson had managed to close on the guesthouse and retrieved his pyro gear from his pack. He began to stick Pyro Putty along the wooden areas of the structure and doorframes. As he worked, he began lighting each gob of the highly flammable paste. It would take a little while for the thick wood to ignite, but he needed the extra time to place the accelerant all the way around the house. As he arrived at the front entrance door, he tried turning the knob. The door was unlocked. He knew the fire would be much more likely to trap the inhabitants upstairs if he lighted it inside, so he went in. He carefully positioned the putty in strategic locations on the first floor including a key one next to the gas stove which he would turn on just before he left. As he placed a final deposit under some curtains in the kitchen, he heard muffled voices coming from the second floor. He couldn't make out what was being said, but the voice was definitely a man's and it sounded a lot like Mac Sisco. *What a break*, Jefferey thought, he was in the house and had the advantage of surprise. He couldn't pass this opportunity up. Sisco might escape the fire and this way there was no doubt about his fate and Jefferey Gunderson would have his revenge. *His father would be proud he finally delivered,* he thought.

He quickly climbed the stairs and went down the hall. The voices had stopped, but there was only one door closed. Gently, he turned the knob, but the door was locked. *No problem,* he thought, this lock was no match for a practiced kick from a 225-pound professional. He stepped back and kicked his size twelve boot directly into the lock with tremendous force. The door splintered and flew open and Jefferey lunged forward, his handgun pointed straight out in front of him. A man stood on the opposite side of the room peering out of the rear window. *It was Sisco,* Jefferey thought, *perfect!* The man spun around as he heard the sound of the door breaking and stared at Jefferey without emotion. Gunderson looked on horrified as he stared back at Joe Sisco.

"Where's your son?" he demanded.

Joe Sisco smiled and said, "not here, but I have no doubt that you will meet him soon enough."

"We'll see about that," Jefferey laughed ominously. "As much as I'd like to have the pleasure of watching you witness his death, I just don't have the time to manage all that, so I'll have to reverse the order." Even as he began to squeeze the trigger, his finger seemed to lose its strength as the slug from the barrel of Winnie Sisco's Smith and Wesson pierced his temple from eight feet away. Joe Sisco looked at his wife in appreciation, nodding his head in thanks.

"Great shot sweetheart. I'm sure glad you took that potty break when you did."

She smiled back and said, "well I've always had a bit of a weak bladder in times of stress. I guess this was one of those times."

Mac smelled the smoke before he saw the flames and took off in a sprint down the slope. The flames on the porch of the guesthouse were just starting to get a hold as he rounded the front porch towards the rear of the house. He raced through the back door and rushed up the stairs where he had left his parents. Seeing the broken shards of the door, he imagined the worst as he flew through the doorway not caring about opposition. Grinding to a halt in the center of the room, he stared in awe as Joe and Winnie Sisco stood across the room arm in arm, two handguns poised in their hands.

"We thought it was you," Winnie said smiling, as she lowered her weapon. No one else would be crazy enough to make all that racket just to save us."

"Especially, when we told him we could take care of ourselves," reminded Joe. In spite of the tension, they all laughed and hugged each other, thankful for the outcome.

"It's not over yet," Mac said, as he pulled away. "We've got a rogue Mossad agent out there and I don't know which one, but I've got to stop them."

"Well what are you waiting for?" Winnie said, as she pushed him gently towards the door. In the kitchen Mac pulled the fire extinguisher from the wall by the stove and went out the rear door. He circled the guesthouse quickly smothering each budding fire with the foam retardant and then crossed the driveway to the main residence.

He still hadn't seen Bakman and decided to keep off the comms for now. He also wanted to maintain the element of surprise with Alan

Belks, as he wound his way around to the end of the house where the Guest suites were located. Staying low, he hugged the exterior wall until he came to the large picture window of the guest suite where Belks and the Prime Minister had hidden. He stooped down and cautiously peered through the partially open slats of the plantation shutters. Belks was sitting with his back to the far wall in a wing-backed chair. His gun rested on a small side table next to him. The PM was next to him in a matching chair only six feet away. Joe was lying prone on a couch along the adjacent wall behind a rustic coffee table, his eyes closed, and Jasmine was beside him in a large leather chair her eyes focused intently on Belks.

He could hear her begin to speak, "Alan," she said, "we haven't heard from Mac and I am concerned. We also need an update on what's going on. It's not like him to stay silent so long, unless there is a good reason, but we are sitting here blind."

"I agree," said Belks, "go ahead and call him."

Jasmine put her hand to her ear and selected Mac only and said, "Mac, we're all together in the suite are you OK?" Mac remained silent and waited. He wanted to see how Belks responded to the situation.

"Mac, please respond," Jasmine repeated, genuinely concerned.

Belks chimed in, "try to get Victoria, maybe they're together."

"OK," answered Jasmine and made the call with the same result, no answer.

"Bloody Hell," she said. "This doesn't look good; someone has got to go out and find Mac and find out what the shit is going on."

Snow began to get to her feet, but Belks said, "Jasmine, I should be the one to go. You need to look after Joe, and I know you can protect the Prime Minister as well as I can. Besides, my partner is out there too and could be in trouble, so I really feel an obligation to help her." Jasmine considered the man's request and turned to Prime Minister Cohen.

"Sir," she asked, "how do you feel about Alan going out?"

Cohen didn't hesitate, "I'm fine with it Jasmine. I've been in his shoes and completely understand the need to protect your partner. I would expect nothing less. Besides, I am confident that you and I are more than capable of handling the situation," he concluded as he placed a lethal FN 5-7 on the table next to him. Alan certainly sounded sincere and she really had not wanted to leave the PM alone with this guy knowing that there was a chance he could be the assassin.

"OK, Alan, that makes sense. I'll let them both know that you are going out onto the grounds. Please stay on comms and keep me updated so I know how to manage the situation here," she requested. Belks nodded and headed for the door of the suite as Jasmine got back on comms and broadcast their plan to Mac and Bakman.

Mac watched as Belks left the suite and hurried to the rear of the house to follow him. His situation had grown more dangerous than ever. There were three highly trained operatives out on the property and two of them would like nothing more than to eliminate him on the spot. As he came to the back patio, he expected to see Belks exiting the French doors, but he was not there. *Damn*, thought Mac, he must have left by the front door, but that didn't make sense. He would be wide open with no cover. The shortest distance to the front was through the house, so he sprinted through the patio doors, through the great room, down a long hall to the front foyer where the front door was slightly ajar. He burst out and scanned the compound. Nothing! Even as he felt a growing sense of unease, he felt there was something he was missing. He needed to act, but he had no idea which way to go or what to expect. Then, like a lightning bolt, the answer jolted him into action. He sprinted back through the house and out the French doors rounding the corner towards the PM's guest suite. In the darkness thirty feet away, he could see a figure outside the window he had just left, an outstretched hand gripping a weapon, its barrel inches from the glass. Even as he reached for his own weapon, he knew he was too late, as the report shattered the night.

Mac's jaw dropped in surprise as the figure crumpled to the ground in front of the window. Still unaware of who shot whom, Mac dropped down and waited. His epiphany minutes ago had been that Belks had purposely volunteered to leave the residence so that he could sneak around to the rear window and shoot the PM without having to deal with Snow inside. But now, he wasn't so sure. The corpse under the window could be Bakman and Belks might have come upon her and taken her out before she could kill Cohen. It might even be Peter Gunderson lying there, having been eliminated by either Mossad agent. The game, apparently, was still afoot. This mission sure had its twists and turns, he thought as he began to crawl forward towards the corpse.

A familiar voice suddenly broke the silence, "I wasn't sure you were alive when your comms went silent Mac," Victoria Bakman said softly, from only a few feet behind him. Mac froze, and then slowly turned to look up at the Mossad agent, towering above him holding her sniper rifle with the barrel pointing at the ground just in front of him.

"You as well," Mac replied. "Where have you been Victoria and what are you doing here?"

"Just doing my job Mac," she answered. "Whoever I just killed was about to take out my PM and I couldn't let that happen, now could I?" she answered seriously as she reached out a hand and helped him to his feet.

"So you don't know who that is, up there?" Mac asked, pointing at the corpse shrouded in the darkness.

"Not a clue," she answered, "but there are only two possibilities," she said.

Mac nodded, and said, "Peter Gunderson or Alan Belks, your partner."

"Yep," she agreed, "and I guess we better see who got the short straw."

After Mac and Victoria had confirmed the corpse's identity as Alan Belks, he contacted Jasmine.

"We are OK. That last shot you heard was Victoria taking out Belks, as he was about to shoot the PM from the rear window."

"Mac, what about Krishinko and Jefferey Gunderson?" Jasmine asked.

"I took out Krishinko up on the ridge and Winnie nailed Jefferey when he was about to shoot Dad in the guest house."

"Well hello," exclaimed Jasmine joyfully, "good for your Mom!"

"And Peter Gunderson?" she asked finally.

"Still at large, and unless Gunderson brought in some reinforcements, which I doubt, he is the only Typhon agent alive on the premises. Victoria and I will search the property and clear it. You guys stay put."

"OK, Mac, but you guys be careful. He's a real son of a bitch and dangerous."

"Thanks Jas, we'll get back as soon as we can."

As Mac and Victoria set out to hunt down Peter Gunderson, Victoria turned to Mac and said, "I figured that was you who saved my bacon on the ridge, thanks."

"I got lucky," he responded. "He was so intent on you, I got so close, I couldn't miss. Besides, you sure did your share of saving asses," he complimented. "You saved the life of a good man, a good friend and a great Prime Minister."

"Thanks," Victoria beamed, "I guess we both have had a pretty good day, now let's go find that bastard Gunderson." They scoured the property around the compound and then moved outward, finding nothing. Eventually, they came upon the area where Gunderson's vehicle had been parked. The tracks in the dirt were fresh and showed both incoming and outgoing tread marks. There was nothing else there. Gunderson was once again in the wind.

CHAPTER EIGHTEEN

AFTERMATH

In the days that followed everyone at Agave Ranch visited the NSA complex at Ft. Meade, Md. All Team Apogee's members, the Sisco's, Prime Minister Cohen and Victoria Bakman were part of the Individual and collective briefings that were conducted for several days to begin to understand the scope and reach of Typhon. It was a grueling task, but piece-by-piece the picture became clearer. As predicted by Gunderson himself and reinforced by Admiral Clausen, the NSA more than lived up to its reputation, as its cryptologists and technical analysts began unraveling Gunderson's briefcase's secrets. The workings of the Chaos activation device were discovered and used to neuter and dismantle the planned fractal catalysts.

Once decrypted, the terabytes of files detailed Typhon's organization structures, contacts, financial resources and intricate operational details across the globe. NATCOG meetings were held and plans were developed to expose and terminate Typhon operations and arrest its members and supporters. It would take years to flush out and bring to justice those involved in the United States. The breadth and reach of Typhon's tentacles were enormous. Major players in every segment of American society, business, high tech, academia, banking, the media and the local and federal government 'swamps' were deeply entrenched in corrupt activities and had been for decades. The task seemed insurmountable, but the cause was just and the very thing that made Typhon so powerful, it's tightly controlled secret cabal, had ultimately been its greatest vulnerability. Once that was dismantled, the entire artificial infrastructure of disruption began to collapse.

But the world wasn't fixed. Typhon had been working for decades to manipulate societies world-wide. Their subtle changes were slow but indelible and had morphed and grown and their roots were deep. The destruction of Typhon only served to eliminate new artificial stimuli, but the seeds of disruption had been sown long ago and had developed their own inertia. Now, the really hard work would have to begin, and it would take many years to turn the ship away from the falls and probably a few miracles to keep the frog from boiling to death.

One week after the takedown of Typhon, a full debrief had been chaired by the POTUS on the Apogee mission in the Situation room.

As the room cleared, President Holbrook pulled Admiral Clausen aside and said, "Jim would you mind accompanying me back to the Oval Office? I need to chat with you about all of this for a few minutes."

"Of course not, Sir," responded Clausen, intrigued.

Once seated around the colonial coffee table, the President wasted no time. "Jim, I would say, we dodged a bullet, but the battle has yet to be waged. What Typhon started a half century ago has a will of its own. We may have killed the rapid acceleration that Chaos would have initiated, but we have done little to really impede the global threat. Here in the U.S. we have hardly dented the increasing divisions that threaten to tear our country apart. What are your thoughts on how we deal with this growing crisis?" Clausen cleared his throat as he contemplated his response.

"Sir, first let me say that I agree with your assessment. We really have two dangerous fronts to deal with. The first, as you point out, is our own national situation and the second is the ever-growing possibility that another bad actor will pick up where Gunderson left off."

The President nodded and said, "you are right Jim and both issues are existential threats to our nation."

"At the risk of putting you on the spot," Holbrook continued, "I would be very interested in your current thinking on how we deal with each."

"On the contrary, Mr. President, I wouldn't be much of an intelligence officer if I hadn't gotten out in front of this, at least enough to form an opinion," Clausen responded. "In terms of interventions, Typhon's plan provides us with the best guidance on how to mitigate the societal disruptions nationally and globally. Essentially, we need to use it in reverse to identify priorities and develop counter actions. On the second issue of bad actors appropriating Typhon's position, I believe that may already be happening."

President Holbrook looked stunned as he leaned forward and asked, "by whom?"

"There is only one organization that is motivated and resourced for such an undertaking, answered the Admiral gravely, "China!"

"Do you have evidence of this Jim?" the President asked.

"Yes Sir, we do. In fact, before we discovered Typhon's operation, our best guess was that China was behind all the anomalies. The evidence we gathered still points at significant Chinese global activities from their Belt and Road economic initiative to their interventions throughout the world to gain influence and control over sovereign nations, including our own."

"And your recommendations?" Holbrook asked anxiously.

"Well, to start with I have three immediate actions we should take," Clausen answered. "First, maintain the NATCOG structure, second, launch a new mission to address this growing global and national threat."

Before, he could finish, Holbrook interjected, "and the third, Jim?"

"Re-constitute Team Apogee, at the appropriate time, to head up the mission." Holbrook stood up and extended his hand to his friend and said, "thanks Jim, as usual, you're right on the mark on all counts. With the upcoming election, I have a feeling things could get dicey, but whatever happens, I will get the ball rolling, so start putting your plans together."

"Yes Sir," Clausen answered with a nod, "I already have!"

♦

Three months after the Agave Ranch episode, Mac was back in D.C., having some coffee on a rare non-working weekend, when his mobile rang.

Checking the caller ID, he smiled to himself and answered, "hey Joe wassup?" He could tell immediately that his old friend was excited.

"Mac, did you check your mail," the Seal asked.

"Not today," Mac responded, "why?"

"Well, go check and call me back," Joe demanded.

"C'mon Joe, what's this all about."

"Humor me Cap," his friend begged and hung up. Coffee in hand, Mac walked out the front door and checked his mailbox. There was the usual assortment of bills, magazines, flyers and a few standard letters. As he walked back inside, he flipped through the stack and came upon a smaller square envelope with no return address. Curious, he opened the envelope and retrieved a folded insert. At the top was the imbedded Seal of the President of the United States followed by the words, *The President and Mrs. Holbrook request the honor of your presence at a reception and dinner at the White House on Wednesday The Seventeenth of June Two Thousand Twenty. Well, I'll be damned,* thought Mac, as he dialed Joe's number.

♦

It was a glorious reunion to say the least. Everyone was there who was part of the mission, from the NSA team to Prime Minister Cohen and Victoria Bakman. He even spied the General from Auckland and the pilots that had dropped them on both ops there. Of course, Mac's parents happily renewed their old relationships with The President and Mrs. Holbrook and Admiral James Clausen. Team Apogee sat together at table number two. Mac and his five teammates were all together again, at least for one night, and to his delight Jasmine Snow was seated just to his right. Among the most rewarding aspects of the mission had been Jasmine's transformation and her loyalty and valor had been rewarded when President Holbrook had contacted the UK Prime Minister and requested that Jasmine be reinstated at MI-6 and her contributions to the Apogee mission be recognized.

The team couldn't help but reminisce about the mission while skirting the sensitive areas because of their classified nature and sources and methods, but they did their best to get up to speed on all the juicy stuff. They were especially interested in the outcomes of some of the major players. Because Mac was still the closest to the action, they all turned to him, when the question came up.

"OK, OK," he said, "here's what I know. Both Stabler and Fowler are currently being held without bail as obvious flight risks awaiting trial on multiple counts. A couple other moles in NSA and elsewhere were identified and have also been charged."

"Wasn't there a senator that was also arrested?" asked Peter Singe.

"Yeh, I heard about that too," chimed in Carrie Swan.

"Yes, that was certainly a shocker," answered Mac.

"Senator William Billings, a member of the House Intelligence Committee, is currently under investigation. He has denied everything of course, but they have some serious evidence against him."

"What about Peter Gunderson?" asked Pat Curry. "Can you share anything about him, Mac.?"

"I would if I could," answered Mac gravely. "He's the one real piece of unfinished business. We do know from the briefcase files that he has numerous global underground connections including heads of state in non-friendly U.S. countries. My guess is that he is licking his wounds in one of those."

"And re-grouping no doubt," added Elaine Warsaw.

Mac frowned and said somberly, "of that I have no doubt. I'm afraid we have not seen the last of Mr. Peter Gunderson!"

The sound of a spoon tapping on crystal brought silence to the large room, as the President stood up to address his guests.

"First, let me thank you all for making the trek here tonight. For some of you it was a short trip and for others, you're very far from home and I sincerely appreciate it. The purpose of tonight's event is to recognize each and every one of you for your extraordinary contribution to our collective mission. You made great sacrifices, took great risks and a number of you endured painful injuries in the line of duty. I stand here representing all NATCOG member countries across the world who, because of your efforts, are now armed and able to defend their societies and begin to eradicate the cultural and ideological corruption that threaten their values and their very existence. So, on behalf of a grateful world, thank you all.

"Finally, before I close and open up the bar for some after dinner celebratory libations, I would like to recognize one group of people who were especially instrumental in the success of our mission. That is the field operations team who really was on the front line and who exhibited exemplary courage under the most adverse conditions. As you all know, since this was a highly classified operation, I can't describe their specific acts of valor, but I can assure you I have never been prouder to award the Distinguished Intelligence Cross to these worthy recipients. The cross is America's highest clandestine service recognition and is awarded for voluntary act or acts of extraordinary heroism involving the acceptance of existing dangers with conspicuous fortitude and exemplary courage. When I call your name, please come forward and receive your cross," the President concluded. "Mr. Joseph Franklin, Ms.

Carrie Swan, Mr. Peter Singe, Mr. Pat Curry, Ms. Elaine Warsaw, Ms. Jasmine Snow and team leader, Mr. Mac Sisco."

Once the thunderous applause, which lasted embarrassingly long, and the handshakes and pats on the back were graciously accepted, the team moved into the reception area. Mac found himself standing off to the side taking a breather when Jasmine approached him and handed him a flute of champagne.

"Well, that was a bloody shocker," she said in her wonderful British lilt. "I think I was more nervous walking up to receive that award than I was when we did our HALO jump at 25,000 feet."

Mac chuckled and asked, "how long are you in town for?"

"Well, I love D.C., so I figured I'd act like a tourist over the weekend and take a red eye back Monday night so I can sleep in Sunday and recover. Why?" she asked.

"How would you like a free tour guide?" Mac asked smiling.

"You know Cowboy, I'd like that very much indeed," she purred as she tapped her glass against his.

255

THE TYPHON AFFAIR

AFTERWORD

The Typhon Affair is the first sequel to *Apogee*. To be transparent, it didn't start out that way. As sometimes happens in storytelling, it evolved almost on its own. It is a rather intriguing phenomenon that when the story is in charge, it doesn't like to stop telling itself.

So it was that Apogee didn't want to end and frankly, I was OK with that. Ultimately, it became apparent the best way to complete the story was to split it into two volumes. And thus, *The Typhon Affair* was born. I worried some about how to transition between the two, and I feel I did it well. If you are reading this epilogue, I know you stuck with it and for that, I am grateful. The Mac Sisco Trilogy continues with book three, *The Maslow Conspiracy.*

—*Lou Earle*

ABOUT THE AUTHOR

Lou Earle is a writer, entrepreneur, and business executive with roots in corporate America. He graduated from the University of Pennsylvania and served four years in the United States Navy as a member of the Naval Security Group during the Vietnam War. He spent his final two years of service at the National Security Agency (NSA) in Fort Meade, Maryland.

Lou was the founding Chairman of Badgerdog Literary Publishing Company, a not-for-profit that published the literary digest American Short Fiction and provided outreach writing courses through Youth Voices in Ink for disenfranchised children in central Texas. He is also the owner, CEO, and publisher of Austin Fit Magazine, a health and fitness publication.

Lou is married with three children and three grandchildren. He and his wife Lynne live on a ranch in Wimberley, Texas with a menagerie of furry friends including two horses, one mammoth donkey, two miniature bulls, five dogs and five chickens.

For more information, visit louearle.com.

LOU EARLE